CW00767644

Margaret Garth

A Step Towards Unity

A Tale of Salima

Limited Special Edition. No. 23 of 25 Paperbacks

Margaret Garth was born in Manchester and studied Chemistry and Mathematics at St Andrew's University, Dundee, despite her interest in history and her love of stories.

She married and moved to Norfolk and kept her imagination lively by telling stories to her four children, and later to her grandchildren. Gardening and sewing are her main hobbies.

Somewhat late in life, she finished a novel, A Tale of Salima. This book is fourth in the series.

Other tales of Salima:

- *The Witch of Bellue*
- *The Battle of Felten*
- *The Beginning of Unity*

This book is dedicated to my staunch and steadfast daughter-in-law, Tracie.

Margaret Garth

A STEP TOWARDS UNITY

A TALE OF SALIMA

AUSTIN MACAULEY PUBLISHERS™

LONDON • CAMBRIDGE • NEW YORK • SHARJAH

A CIP catalogue record for this title is available from the British Library.

ISBN 9781788789981 (Paperback)
ISBN 9781528956574 (ePub e-book)

www.austinmacauley.com

First Published (2019)
Austin Macauley Publishers Ltd
25 Canada Square
Canary Wharf
London
E14 5LQ

Chapter 1

Princess Indola stood at the window and watched her son as he strolled with his friends in the palace garden. She frowned. He ought to have attended Assembly today. There was not a long agenda, but one or two of the topics were of importance. State affairs were not discussed with her. She had no particular interest, but she did have her own ways of finding out what was happening. Her husband indulged his son but she did not, and though he went to most Assembly meetings, she knew that he rarely offered an opinion.

She was a formidable and ambitious woman, named after the granddaughter of Nikkor and Kaealestria[*]. She did not possess the intellect of that Princess, but she was shrewd and had fought to be the Chosen Woman of the High Prince of Westland despite some opposition and a great deal of competition. For all her determination and her talents, they had had only one child, Darmon, and he was not maturing as she had planned. He was four and twenty, but she felt that he still lacked a proper appreciation of his duty. He disliked the formality in which she revelled and had shown no inclination to select a Chosen Woman.

Her frown deepened as she watched. He was going with his friends to the 'children's garden' and she could not see him there. She had never managed to persuade her husband to cut down the trees that shielded that place from view.

"All children," he had said, "and possibly Princes more than others, need a place where they can play and fight and test their courage as they choose, without being supervised and worried by adults."

---

[*] The Beginning of Unity.

"It is the adults who do the worrying," she had protested, but he had merely told her not to fret and had, she was sure, made certain that those who tended the palace gardens knew exactly which trees they might cut as they felt appropriate and which they must leave alone unless they had his personal permission to trim them.

Whether or not that was the case, the trees had grown unfettered and now concealed all parts of the 'children's garden' from every vantage point in the palace, even the scullery maid's attic.

Darmon was well aware of the privacy offered and its limits.

"Do not start practising your leaps just yet, Jon," he warned.

"We are not small boys any longer. Heads are visible until we pass Seabee's bush, and my revered Mama will be watching. She already considers you frivolous; do not give her proof of it."

"And do not turn your head to look for Her Highness," added Ped. "She has sharp eyes."

Pedan was the eldest of the three and was already in possession of his lands and title, but despite the considerable efforts of eligible young women, their parents and their friends, the handsome Lord Pandour was still unattached.

Jonal Tesher, third son of Lord Barre, waited until they were safely past the bush, named for the cat whose grave it marked, before he informed Ped that he was not a fool, and he emphasised the message with a friendly thump. He then leapt into the air and began to run towards the 'rope' tree.

The informality of the children's garden extended to names. Titles were abandoned and even the Prince was addressed, without deference, as Dee.

The 'rope' tree was old. Its strong branches spread wide, and it had been used by generations of children for climbing. Three sturdy ropes hung low, ending at various heights from the ground, and the remains of others, long since broken, were half-hidden in its high crown.

Climbing the ropes was no longer a challenge for the young men but leaping high enough to clasp a certain branch and swing oneself up to straddle the stouter branch beneath it, was, and Jon, shorter and more sturdily built than the others, sometimes struggled.

"He has been practising," noted Ped. "Do you think that today he will make it first time?"

"Perhaps, but it is not easy. Even I have been known to need a second attempt, on occasions."

"Many occasions," returned his companion with a grin, "and you can practise whenever you choose."

"Indeed, I cannot!" protested the Prince. "I have official duties, social engagements of the dullest kind, and I am obliged to attend Assembly meetings. They are so tedious. The most trivial of decisions always generate the longest discussions and meetings always seem to coincide with pleasant social occasions such as race meetings and beach parties. How I am supposed to meet informally with young ladies of quality, I do not know."

Ped gave an unsympathetic laugh as they came in sight of the tree. Jon was waiting, sitting smugly astride the favoured branch.

"Best make it first try today," he warned, "or Jon will never let you forget."

"Come," that gentleman shouted. "Last is hardest!"

As this was undoubtedly true, both began to run. As they were evenly matched at running and jumping, they reached their target at the same time. The branch bent alarmingly under their combined weight, and though the lower limb was sturdy enough not to sway, they landed beside Jon in an ungainly tangle.

As this was a common occurrence, they seated themselves more comfortably without difficulty and Ped initiated the discussion as to whose turn it was to provide the refreshments, for it was unthinkable that they came to the garden without food or drink. Long ago, it had been fruit juice and cakes or sweetmeats, now it was wine and savouries.

"No bags," exclaimed Jon and added with a touch of anxiety, "I don't think it was my turn."

Dee, balanced at the narrow end of the branch, reached up and pulled down two lengths of trailing greenery.

"My turn," he said as he tied a couple of flexible twigs together. "All we need is safely stored in the hollow."

Jon hauled himself upright with the aid of the catching branch and reached upwards to retrieve a small basket. He handed it to Ped and settled back in his place.

"I was free this morning," continued Dee, adjusting the living sling behind him and gripping it beneath his arms. "Unexpectedly, as I thought there was an Assembly meeting. It seems that the time had changed, though not the agenda, and although my diary had been updated, I had not been told. It is now in session, but by the time I discovered the change, I had – so sadly – made other arrangements."

He accepted a wooden cup of wine and grinned contentedly. "I shall miss this when I choose a woman."

"Under pressure?" inquired Ped with careful disinterest.

"My father," replied Dee. "He has been told by one of his doctors that his heart has been strained by his responsibilities and that unless he takes great care, he will be dead in five years. I do not believe it, but he is worried. He has said nothing about my taking a Chosen Woman, but he has reminded me that parents do not accompany their children into this garden. It is the privilege of the grandparents to introduce the first born to its delights; and he looks forward to doing so."

The even tone did not deceive his friends. Jon burst out indignantly almost before the last words were spoken.

"That is dreadfully unfair; an underhand way to try to influence you. He knows how much you love this place!"

"Subtle," commented Ped quietly and did not add that it was more likely to persuade than the Princess's blunt and dictatorial statements on the subject.

"I do love it," agreed Dee, answering Jon rather than Ped, "but so, I am sure, has every other young prince and princess and all have been obliged to grow up and leave its pleasures to their children.

"I am surprised," he continued thoughtfully, "that none have made an 'adult's garden' for themselves. Perhaps I shall create one. If I do, what shall we have in it?"

Jon made an immediate suggestion and they fell into an animated discussion. It was, thought Pedan, an admirable way of avoiding the topic of women, love and the duty of Princes, and to a lesser degree of lords and landowners, to produce heirs.

Jon was diverted, but he had not forgotten the topic. He did not, however, raise it until he and Ped had left both Prince and palace and were strolling across High Square.

"The Prince," he said, for the informal 'Dee' was used solely in the garden, "must choose a woman soon, but I do not envy him the decision and he does not seem to have any great preference for one lady over another."

"He keeps his heart encased," replied Pedan. "He must. The situation is complicated enough without a love affair intruding."

"The hot money is on Bordilen's daughter, but I have not bet."

Jonal put on a virtuous expression which did not deceive his companion for a moment.

"You would lose your stake if you did, I think. That family is powerful already and even some of their supporters would not want to see their daughter in the palace."

Pedan paused and contemplated the political situation for a moment before asking with a grin, "And where have you put your money?"

Jonal laughed. "In truth, I have not bet. The Prince is my friend, and though I would happily back him in a horse race, I do not much care to bet on such an important matter. Nor," he said with a sigh, "do I know where to put my money.

"He must find a Westlander, for no foreign lady of quality will consent to being sent home if she does not have a child with him, and there are many young females here who would sympathise; they are not happy with idea of being Chosen either.

"Poor man! If he chooses a northerner, those in the south will be unhappy for the last three Chosen Women were from the north; and most of the eligible ladies of the southern and midland areas are from families who are known to be allied to, or positive enemies of, Lord Bordilen. Mountain girls are not sufficiently high-ranking; nor, I suspect, would they cope with our complicated society."

"The Princess Kaiealestria was mountain," noted Pedan, "and she coped; in fact she did more than cope – she changed things."

"That was years ago, and she was exceptional. She was also an Elander."

Jonal considered his own words. "I suppose, the Prince *could* approach Eland," he continued. "The Princess Andrela is a well-favoured young lady according to photographs and relays, and she is reputed to be –" He hesitated. The Princess Andrela was difficult to describe, impossible to categorize. He decided that 'outgoing' would come close enough and settled for that.

Pedan laughed. "How unlike you to be so tactful, Jonal," he answered. "From what I have heard, depending on the speaker, the Princess is wild or very lively; tactless or inclined to be forthright and unmanageable or independent minded. All consider her to be heedless of her reputation and some even call her promiscuous. Whatever she is, I do not think that she, or Eland, would accept the position of Chosen Woman, and Westland will not change for such a one."

"No. I agree on that. The Assembly is bound to its traditions. You are one of the young and forward-thinking members, but you do not like change; or lively girls. The Princess is fond of sport and has a great many friends, but I doubt that she is promiscuous."

Pedan objected. "I did not say that she is. It is hardly possible to obtain firm evidence of that, but you must own that she shows no respect for convention. It would not matter if she were not a Princess, but she is, and in my view ought to realise that she is always in the public eye. Skimpy swimming suits are not appropriate."

"They are not seen here, that is true, but Eland allows women to swim in public, and she does have a wonderful figure. I suspect that she was teasing the photographers who follow her everywhere. When she emerged from her supposedly naked swim, she was swathed in enough towelling to satisfy the strictest dowager in Westland; even her head was wrapped. They will lose interest eventually and she will change."

"She may settle down in time, it is true, but meanwhile our good Princess Indola has long since abandoned any plans she had for encouraging a match between east and west."

"Did she have such plans?" asked Jonal in surprise.

"I believe so," answered Pedan and regarded the younger man kindly. Esquire Tesher had travelled far more widely than most of Westland's aristocracy, including himself and Prince Darmon, and he knew trade, but politically Pedan considered him naïve.

"She was supported by Prince Maldon, but their enthusiasm wavered around sixteen years ago when Prince Fidel was born. You may not remember."

"Ahh!" said Jonal, understanding completely. "No, I do not remember. At that time I was far more interested in the ships that sailed the north seas and called in at New Stannul. I am still of the opinion that it is trade that is important. Rulers come and go, but for most people what they grow or make and sell determines their prosperity and their future. Those in charge who help them are admired, those who do not are regarded with contempt; and if they can avoid it, they see no good reason why they should pay taxes."

Pedan frowned. "It is not right to avoid paying tax. Even an unpopular ruler must organise the large scale projects: defence, the maintenance of law, support of hospitals and roads and just now the new rail tracks."

"The new rail tracks will benefit the people of Kaldor, Ostara and Blau and perhaps the mountain folk if they ever reach that far. It is of little interest to those who will see them only on the relay; as they see the grandeur of our High Prince and his Princess and the noble Lords who gather for Assembly."

He spoke lightly, and his smile softened the harshness of the words. "You should travel more. So too should Prince Darmon, but I dare not suggest it. We do not talk of politics often. It is banned in the garden and best not discussed too frequently amongst friends. It can destroy friendship and it almost always ruins conviviality!"

"Nothing affects your conviviality, Jonal," Pedan replied warmly and with no trace of the envy that he felt for his friend's joy in living, "not even unrequited love; and that is fortunate, for I see Lady Vealla approaching, and she does not seem pleased."

"Shades! I had forgotten!"

Exactly what he had forgotten was left unsaid, for Lady Vealla quickened her steps and greeted them boldly when she was still too far away for easy conversation.

"Lord Pandour, how very pleasant to see you!"

She lowered her voice as she came nearer, but continued without pause. "Unexpected too; whereas I *was* expecting to see Esquire Tesher, some half an hour past, at Raikes Coffee House."

Lord Pandour returned her greeting coolly, but with exquisite politeness, and waited. He was curious to know how his friend, whose popularity with young ladies was legendary, would excuse himself. He was not disappointed.

13

"How very elegant you look," declared Jonal, and he surveyed the lady with great care and obvious admiration. "We were in the palace gardens, but it was Prince Darmon who delayed us. The gardens could not, for though they are full of beautiful blossoms, none are as lovely as you."

"You pay extravagant compliments, Mr Tesher, but I am not sure that I believe you," replied the lady. "Nor am I ready, on an instant, to forgive your tardiness, but I will allow you to walk me around the square." She held out her arm.

Lord Pandour bade them both a cool farewell and walked away. Mr Tesher took the proffered hand, but before he could embark upon his chosen topic of conversation, she spoke.

"Lord Pandour does not approve of me. Do you think that my skirt is too short for his sense of propriety?"

"If it is, he will be shocked by every fashionable young lady, for your skirt is at precisely the length decreed in the latest edition of 'Dress' and reveals a delightful pair of ankles, as intended."

She teased him on his choice of reading and they began by discussing fashion as they strolled around the great square. That topic was soon supplanted by an exchange of the latest gossip. Both were too young to know much of the current suspected infidelities amongst their parents' generation, but they were well informed of the current courtships and whether or not they might result in marriage.

They had almost completed a circuit of the square when Lady Vealla sighed. Mr Tesher noticed at once.

"What troubles you?" he asked, "Surely not the probable disappointment of Mr Wensham?"

She shook her head. "It is my own problems that trouble me – on occasions."

"And they are?"

There was a long silence. Lady Vealla was not given to serious conversation, or indeed to serious thought, but she had recently celebrated her twenty-second birthday and her parents were pressing her. She did not have a special friend in whom to confide. Indeed, she did not trust any of her female acquaintance to keep a private comment to themselves. Men, and her present companion in particular, were different.

"My mother wishes me to marry; and in the near future. She thinks me frivolous and wishes me to 'settle'." The word was pronounced with great contempt.

"It is not an unusual desire for mothers," observed Mr Tesher mildly.

"No," agreed the lady with an impatient sigh, "but she and my father are talking of 'making approaches', as if *I* had no opinion in the matter at all! They have made a list of suitable gentlemen!"

Her indignation was evident and he hid his laughter.

"You have seen it?" he queried.

"Yes. It was offered; and my comments were invited."

She sighed again, regretfully. "I believe that *they* felt that that was considerate, but I did not agree. I am afraid that I was not polite, either to them or in my expressed opinions of the gentlemen. The list was headed by Lord Pandour."

"Namier's blessings upon your parents, my Lady!" he answered. "They are very foolish. They ought not to have shown you a list, nor placed Lord Pandour at its head. Ped will not marry you, no matter what incentive is offered. He does not seek greater power or wealth. He is contented and will marry only if he falls desperately in love with an unmarried female who returns his affection. If he has the misfortune to become fond of a married one, he will remain faithful – and unwed."

Lady Vealla did not answer immediately and when she did, she preceded her words with an uncertain laugh.

"Do you always call Lord Pandour 'Ped'? It does not suit him. 'Pedan' is perfect for such a rigid and disapproving man."

"No, I do not. Not always." Mr Tesher was annoyed with himself for the slip. "We use shortened names in private. In company we are formal; but you are wrong about his character. He is not rigid, though he is precise, and I do not think that he disapproves of *you*. He thinks it foolish of *me* to keep your company so often, but that is because he fears that I am becoming enamoured of you, and he knows, as I do, that you will not marry a mere Esquire."

This time the laugh that preceded her words was genuine and affectionate.

"Oh, my dear Mr Tesher, you are not a 'mere' Esquire; you are a sophisticated, well-travelled, amusing and utterly delightful man; and you dance well. You are not on my parents' list, but I would marry you regardless of that, if I loved you. I like you more than any other man whom I have met, but I do not think that I love you – or that you love me."

She sounded regretful.

"No," he agreed happily. "Our friendship is not complicated by such emotions. We will remain friends, I trust, for many years. Sometimes one needs friends."

"Yes." She replied without hesitation. One did need friends.

As daughter of Lord Marishen her position in Kaldor society was assured. She knew all the aristocracy, rich and poor and those wealthy families who hung around the edges, hoping for advantageous marriages. She had taken their acquaintance for granted, but whom did she count as friend?

"I must go," she said suddenly. "Lady Senegar has passed by twice in her carriage and will have noticed us on both occasions. I do not know what scandal she can create about our walking together in High Square, but she is very inventive."

"And talkative," observed Mr Tesher. "Best that I take my leave at once. I shall see you at Jared Freckland's party if you honour his coming of age with your presence. The *food* will be excellent."

He bowed politely and walked away before she had time to laugh at his comment. The Frecklands were impossibly rich and notoriously vulgar, but the food *would* be excellent. If she wished to attend, however, she must find a chaperone or at the least a companion. Her mother would not go and she was not bold enough to arrive alone.

She sighed at the restrictions that society placed on young single women. Mr Tesher would be at Freckland House and most likely she would not; but he was her friend.

He would be a good friend, she thought, and probably a permanent one. She found that comforting.

Chapter 2

Prince Fidel glanced at the splendid clock that graced the mantle-shelf in what was officially named his study. His term for it varied, the most flattering being 'school-room', the worst 'dungeon', but he did not use the latter in his sister's hearing. She was, on occasions, annoyingly precise and had pointed out, more than once, that no dungeon worthy of the name had a view.

He sneaked a quick look through the window, but little more than the tops of trees were visible from his desk. To see the gardens, the river, the spreading city, the towers and the castle ruins on the far bank, one must stand or sit closer to the glass. It lacked three minutes to the hour, so he bent his head again and dutifully continued writing.

He was a quiet young man and did not rebel against his elders though he frequently found them dull and their demands tiresome.

He wrote, 'The great ring with the oblong ruby is worn only when a new Lord is granted his title and lands. The last Lordship created was that of Handrell. No Crown land was given, but several of the mountain valleys had gathered under one leader and he was granted the title of Lord in place of the traditional title of Theale. For the first time, a mountain man was able to attend Council'.

Fidel put his pen down carefully in its stand and stood up as the clock began its chime.

"You may go," allowed the elderly gentleman who had apparently been asleep. "If you have recorded all that you learnt this morning, we shall not need to study the Ceremonial Jewellery again."

Fidel bowed in reply and left swiftly. He had not quite finished, but the final item, an ornate gold brooch set with a large cabochon ruby, was so famous that everyone in Eland had seen pictures of it and knew its history. It had been given by King Cendara to his son when that Prince had married Lord Parandour's granddaughter and Eland became a Princedom. Few had seen it for it was worn only at coronation ceremonies.

Lord Geraish rose and picked up Fidel's script. He saw at once that it was incomplete, but made no attempt to call the young man back. He considered that Fidel was a good conscientious boy, respectful and steady; not at all like his sister. The elderly lord had not yet decided whether or not those qualities would make him a good ruler. The Lordship of Geraish was an ancient one and some of his ancestors were considered strong and some weak. Much depended upon what had happened during their time.

Fidel sped down the stairs. He was hungry, but the morning had been devoted to study with no chance for exercise other than walking slowly beside his instructor. There was time for a swim before lunch.

The palace pool had been completely rebuilt for his grandmother, an imperious woman who believed that swimming was essential to good health, but did not feel it appropriate that a Princess should appear in public in a bathing dress. It was now longer, wider and boasted heated water. Broad steps allowed for an easy descent into the shallow end and a glazed roof admitted daylight, but retained privacy. The many cubicles were fitted with cupboards, seats, showers and hot air driers for those who disliked towels.

Fidel scarcely noticed the water. He went straight to his own cubicle, fastened the door against the cleaners, who came at most inconvenient times, and was pulling on his costume when he remembered the splashing at the far end of the pool.

He emerged cautiously. His parents were not keen swimmers, but they did occasionally indulge in 'paddling about' as he termed it. Either would disturb his swim by asking questions about his morning.

He breathed a sigh of relief when he saw the head in the water. Long hair floated out behind it. Father did not have long hair, in fact he had very little hair at all, and Mother always wore a frilly cap when she swam. It was Andrela.

He dived into the water and swam towards her.

"Race you to the far end," he shouted, and, disregarding the fact that she was swimming in the opposite direction, he started immediately.

His advantage was insufficient. One hand touched his as he reached for the wall and with the other she pushed his head firmly beneath the water. He was gasping for breath before she allowed him to surface.

"That will teach you manners," she said with a grin, "A gentleman ought to give a lady the advantage, not try to sneak a lead for himself."

"Hadron's Shades, Drey, you almost drowned me!" protested Fidel when he was able to speak. "Besides, you are my sister. I do not count you as a lady and I need every advantage I can get when I race with you. I cannot understand how you get through the water so fast without seeming to try."

"I won't drown you, Fid. You know that. If I did, I would be Heir to the Throne and be obliged to learn about Ceremonials and attend Council Meetings."

"And you would be executed for high treason if anyone found out," he noted and returned her grin.

"I might well prefer that to viewing the Royal treasures in the company of some doddery old Lord," she retorted and swam away in a leisurely manner.

He did not challenge her again, but covered the ten lengths that he had planned to do at his own pace. She was still in the water so he did not speak to her again until he had showered and dressed in readiness for the mid-day meal.

She was walking towards her own cubicle, but she turned when she heard his step.

"Don't mention that you have seen me," she said. "I returned last evening and have seen Father, but he believes that I am locked in my room. He and mother would be disturbed if they knew I can get out."

"Do you still have the key?" he asked. "It is years since you have been in such trouble that you were locked in."

She grinned so wickedly that he wondered about the key to the schoolroom, the round house in the garden and the old dungeon in the cellars, where once His Highness had threatened to confine her.

"It pays to be prepared," she said gaily, and he wondered no longer.

"I cannot imagine why you did not stay in the mountains for a few more days. You must have known what an upset you had caused. Is that the costume that made its appearance in all the news sheets? It looked blue in the pictures."

"No. Sadly the blue one was confiscated, but I bought this in turquoise and another in crimson, and I was kindly given a fourth in black and white for promising to wear one in public. I gave them good value, don't you think? It was in nearly every news sheet.

"And I returned from the mountains because it is Grizzie's party tonight and I would not miss that for all Erion."

She walked away as she spoke and an appalled Fidel found himself addressing the door of her cubicle.

"You cannot go to that party! It's an important event and has been on the calendar for months! Everyone will be there, including the parents! The place will be awash with news men and photographers!"

"You have forgotten that it is fancy dress. I have a splendid costume and will fool the photographers again! No one will recognise me. I will be able to flirt outrageously with anyone I choose and talk scandal about myself, which will be great fun."

The noise of the shower drowned some of her final words, but Fidel had heard enough to sink his spirits. His sister was irrepressible. She was also clever, but he was not as confident as she appeared to be in her ability to pass unrecognised. He considered what possible fancy dress would ensure anonymity and dismissed them all.

A Shade of Hadron costume would cover the face, but would not allow flirtation; a Witch outfit would disguise, but not show off his sister's undoubted attractions. She would not like that. There would be Flowers of Krundel by the dozen – girls in green dresses with flowers in their hair – and there was a degree of safety in numbers, but he could not imagine a flower headdress that disguised the features.

His own costume was of a character from a classical play staged recently at one of Bosron's theatres, but a careful consideration of the well-known female characters in current and classical plays did not supply an answer. None appeared in clothes that hid their faces and Andrela's face was eminently recognisable, especially to her parents.

Fidel was subdued at table and ate sparingly. His father did not notice. Prince Roddori was occupied with his own thoughts, unpleasant thoughts about what to do with his daughter, but his mother did. The Princess Margren was ever conscious of her son's health. She had been disappointed that her first child had been a girl and had waited several anxious years before she conceived again. Fidel had been a sickly babe, but he had survived and was a much easier child to rear than her rebellious daughter.

She regarded him tenderly and was partially correct in her assessment of what troubled him.

"Do not fret about tonight, or about your sister," she reassured him. "It is your first appearance at a large ball, but we will not stay long and Andrela is, and will remain, safe in the palace. Do not fear that you will have to make excuses for her. There will no doubt be many commoners present, for Lord Campenden allows tickets to be sold anywhere in the interests of his charity, but *we* will not encounter them. None whom *we* meet will be so ill-mannered as to comment upon her latest indiscretion."

"I trust not," replied Fidel meekly, "but does not Andrela wish to attend the ball? I saw her calendar months ago with the date marked and 'Grizzie's party' written by it."

"Andrela's wishes are not, at the present moment, being considered," the Princess's voice was severe, "and though *she* may refer to Lady Annia by that ridiculous nickname, it is not proper for *you* to do so. They met when Lady Annia was still Miss Grishley, before her father had succeeded to his title and become Lord Campenden, and **That School,** which your father permitted her to attend, allowed the children to address one another by nicknames."

"How dreadful," murmured Fidel, which was his stock answer to his mother when she spoke disparagingly of something with great emphasis.

She looked at him sharply and he realised that it had not had its usual soothing effect, but he had no need to find another. His father spoke.

"The school was a great improvement on the governess whom you employed, Margren. I think it a pity that you did not encourage Andrela to attend university. She might then have occupied her brain with learning rather than devising schemes to shock and to deceive."

There was silence. Only Andrela replied or retorted when Prince Roddori spoke in that particular tone, and she, thought Fidel, would have returned to her room to ensure that whoever brought her food found her there as expected, but she would have left again as soon she was able, and might now be anywhere in Bosron.

He was right and wrong. Andrela had returned to her room and had left it again, but she was not 'anywhere in Bosron'. Dressed in a maid's uniform, purloined long ago from a linen basket, she had left the palace through one of the garden gates, hired an electric car and was driving, somewhat erratically, towards Measham.

She began to hum when she passed the city boundary and reached the countryside. Her 'escape' had been easy. As a child, she had enjoyed history and her father had allowed her to read anything, however ancient, in the palace library. Somewhere she had read of Kaiealestria's opinion of the palace security and she had tested it. Much had been updated, and she could not find her way into every room, but some of the old keys that she discovered opened, and closed, several locks. One such opened the old garden gate that led into the park. Shrubs now covered the gate on both sides and she had only come across it when playing hide-and-seek with some friends. She had kept it secret even from Grizzie and used it rarely. It was too precious to risk using often.

It was only the second time that she had hired a car and she had returned to the same place, but it was manned by different people and she saw no sign of recognition in their faces. It was surprising how few people noticed her when she was alone and dressed in ordinary clothes.

They would notice tonight, she thought. She would be dressed in extraordinary clothes, but she was confident that she would not be recognised. She gave a bounce of excitement and almost missed her route.

She was not going to Measham. That town was far too busy to risk visiting, but there was an excellent dressmaker in a village only a league or two from the main road. She worked from home because she had bad legs, she did not charge extortionate prices and she did not gossip. The disadvantage was that the village was not served by a good road. It was little more than a cart track, but carts were difficult to hire and were open to the air and to the view of passers-by.

Andrela was concentrating on avoiding a large pot-hole on one side of the track when a large bird swooped down to seize some poor rodent hiding ineffectually in the undergrowth by the hedge. The bird flew safely away with its prey, but Andrela had been startled. She swerved sharply and the front wheel bounced into the hole. The car tilted alarmingly and came to an abrupt stop. Her head hit the front window and the steering wheel bruised her ribs.

She was not seriously hurt, but it was several minutes before she was ready to drive again. The engine started easily enough, but the car did not move forward steadily. It lurched, made an unpleasant noise and settled back into its previous position. She took a deep breath and scrambled out of her seat to survey the scene.

It was not good and she expended more breath than was advisable on expressing her anger.

"It is useless to swear," she told herself firmly after a while, "or to cry," and she brushed away the drops that had gathered in her eyes. "There is no help to be found nearby, so you must walk, or you must push."

She could not decide in which direction to walk, so she tried pushing. First she tried with one hand on the steering wheel, later she pushed from the back, hoping simply to jerk the car out of the hole, but she achieved no more than a torn skirt and soiled hands.

"You appear to have a problem," observed a laconic voice as she picked herself up from her latest stumble.

She turned. The speaker was a man, a well-dressed man with polished boots seated upon a fine horse. She was annoyed that her exertions had prevented her from hearing his approach, but she found herself hoping that he had not heard her last exasperated exclamation.

He edged his horse around her and stared at car.

"You waste your effort trying to move that," he stated. "I might succeed, but it would do no good. The axle is bent or broken. The car must be lifted and the axle repaired before it can be driven again."

He turned his penetrating gaze upon her.

"Are you hurt?" he asked and when she shook her head, he questioned further. Where was she going? And was it to her home?

She explained that she was on her way to collect a dress for her mistress. It was needed for tonight, for a fancy dress ball in Bosron.

"Your mistress will have to find some other costume, for that car will not be repaired in a hurry. It is better *not* to drive into deep holes, or indeed to drive at all along a track such as this."

"I do not need to be told that!" retorted Andrela. "I was proceeding very carefully, but a bird distracted me."

He started to answer, but she anticipated him. "And do not tell me that I ought not to have been watching birds! It was a bird of prey, a large one, bigger than a hawk, and it swooped down just in front of me. If all you are able to do, sir, is to make foolish remarks, you had best ride on, and I shall seek other help."

He laughed at her indignation, but it was gentle laugh.

"No, I shall not abandon you. This is not a well frequented track and I am travelling to Morehallangard. Are you happy to ride with me?"

She was not, but she needed help. He was right about the lack of traffic and she knew of no habitation until the village was reached, so she nodded.

He dismounted, tossed her onto the horse's neck without ceremony and pulled himself up into the saddle to sit behind her.

"This is not comfortable, but it will get you to the dressmakers. Do you know if there is someone in the village capable of repairing your car?"

"There may be," she answered cautiously, "but there is no charging station. I know only the dressmaker. She keeps an oil lamp by her, and candles, because the electricity supply is not entirely reliable in bad weather. It is a small village – but you will know that."

"I know it as little as you do. I am going on business, but it may not be worth the effort. I might have guessed. In Eland, the tiniest villages boast the longest names."

"Are you not from Eland, sir? You have an accent, but I cannot place it."

"I am from Shyran," he answered, and they talked of that island until he set her down where she requested.

"Half-an-hour?" he queried and promised to return to collect her after that time.

The dress was as daring and as concealing as she had hoped. She thanked the provider profusely and willingly paid the bill, but she did wonder, as she prepared to leave, how she was to return to Bosron.

The gentleman, however, was true to his word and she saw him approaching as she stepped out of the front door.

"You are on time," he remarked, "how very unusual for a woman at her dressmakers."

"My mistress's dressmaker," she corrected, and he said, "Ah, yes," and smiled.

"No one in the village can repair the car, but I have arranged for a farmer to pick it up in his cart and return it to the hire company."

"But he will not know –," she began and he smiled again in that superior way he had and informed her that the name and address of the company was displayed, albeit discreetly, on the rear of the car.

"You, however, if you wish to return to Bosron in good time for the ball tonight, will be obliged to travel with me on my horse. I regret that I could not find another mount."

She suspected that he had not tried very hard, but she could not criticise. He had come, so far satisfactorily, to her aid. She duly thanked him, handed him her precious parcel and walked a few paces to a large milestone. By stepping on to its flat top, she was able to mount his horse with more dignity.

The journey back to Bosron was uneventful. The Measham road was busy, but he rode along bridle paths which avoided traffic and supposedly were shorter. Certainly, they arrived in Bosron earlier than she expected. She was duly grateful.

"Where is this ball tonight?" he asked as he set her down a short distance from the park. "And what is the costume we have brought? I would like to see your mistress and the other guests arrive."

"The ball is not in Bosron. It is in the Great Hall near Senby."

"And the costume?"

"I cannot tell you that. All the ladies, and I believe many of the gentlemen, prefer to keep that secret."

He expressed his disappointment and she took pity on him. He had been helpful.

"If you tell me your name and where you are staying, I might be able to send you a ticket."

He laughed. "I would not be allowed in even with a ticket. I am a man of business not one of the nobility."

"Everyone with a ticket is allowed in. It is fancy dress and faces are hidden. There will be many there who would not normally be invited to society parties. They usually come as Shades of Hadron or ghosts, for those are easily made costumes and conceal identity very well."

She gave a mischievous smile and added, "I might even be there myself."

"You tempt me to try," he responded. He produced a card from his pocket and handed it to her. "I am staying at the Westgate Hotel in Black Street, but you now have the advantage of me. I do not know your name."

'Caston Ambril' she read, 'Import and Export'. The address in Shyran was given also, but it meant nothing to her for she had never been to Shyran.

"My name is Margren," she said and hurried away without a backward glance.

Chapter 3

Fidel was worried. He loved his sister and he admired her many talents, but he did wish that she would not involve him in her schemes. The letter in his hand was from her, marked 'PRIVATE' in her own distinctive capitals. It was as well that he had found it, rather than his valet. Venth was a good man, but had he recognised the hand, he might easily have considered it his duty to take the note to father.

"That", thought Fidel, "would almost certainly have caused a problem."

He slit the envelope and sighed with relief. It would have caused a problem had it been handed to Prince Roddori, but it did not ask the impossible. He did have his invitation, it was to hand and Andrela had enclosed an addressed envelope in which to put it. She had also enclosed an accompanying note to someone by the name of Caston Ambril.

That was not labelled private, but he did not unfold it. Andrela trusted him. Long ago, she had asked him to keep silent about some matter and he had stared at her in surprise. She had smiled, clapped him approvingly on the shoulder and had never asked again.

A few minutes' thought and he found a way of obliging her without lies; a little deception maybe, but not a lie.

"I met with Benel and some others this afternoon," he told Venth truthfully. "Someone needs an invitation for tonight. I do not know the 'someone', but I do have an invitation," and he waved it. "*I* will not be in disguise and will be with my parents. I doubt that Their Royal Highnesses will be asked to produce their invitations in order to be admitted."

His valet smiled at the pleasantry and promised to have the letter delivered by hand and at once.

Thus Caston Ambril received his invitation and a note (signed Margren) from Andrela.

He pondered, tapping the invitation against his thumb for some time. The ball was unimportant, but the lady? He was uncertain about the lady and felt that this decision could be momentous.

He compromised. If he were able to hire a suitable costume, he would go; if not, he would forget those sparkling eyes and spend some of his profit on a splendid meal.

His tentative queries were met with enthusiasm. If Sir had an invitation for the ball tonight, he should go. A coach might be hired, but there were plenty of public coaches to take the revellers to the Great Hall just this side of Senby. People went in costume, but there were places in the Hall where folk could change their clothes, either before or after the ball.

They would happy to find a costume for him. At this late stage it might be expensive to find something other than a black cloak and mask, but it would be worth it. The lower classes of society, he learnt, were invariably dressed as Shades or Spirits and should be avoided. The older members of the aristocracy were easily recognised, and those 'in between', so to speak, were interesting, enterprising, or out for fun.

The implication was plain; a well-disguised gentleman might find amusement, advantage or various types of fun – whatever took his fancy.

Mr Ambril desired the helpful receptionist to find him a suitable costume and it was duly found.

Fidel was disappointed with the start of his evening. The costumes were conventional; expensive probably, flattering in some few cases and exciting in none. He did not discern any women in exciting or 'adaptable' dress even among those outside the 'quiet' area, where he was expected to stay. He recalled the costumes that Andrela had shown him before the last two balls. They had had pieces that could be removed later in the evening to add more interest.

She had told him to look for such items when he attended his first fancy dress party, but he saw nothing. He felt middle-aged and unsophisticated at the same time. It was a dull start.

Having stood up with several suitable young ladies for a few dances, he was sitting nursing a glass of wine, when a remark from one of the stricter matrons caught his attention.

"Lord Campenden," she noted, "ought to monitor his ball more closely. A ban on public coaches would certainly improve matters!"

Fidel glanced at the new influx of revellers. Shades and spirits abounded, but were worth a closer look. He sipped his wine carefully, hoping that the action would disguise his interest.

One spirit costume was so flimsy that the frills and lace on the wearer's underwear were visible; another, more subtle, was almost worthy of Andrela. A Shade with a spangled mask caught his eye, and one with huge sleeves that did not quite hide the tightly fitting gown beneath the over garment.

"Detachable!" thought Fidel, and instantly felt happier.

The next arrivals were equally interesting and more inventive. There was a wrestler whose heavily muscled chest was inadequately concealed by his cloak, a Wild Man of Coron plentifully covered in hair, but very little else, a mountain girl with paper fish and strings of coloured stones adorning her scanty clothing and a woman dressed as the Third Temptation of Namier.

She wore a mask in the shape of two 3 s, and was draped in transparent fabric of palest grey, embroidered so cleverly with Temptation 3 in a variety of scripts that it was difficult to see what, if anything, she was wearing beneath her garment. It was certainly a splendid costume, but it was very revealing. It could be Andrela, but he rather hoped that it was not.

Almost all the later arrivals were dressed dramatically. They had waited, intending to make an entrance. Fidel watched in delight as the expensively clad historical characters vied for attention with the more daring costumes.

"Namier's moons!" exclaimed one of the well-bred young girls seated nearby. She blushed richly and swiftly denied swearing. It was the costume. It represented the thousand crescent moons that Namier had sliced from Erion's moon when it had been covered in cloud.

The girl protested that it must be a 'good' costume for Namier had vanquished the evil things of Hadron with his curved weapons, but Fidel hardly heard.

Whether it was a good or an evil costume, it was certainly fascinating. Swathes of white muslin drifted over the golden moons that hung in profusion from the deep blue undergarment. More moons and muslin fell from the headdress and concealed the face and hair so well that a mask would have been superfluous.

Impressed, Fidel added it to his 'maybe' list.

His list changed as the evening progressed. A showgirl and Third Temptation were removed for their wild dancing, but were re-instated when others were eliminated for worse behaviour. He recalled that his sister had almost rejoiced in her supposed confinement, and he worried. Their parents believed that she was safe at the palace, and she was convinced that no one would recognise her.

She was right about that. He had seen through Lady Annia's fetching mask, Lord Kalver's helmeted warrior and Mr Delton's foolish clown, but he was not at all sure of his sister. He took no credit for recognising Lord Collingwade – he was half a head taller than most other men – but he did take comfort in that gentleman's presence. Colly looked after people. He was no more than two years older than Andrela, but he would take care of her.

The High Prince and Princess left a little before eleven and Fidel was obliged go with them. He took a last long look around the room before he followed.

Namier's Moons was standing with a man. She had been standing or dancing with the same man for almost the entire evening, and Fidel had concluded that she was not Andrela. His sister liked variety. She would, however, appreciate the costume.

The man was dressed as Prince Atture II, more commonly known as the Peacock Prince. He had an accent. Fidel had heard him speak as they passed on the dance floor.

It was a superb outfit, copied from a portrait, and Fidel was sure that it was exact in every detail, the only addition being the elegant mask; but it was a strange choice for a foreigner, he thought idly as he made his way out. Perhaps it had been hired at the last minute. If so, ticket and costume must have cost a considerable sum.

Perhaps Namier's Moons was worth it, he mused and almost bumped into Lord Collingwade. That gentleman bowed low in apology and said in an undertone, "I will take care of your sister if she is here."

Fidel was reassured. Colly was not a great Lord; his Command was no bigger than many an estate and certainly would never merit a place on Council, but he was.

Fidel thought of many words that described the virtues of the young lord, but he settled on 'reliable' as a summary. Andrela would be safe with him, and she liked him. In fact, he wondered that she did not marry him. She would not care that his Command was so small that some laughed at his title.

Pondering on this topic, he forgot all about the man with the strange accent who was dressed as the Peacock Prince.

Chapter 4

Caston, having been given his ticket, had hesitated only a second before agreeing to pay the exorbitant price for the hire of his costume and, when he donned it, the fear that he had been overcharged receded. It was well made, of good fabric, and it fitted. Several sizes of the elaborate buckled shoes were also brought for him to try.

"Part of our service," said the man. "The shoes are part of the costume and no one is able to enjoy themselves if their feet hurt."

Caston agreed wholeheartedly, made his choice and gave the man a generous tip.

He attracted several admiring glances both on his way to the Great Hall and as he stood outside to watch the guests as they entered. He had come early. He did not want to miss the arrival of the intriguing 'maid' who had sent his ticket.

As Fidel had done, he noted those with interesting costumes, for it was surely a special outfit that had caused such secrecy. He also sought for bright eyes, grey-green he thought them, but could not remember exactly.

He spoke to more than half a dozen and danced with three before he approached the lady of the moons. He could not see her eyes, but he knew at once that this was his 'maid'.

They danced and danced again. Whilst they rested, she was approached by another. He made no objection. He smiled and told her gently that he would wait; she might return if she chose to do so. She did so choose.

After eleven, when the High Prince and most of the older nobility had left, the party became much more informal. Some abandoned their masks, capes that had hidden bare torsos were discarded and various bits of drapery were removed from many of the ladies' costumes. The musicians played with greater verve and at a greater volume.

Refreshments were still available, but they were more substantial, less sophisticated and were not free. Indeed, the better offerings were decidedly expensive. Caston was glad that he had filled his purse. He did not care for cheap wine or heavy pastries.

Neither, he discovered, did the lady. She agreed that she was hungry and filled her plate with delicacies. She chose the finest sparkling wine available and she did not offer to pay. She did, however, thank him very prettily.

She also managed to eat and drink without removing the veil that covered the lower part of her face.

Andrela did not want to be recognised by anyone. If that happened, she would have to leave and she was enjoying the company of this man from Shyran. She hoped to watch the sunrise with him.

Only once before had she walked to the beach and that had been with a group of young aristocrats. They had been accompanied by several bodyguards to ensure that no harm befell them. She would not miss that protection; she did not feel that any harm would befall her in the company of Caston Ambril.

She was right. In the early hours of the morning when the dance floor was sparsely populated, she indicated a couple in a close embrace.

"I do not do that," she said, "but I would like to watch the sunrise with you."

"I will be delighted to accompany you," he replied, "and I will keep whatever distance you desire."

Later, standing on the beach in the flickering light of old-fashioned fire torches, the distance between them was greater than she desired, though it was a trifle less than strict protocol demanded.

The night air was cool and she shivered. He noticed at once and took off his short cloak to put around her shoulders. Their hands touched as he helped her to fasten the clip.

"Your hand is cold," he said and rubbed it gently.

Somehow it remained clasped in his as they waited for first light.

As a spectacle, the sunrise was disappointing. The sea mist persisted. It blotted out the rising of the orange orb and dampened the sound of the waves. No red lined the horizon, no golden path led east across the bay and the brightest lights were those that shone softly along the shore.

Caston asked what they were, as he thought that the Bellue peninsular was almost uninhabited.

"There are some who still live in Bellue," she answered, "but they do not have electricity. Those lights are from the hotels near Senby. There were six or seven at one time when it was fashionable to stay and watch the sunrise from there. Now people go to Corbay and there are fewer here. One has a terrace where guests can sit, but the best rooms have balconies so that sunrise may be seen without the effort of rising early, or of staying up late."

He could not see her face, but her voice was full of laughter.

"I have not found staying up a great effort tonight," he replied, squeezing her fingers gently, "though I have seen more colourful dawns."

She asked whether Shyran had resorts dedicated to watching the rising sun.

"Ah no. Shyran is long and thin and has a very short eastern coast. The western end is broader, however, and boasts a port with an hotel. From there one may see the sunset without any effort whatsoever."

She laughed, and they talked of Shyran; its Lord, its people, its scenery and its famous rugs.

A watery sun finally appeared and they realised that the crowd on the beach had all but disappeared. It was time to go.

He wanted to see her safely home, whether on foot or in the public coach, but Lord Collingwade appeared and offered a place in his coach.

Andrela accepted.

"It is best," she said to Caston. "It has been a delightful evening and I do not distrust you, but Colly knows me and knows Bosron. He will take good care of me."

"I know most of Bosron," he answered, "but I do not know you and perhaps not the area where you live. I stay always at the same hotel."

He bowed and relinquished her to the tall young man she had called Colly. There had been no introductions. He had no idea who the man was and no idea of her true identity. For him, she was Margren. It was not an uncommon name in Eland though it had originated in Shyran. It meant 'The Wanted One'.

He made his way slowly back to the public coach.

Lord Collingwade guided Andrela to his private coach, a plain vehicle, waiting unobtrusively by the Great Hall. There she collected her holdall from its hiding place.

"Sensible clothes," she explained to her companion.

"I shall ride with the coachman," he told her. "There are already four passengers, but there will be room for you to sit in comfort."

There was, and she took her place beside a middle-aged man whom she did not recognise, opposite Lord Brey's son and his twin sister. The girl was silent, but tears were running unchecked down her cheeks.

An anxious question from their rescuer prompted a disclaimer from the boy.

"Not ill," he said carefully. "Losht her bag."

Lord Collingwade produced a bundle, a spirit costume from the colour, and unwound it. Within its folds lay a white evening bag.

The tears ceased and a hand stretched out to take it.

"Oh! Thank you," exclaimed the girl. "You are *so* kind."

"You had left it on the beach."

He placed the bundle on her lap, bowed and closed the carriage door. Andrela thought he sounded bored and wondered, as she had wondered often before, why he took so much trouble to look after those who had not made adequate arrangements.

The twins were very young and silly, but the older girl sitting next to them ought to have been more careful. She was high on some drug or other and was singing softly to herself completely oblivious of her surroundings.

Andrela glanced at the man beside her. He, she thought, would not have been unduly concerned about his picture in the news sheets; nor would the photographers have chased him.

He noticed the turn of her head.

"I twisted my ankle," he explained. "I was not even dancing; I tripped over a step. Very uninteresting, but unfortunately very painful. I had planned to return on the public coaches, but I could not make my way to or from any of their stops. The gentleman, whom I have never met before, noticed my problem and offered to take me to my home. He is indeed very kind."

She agreed softly and did not speak again. Voices were recognisable. She was known to all three who were sitting opposite to her, and she could not rely upon any of them to be discreet. She was glad that Colly bade her alight at the first stop.

"Walk into Sun Crescent," he advised. "If any of my other passengers notice they will think that you live there. Cross to the square only when we are out of sight."

She did exactly that, though she considered it an unnecessary precaution. It was not unusual for those returning in the early morning to pay a visit to the conveniences in the square. The public coaches stopped there for that very reason.

Colly had timed their arrival exactly. They were between coaches and the square was deserted. She slipped in unobserved and changed into clothes more suitable for a safe return to the palace. She also needed to concentrate and she did not think again of her evening until she was lying in her own bed.

She did not sleep for some time. Every detail of the past hours must be committed to memory. She would not meet Caston again. He could not contact her, and she ought not to contact him, though he had said that he always used the same hotel.

As she was drifting into sleep, her thoughts turned to the afternoon and she realised with a shock that she had forgotten about the hired car. She had not returned to the hire company to ask about it, nor had she questioned Caston as to how much he had paid the farmer.

He must have paid the farmer, she reasoned. People who lived in small villages did not trust strangers; they did not easily trust one another. She had trusted Caston, but he might have been lying. She did not want to think it, but the suspicion would not go away.

It was foolish to attempt a third secret outing, but she did not sleep until she had decided to do just that. She would not seek Caston, but she ought to check at the hire company and discover what had happened to the car. They asked very few questions, which was why she used them, but they did demand large deposits in cash.

She hoped that the deposit would cover any costs, for she had emptied her account to raise it and her quarterly allowance had only just been paid in. Her behaviour for the next few months, she concluded with a sigh, must be impeccable, and with that worthy thought in mind, she finally fell asleep.

The following day brought a surprise summons from her father. It was for late morning, so even had she wakened early, which she did not, she could not have risked the outing that she had planned.

He father was predictably censorious and she responded in her usual meek and seemingly repentant manner. They understood one another. This meeting was primarily to satisfy her mother, with whom she had little in common.

She was relieved that no mention was made of the previous evening. She was sure that her parents had not recognised her, but it was possible that her absence from the palace had been discovered.

It appeared that it had not. Her father did not mention it.

"You have upset your mother again, Andrela," he finished. "You really ought not to tease her so. I do not like to restrict you, but I must remind you, once again, of your duties as a Princess.

"You may leave your rooms now, but you are to remain within the palace and its grounds until your next official appearance, which is, I believe, the wedding of Lady Emma and Lord Orand."

She nodded. She was to be a bridesmaid at the wedding. Lady Emma was not a particular friend. She was young and rather shy, but her Mama was not. It was her mother who had instigated the match and she was highly delighted with it. She wanted her daughter's nuptial celebrations to be the event of the decade, or at least of the year, and had persuaded every great family in the land to take some part in it. The whole affair was to be very grand; the sort of occasion that Andrela avoided if she possibly could.

Her feelings must have shown in her face, for her father dismissed her with a plea.

"No foolishness, please, on that occasion. It may not be to your taste, it is not to mine, but it is Lady Emma's day. Do not spoil it."

"No, Father," she answered. "Thank you for allowing me to walk in the gardens. I shall take a long stroll after lunch."

Her stroll was much longer than she intended. She had planned a swift visit to the hire company and a brisk walk to note any great changes in the garden, followed by a swim.

The first was managed without difficulty, but it surprised her. She returned in a contemplative mood and with a large amount of money.

Her deposit had been returned in full. The car had been brought back on a cart and the gentleman who called later, had asked about it and had paid for the repair. The young man had handed her the money and given her a broad grin in answer to her question.

"I suppose your mistress's friend paid for the cart too," he had said. "The driver didn't ask *us* for any money."

This gave her a problem. Caston Ambril had paid for her accident and that was before she had sent him the invitation. At the party they had not talked of the afternoon. She had assumed that costs would be deducted from her deposit, but now she was indebted to him. Worse, she could not reimburse him for she had not the least idea how much the cart journey had cost.

She walked several times around the garden pondering the situation and came to no decision. Later, she wondered what she would have done had not the talk that evening turned to debts.

Her parents had no official engagements and, as always on such rare occasions, Prince Roddori insisted on an informal dinner. The dishes were placed in the centre of the table and the family served themselves. A bell was rung when they were ready for the next course.

Andrela usually enjoyed such meals and often led the conversation, but that evening she was cautious. Her mind was in turmoil and she feared that she would make some careless comment and give away her secret. Fortunately, Fidel seemed happy to talk and did not once mention the previous evening.

He did speak of a friend who had financial problems and when the Prince warned of the dangers of running up debts that one could not pay, especially if one were Royal, Andrela was able to agree wholeheartedly.

"For if one likes the person one owes, it is difficult to refuse a favour; and if one dislikes them, they are more likely to make impossible demands."

Her parents nodded approvingly, but she saw a questioning expression on her father's face and added hurriedly, "Some debts are not simple to repay, though. If they involve assistance, say a place in a carriage when one is caught in the rain, the value is difficult to estimate."

"I do not think that a lift in a carriage constitutes a debt," said her mother with a smile.

"It can," said Fidel. "Once Benel and I were riding out near Measham and were caught out in a thunderstorm. The horses were unhappy and we were both soaked. He found an inn, dry clothes and food and hired a carriage to bring us back to Bosron. I felt indebted to him. We ought to have shared the cost."

"How did you repay him?" asked Andrela, sure that her brother would have done so.

He had. He had asked Brand, their chief steward, for an estimate of the cost and had pressed near double the amount upon his friend. Benel had mocked his innocence and had let slip the true figure.

Fidel had counted out exactly half of that figure and had placed the money on the ground to be picked up or left for the next passer-by. He had paid his debt.

"Benel did pick it up," he added, "but I suspect that the next few beggars benefited as much as he did."

Andrela turned the conversation neatly to the subject of beggars before either parent thought to question where Fidel's bodyguard had been during the thunderstorm.

She did not think that he often threw off his constraints, but when he did she would support him, as he had so often, and so subtly, supported her.

Chapter 5

Brand proved helpful. She asked him about the comparative costs of carts and of electric cars and of the problems that might arise whilst using them. He gave answers without expressing any curiosity. He was not uninterested or unimaginative, but thought it would do more good than harm if the young Royals were aware of the cost of transport. He had his suspicions as to why they had enquired, but he did not feel it necessary to tell anyone about them.

Andrela was intrigued by his attitude, but said nothing. Fidel trusted him and Fidel was a good judge. He was not yet seventeen, but she sometimes felt that he knew her better than she knew him. He would make a good ruler.

She followed his advice on method also, calculating as best she was able the cost of the cart and doubling it. She added the cost of the repair and put the money in an envelope. The accompanying letter took longer to write, but at last she finished one and burnt all previous attempts. The cleaning staff in the palace had been known to explore the waste baskets.

She waited for a few days before seeking to deliver the envelope, choosing the opening day of the Royal Bosron horse races. She had once wanted to ride in races, but she had no interest in watching them or in betting on the results.

Her parents, however, were avid race goers and Fidel was almost as keen. So were many of the aristocracy and their retainers. The palace would be quiet, except for the visi-screen room in the servant's quarters, and the city would be almost empty of those who knew her best.

So it proved. Black Street was in the commercial area of Bosron, and she had some difficulty in finding it. The Westgate Hotel, however, was easily seen and, though much less opulent than the hotels she knew, it did look respectable. She walked in without hesitation.

The young man behind the reception desk was helpful. Yes, Mr Ambril was still here. He had just finished lunch and would probably be taking coffee in the sitting room. It was just through here. They could go and find out.

Andrela would have preferred to have left her letter, but the young man was as quick as he was helpful. He shot from behind his desk as he spoke and set off in the direction of his still waving hand. Feeling a little overwhelmed, Andrela followed him.

Mr Ambril was seated in an armchair reading a news sheet devoted entirely to business. A small table stood beside him bearing a tray with a single cup and a jug of coffee.

"A visitor for you, Mr Ambril," said the young man. "Shall I fetch another chair and a second cup?"

The chair was brought almost before Caston had risen to his feet and the bringer disappeared to fetch a cup at the first hint of assent.

"He leaves one breathless," observed Caston as he gently guided her into the chair, "and I am also a little stunned to see you. I cannot even greet you, other than by a given name, or Miss 'Unknown'."

Andrela almost told him that it was better that way, but she collected herself and said instead that he might call her Miss Welton. It was not a common surname, but it was her mother's maiden name. She would remember it, and few others associated it with her mother because her uncle, the current Lord and his forebears had always used their title name, Bune. Mama thought that it simplified things, but she considered it arrogant. It was, however, useful just now.

The young man returned with a dish of sweetmeats and a second cup. He offered to pour and was politely informed that that was not necessary.

Andrela watched him and waited until he was well out of earshot before she spoke again.

"I have come only to repay you," she began. "You ought not to have paid for the repair to the car or indeed for its transport to Bosron. The deposit that they insist upon would have covered it. Here is the money."

He finished pouring coffee and placed the dish of sweetmeats in front of her before he took the proffered envelope.

"I had paid the farmer before he set out and I was so charmed by your company on the return journey that I completely forgot that you would have been obliged to pay a deposit. Please forgive me."

He smiled as he spoke and Andrela took a small biscuit from the plate to cover her confusion. It was a concoction of chopped nuts and fruit and tasted delicious. Too late she realised that it would be added to his bill.

He opened the envelope and glanced inside. He did not count the money. He merely observed that it was far too much, as she probably knew. Besides, he added, he had been amply repaid by the ticket to the ball. He had enjoyed that evening very much.

"So did I," she owned, "but that does not alter the fact that you ought not to have paid for my accident. *You* did not cause it. Please take what I owe you, including something for the coffee and a tip for the energetic young man.

"I did not expect to meet you again. I intended to leave the envelope at the desk for you. That has its dangers, but I could not trust so much in the post to Shyran and I do not like to be beholden."

He was surprised by her earnest expression. He had thought her to be well bred, but thoughtless and frivolous, amusing herself by spending time with a man far beneath her status.

"Very well," he answered, "but only if we finish the cakes and coffee."

She laughed at that and they spent an agreeable half hour together before he mentioned an appointment that he must keep. It was at the docks and he had ordered a carriage to take him there. He offered to take her for the ride. They could then complete their transaction in the privacy of the carriage.

Andrela accepted the offer and, more reluctantly, accepted the money that he returned to her. She thought it too much.

He returned it in the envelope, but she noticed that he kept her note.

He also took her to the docks, though he warned her that his destination was to the commercial docks. The ships there were cargo ships with chipped paintwork and stained decks, not the smart sleek leisure yachts that she knew and might expect.

She admitted that she never seen a cargo ship before, but she declared her interest in them and a desire to widen her experience. With that noble aim in mind, he had consented.

The ships were as he had described and there was little to interest her, but the cargoes she found fascinating; iron from Regan, exotic sweet smelling timbers from Irrok, nuts from Coron, where most of the wild men had ceased fighting and taken up more peaceful pursuits. She saw cases of fine table ware from Zorrenna being carefully unloaded, thick beaver skins being carelessly flung onto untidy heaps, and fine carpets and fruit from Shyran.

That surprised her.

"Fruit from Shyran?" she queried. "Is not Malport nearer?"

"In terms of sea leagues, yes," he answered, "but the best market for salt pears is in Bosron and they are easily damaged by the journey overland."

His interest was in the cargo from Shyran, and while he dealt with his affairs, she was provided with a chair on the deck, a mug of Sulland tea and dish of salt pears. The mug was thick and she was accustomed to delicate cups, but she did not complain.

She was troubled by the beggars huddled by walls. City beggars did not appear either healthy or prosperous, but these were little more than skin and bone, inadequately covered by their torn clothing.

Caston would not allow her to give money.

"Many are addicts," he explained. "If they have money, they will buy drugs or cheap brandy. Better to give them food."

They bought bread, cheese and some pies and she distributed them as fairly as possible, for more came pestering whenever she gave to one.

"You have spent a good deal of money," he noted mildly. "Even the shop-keepers will be hoping for your swift return."

"It is no more than I would spend on a pair of shoes; and I did not know that such poverty existed," she answered.

She looked up at him and sighed regretfully.

"Oh! I know that no one can solve all the problems of a country, or even the all problems of single person, but if you do not know that a problem exists, you cannot help at all."

He agreed and led her back to the carriage. Whoever she was, this sincere but light-hearted girl, he wanted to see her again. He was not sure at what point in their acquaintance he had lost his heart, but he knew that he had and that he would not retrieve it easily.

"I shall leave a note with the car hire company when I am next in Bosron," he said as he set her down in the city centre. "Miss Margren Welton may collect it or not, as she pleases."

"Do you know the plant shop in Change Street?" she asked. "A note in their window will be easier for me," and her eyes sparkled with laughter as she added mischievously, "and I do believe that Miss Margren Welton *will* be pleased to collect it."

She collected the note the following month, but not as Miss Margren Welton.

The marriage of Lady Emma and Lord Orand had taken place by then. It had been as stiff and formal as she had feared, but the bride seemed happy and the groom delighted with his new wife. She had led the troupe of bridesmaids with admirable decorum and had behaved in an exemplary manner since, spending much time in the palace gardens.

She had always been interested in gardens and had frequently purchased items from the shop in Change Street. It was thus easy to increase that interest without arousing suspicion. She had decided which shrub to purchase and where to have the gardeners plant it a whole week before she saw the note. She went in at once. Her plan worked to perfection. As she carefully selected her purchase, she succeeded in dislodging the board with its notes. She retrieved it with an apology. As she turned it over, she remarked in surprise at the name; her mother's name. She did not recall another Margren although she knew the Welton family very well. Did they know for whom this was intended?

The proprietor did not, nor did the young assistant who had, she eventually admitted, accepted it from a gentleman. He had been very polite, very open. She had never imagined that it was a note for the *Princess* Margren. Why would she ever think of such a thing?

Princess Andrela had been very understanding. She doubted that the note was for her mother, but she would deliver it to her. If it was for another and the contents were of importance, she would discover the identity of the intended recipient and deliver it with an appropriate warning. She did not care to see her mother's name on a note displayed in a public place; nor would His Highness Prince Roddori.

"Such strange methods of contact could give rise to suspicions of secret assignations," she added in the most disapproving tone that she could manage.

She cut short the humble apologies by giving instructions on delivery of the shrub and she left before elation overcame her. It had been a very successful ploy, but it could not be used again.

Chapter 6

His note suggested two popular tourist destinations for their next meeting and she chose the first. The second was not as convenient regarding the time, and she had been often to the cathedral, but she had not visited the tower since childhood.

On the designated day, she shed her smart hat and her fine clothes in the ladies' room in one of the large stores and she emerged in a cheap dress with a scarf covering her hair and half of her face. She had done that on several previous occasions. In summer she wore a sun-hat and glasses, but the weather was not warm enough for such disguise.

No one noticed. Even Princesses needed to relieve themselves occasionally.

She walked to the tower. Sometimes one's neighbours on public coaches began conversations and whilst they were often interesting, they were never safe.

It was not busy around the tower, and she saw him walking some way ahead of her. She checked her pace. She felt it better to meet seemingly by chance at the top of the tower, so she allowed a party of schoolchildren to pass through the barrier before her.

"You may like to wait," said the girl who took her entrance fee. "It will be noisy."

"But the explanation of the old defences will be very clear," she answered with a smile, and she joined the school party.

It was not unduly noisy and the history of the towers, the one on the southern bank being now a ruin, was given concisely. The children asked interesting questions and tried their hand at turning the great wheel to wind in the chain.

"Well done," cried the guide when they managed to raise a length of chain. "This is a short section, but it is heavy. Think how hard it would have been to raise chains that stretched across the river and lifted a net of chain that stopped the ships from coming upstream."

"But if there were others on the other side winding too, then it would be easier. And if there were enemy ships coming, then everyone would come to help. No one likes enemies."

The boy was enthusiastic and the guide conceded that enemies were generally unwelcome.

The party moved towards the stairs and Andrela followed them up the stone spiral. The steps had been recently repaired and a handrail had been fitted, but it was still a long climb. The occasional slits in the stonework prompted cries from the children as they recognised some familiar building now seen from above.

The youngsters dispersed rapidly when they reached the top and by the time Andrela emerged, there was a group of older people patiently waiting to begin the climb down. She exchanged pleasantries with some of them about the climb, the stiff breeze and the wonderful view. It was simple then to stroll towards the lone gentleman and comment on the sad ruin of the other tower and of the once splendid castle on the opposite shore.

They moved slowly around the platform together and the children ran around them. In time the youngsters were rounded up and persuaded to return to ground level.

Caston led her to a vacated bench and stared down the Bos estuary towards the sea.

"Have you time to sit?" he asked and nodded happily at her answer.

"We will wait, then, for the children to spend their pocket money in the shop and denude the cake stall of its sickliest cream cakes."

They waited in harmony for near an hour before they descended the stairs and went into the shop. He searched for a gift for her, but bought nothing. Everything, even the expensive silk scarves, was decorated with a picture of the tower coloured in lurid shades.

"I do not need anything as ugly as that to remind me of today," she declared.

Instead, he bought coffee, the last plate of smoked fish with salad and bowl of mixed fruit. The coffee was freshly made and they shared the food. It was surprisingly good. There was no waiter hovering at her elbow and no starched white napkins, but Andrela scarcely noticed. Nor did she notice the time.

He did. He was engaged to dine with business colleagues that evening.

"I am not free again until Thursday evening. Are you able to dine with me then?" He smiled and added quizzically, "Somewhere where you are not known."

"I am known all over Bosron," she answered regretfully, "and at dinner one must sit for some time at the same table. This place, filled with children and tourists, is different."

"A pleasure boat, then," he offered. "Dinner on one of the boats that sails out to Bellue."

"Oh! But that will be dull for you. You must have sailed along that coast many times."

"Not in your company," he replied, and Andrela blushed.

She also realised that she was late and had not discussed a new way of contact. Indeed, she had not thought of one. She had half thought that one more meeting would satisfy her desire for intrigue and was surprised to find herself agreeing to meet on Thursday evening on the quay side by the pleasure boats. She could, she told herself as she rushed away, always send a note if she decided not go.

She didn't want to send a note, but it was difficult to get away. She had been late returning from the tower. Hal, her body guard, had waited more than fifteen anxious minutes and had told her plainly that he would not agree to any further lone expeditions.

She was suitably contrite, but it had little effect. In time he might become amenable again, but not before Thursday. She decided that sickness, pretended or induced, would afflict her late that afternoon. Having once retired to bed, no one would worry about her.

Even that was not entirely simple. She had some difficulty in preventing her mother from summoning a doctor and was obliged to take some medicine. Fortunately, remedies for stomach upsets did not send one to sleep.

After such effort it was extremely disappointing to discover that the wind had risen and was driving dark and threatening clouds across the evening sky. The pleasure boats would not be sailing.

She made her way to the quayside slowly, thinking of the alternatives. The nearby restaurants would be crowded with other disappointed diners and in the large hotels she would almost certainly be recognised.

There was no chance of that on the quay. It was thronged with people, some were complaining, some were resigned, but all were wondering what to do next.

Caston found her just as the first drops of rain began to fall.

"This way," he said and led her towards the river. "I have hired a boat and obtained food from a restaurant. It will not be elegantly served, I fear, and there is no choice, but I had to make a decision quickly."

There was no time to assess the situation. She hurried with him to the rather shabby boat and was in the small cabin before she considered the danger.

The cabin provided some reassurance. It was not furnished for seduction. The table was plain wood and was fastened to the floor and a large man was covering the upholstered benches with sheets.

"Not fit for a lady to sit on," he remarked with a nod of his head as greeting, "but these are clean. So are the plates, but the implements may need a polish."

He laid a box of cutlery and a stained, but newly laundered, napkin on the table.

"Mal is fixing the hot plate," and he indicated a younger man whose broad shoulders looked small in comparison with his own. "We shall set sail in few minutes. Up-river will be fast with this wind, but there will be time to admire the scenery when we return. This squall will be over by then."

"Aye, but 'twill still be rough in the Bay," agreed Mal and he proceeded to explain the workings and the limitations of the hot plate to Caston.

"There is a cloth, miss," he said and produced one from a drawer. It was slightly too small for the table and frayed at the edges, but he spread it with great pride.

Andrela helped by removing the cutlery box and the napkin. They exchanged thanks. When he left she began to polish the knives. She had never done such a thing before, even at school, but found it surprisingly easy.

Caston smiled at her.

"Atture, who owns the boat, is a business friend. I met him by chance this afternoon and he advised me that the weather would change. He was dubious about my hiring his boat. It would not, he told me, impress a lady, but I assured him that I have no desire to impress you. I may be wrong, but I do not think that you care much for fancy trappings."

He did not wait for an answer. He set two small plates on the table and bent to retrieve a large covered dish from beneath the bench. Meanwhile she found two matching knives and settled for odd forks.

So began a delightful evening.

The bread was uncut, the paté was served as a slab with no adornment and the glasses were straight sided with weighty bases, but the food was good and the accompanying wine was excellent.

The somewhat turbulent start to the journey did not worry her or prevent her enjoying the stew, which had been kept hot on the plate. The return was calm and leisurely, giving time to look at the passing scenery and to savour the fruit and the rich cheese with the accompanying bitterberries.

From near the mountains, he told her.

"I know," she answered, "it is one of my favourites."

Slightly inebriated and very happy, she regained the shore in good time to return to the palace before anyone knew of her absence.

Caston insisted on seeing her to a central part of the city, and in Cheege Street, where the shops were closed and young couples wandered by the park engrossed in one another, he asked for a kiss.

"Is it permissible in Eland for well-bred young women to embrace?"

"I have never enquired," she answered, "but I am sure that many of them do; and if we move a little further on, out of the lamplight, I will not object to a modest contact."

A few steps later, under the shade of a tree, he kissed her; gently at first and when she returned his kiss with more enthusiasm than modesty, he pulled her close and kissed more passionately.

After a while they walked on.

"There is a notice board," he said, "in the general store in Rine Square. Next time I am in Bosron I will have a card displayed there. It will say, 'Wanted one electric car E-Class 3.5 model for spares' and will give a date, time and place. I will choose a popular place where we can meet unobtrusively; if you wish to meet me again."

"Thank you. I will watch for it," she answered.

She knew that it was madness, but several times he had called her Margren and in a significant tone. She knew the origin and meaning of the name, and he, being from Shyran, would also know. Besides, she did want very much to see him again.

Chapter 7

A notice appeared in the general store ten days later and Andrela duly went to the cathedral at the stated time. Mr Caston Ambril awaited her, but there was no one offering an EClass 3.5 electric car. Few had been made and they were now rare. Their few hours together were undisturbed and they met again, for dinner on a pleasure boat, the following evening.

A mail shop with a notice board was the agreed point for their next contact, and Andrela found herself writing a great many letters, all of which necessitated a visit to the shop. She did not want to miss his message.

Her diary was full at that time. Despite her protests that there were dozens of photographs of her, the famous painter who had painted Fidel's portrait had been commissioned to paint hers. He requested far more sittings, and longer conversations with her, than she considered either necessary or desirable.

Her father, however, had silenced her protests with a smile.

"You are at such a lovely age," he had told her, "mature enough for character to show, but not yet burdened with the cares of marriage and children."

She had other commitments too. Several charities that she patronised had their big fund-raising events in the summer and all wanted her presence to boost support. She worried that her picture would appear too often in the news sheets.

Lady Annia Grishley had also caused her concern. She was a serious girl, an unlikely but dearly loved friend who had, throughout their school days, curbed Andrela's wilder proposals for unauthorised excursions. She also brought an element of sense and practicality to any discussion.

Now she warned that on two occasions she had noticed Hal, Andrela's bodyguard, lingering in the square looking anxious.

"I know that you have an arrangement with him, Drey," she warned severely, "but you must not take advantage. He would lose his post if anyone found out and would not easily find another. Also, it is foolish to return to the same place every time."

Conciliatory murmurs had not impressed Lady Annia. She had issued dire warnings and had supposed in a jesting manner that there was a man involved.

Andrela had responded equally light-heartedly, but she was not sure that she had been entirely convincing and she worried.

Grizzie thought about things and would persist until she came to a conclusion that satisfied her. It was unlikely to be correct in this case, but that was not a comfort. Andrela felt obliged to consider her situation seriously.

She was a Princess, but not the heir to the throne; thus she was in the public eye, but had no influence. She was expected to marry, but the choice was limited, and so far she felt that her suitors had cared more for her title than for herself.

Caston was different. She was *almost* sure of that but not entirely. It was possible that he knew her true identity.

In such an unsettled state of mind she waited for the notice to appear in the mail shop. She waited for three weeks.

By then, her portrait was finished and her diary almost clear of official engagements. Summer lay ahead with its sports meetings, everything from horse racing to rackets, from swimming and diving to baseball and sand ball. She favoured the aquatic events whereas her parents loved to watch the horses. Fidel went with them and had never expressed a preference for one sport over another. The aristocracy liked their horses and Fidel was tactful.

In her view, he was also shrewd, though not many realised it. He hid his talents well for one so young. He would make a fine High Prince.

Caston suggested two meeting places, the first being on one of Bosron's popular beaches north of the city, on a day when a sand ball match was being played. There would be people and transport, even if the weather were cold and damp, and the few pressmen present would be devotees of the game and not of the Royal family.

She was not unduly worried about the myriad of pictures of her that had appeared in every news sheet, following the public viewing of her portrait. It had been a week ago and people had short memories.

Whether that was so or not, no one gave her a second glance. The sun was shining and the place was crowded. The stands were packed with fans, the cafes were full, and the sand was almost covered with families sitting on picnic rugs unpacking baskets.

She did not hurry. She liked to watch the ordinary people at play. She envied their freedom, if not their cramped houses and meagre budgets.

It was not difficult to find the market. A huge banner proclaimed its presence and its offerings: food, drinks, clothes, housewares and gifts. What market offered anything else?

She found Caston by a stall dispensing drinks. He was sitting at a small table by a low wall that separated the market from the carriageway. There was so little room between the crowded tables that she approached from the outside.

"I have bought a selection of cold teas," he told her with a smile. "Will you come round the official way, or shall I lift you over the wall?"

She elected to walk, despite his assurance that no one would turn a hair if he lifted her. He gave her his chair and, as there were no others available, he sat on the wall.

She sipped the herb tea and thought it little different from those served in the best hotels by waiters in white gloves.

"We cannot – I cannot – continue to meet you in this way. I must tell you who I am."

"Yes, I agree. You must, but give me this afternoon," he responded, and there was sadness in his smile. "I have not booked dinner, but I have taken a table for four o'clock. Will you be able to stay until then?"

She was able and did not mind postponing the question of her identity until then.

When they finished their tea, they walked; around the market, where he bought her a string of beads; along the beach, where they helped some children to collect shells; and as far as the buffalo farm, where they sampled the milk. Neither liked the taste. They walked back to the only hotel in perfect harmony.

He had booked a table for six in a secluded corner and he murmured to one of the senior waiters that the rest of the party would not be coming. A note was pressed into a waiting hand and a screen was promptly erected about their table. For this discussion, he said, privacy was essential. She did not disagree, but she did note that money secured the privilege to which she was accustomed as Princess.

Coffee, savouries and cake were swiftly set before them and Caston waited until she had poured the drinks and selected a savoury before he spoke.

"I need privacy so that I may stare at you," he said. "I may not see you again save in pictures."

"Why?" she asked simply.

"I have known from the start that you were not a servant and not usually called Margren; but you are *my* Margren, *my* wanted one. I want you more than I realised I could want. I want your head beside me when I wake, your hand to touch before I sleep, your presence in my house; and not just for a day or a week, but for always."

Andrela smiled. "Go on," she invited, for he had not yet asked the question.

"I hoped that you were a merchant's over-protected child, or the only daughter of some minor member of the aristocracy, someone whose parents I could approach with a request to marry you; but you are not."

He looked at her sadly and continued softly. "You are the Princess Andrela, daughter of the High Prince Roddori and second in line to the throne. And I cannot speak to your father. I would not get past the guards outside the palace gates."

"No, you would not," she replied in a practical tone. "I might invite you, of course, but I doubt that my father would consider you an acceptable suitor for my hand. Fortunately, I am of age. *I* might consider you acceptable, but I cannot do so until you ask."

She selected another savoury and poured a second cup of coffee for herself. His cup remained full. He watched her with amazement.

"I cannot ask you to marry me," he objected at last. "I live on Shyran, and though I have a reasonable income, I must work for it. You live in a palace; you are accustomed to the best of everything, from food and wine to clothes and shoes. You are honoured, your patronage is sought after, your presence attracts attention and you are protected. You probably have a bodyguard. I cannot give you that."

"Yes, I do have a bodyguard and it has been very difficult to escape his attention and come to meet you," she answered severely, but after a moment's consideration she smiled and continued. "I daresay there are things that I would miss if I were no longer a princess, but I would relish others; such as standing on a cold beach waiting for a decidedly misty sunrise and eating in places where one can pour one's own coffee without being fussed by obsequious waiters."

He laughed a little uncertainly and laid his hand on hers.

"The sunrise was certainly misty, but the company more than compensated for the cold. Marry me tomorrow and I will take you to Westport in Shyran to watch the sunset. It may be cloudy and dull, but we can sit in comfort and drink wine to savour the disappointment."

Andrela sighed with relief. He had asked! It was not the proposal of her dreams. There was no moonlit garden, no flood of praise for her beauty and no ardent declaration that the proposer could not live without her; but it did not matter. 'Marry me tomorrow' was good enough.

"I will marry you, Caston," she answered, "and come to live on Shyran with you, but tomorrow is difficult. Will Friday do? Everybody will be going to the races at Measham and no one will expect *me* to be there. I find betting and races dull.

"Were you planning to stay in Bosron until Friday?"

He drew a startled breath; "I will stay in Bosron for ever if you will marry me," he declared and there was all the ardour that she could desire in his assurance.

She squeezed his hand and they sat gazing at one another for some minutes.

She broke the silence, reminding him that his coffee was becoming cold. She also warned him that their wedding would necessarily be quiet. Did he have a friend who could give her away?

He had, but not in Bosron. That remark prompted a discussion about where they would marry. Bosron, and possibly any other place in Eland, could raise problems for a woman named Andrela Helen Margren Palynd. Maybe it *would* be better to marry in Shyran.

They did not argue, not at the table, nor later as they walked towards the public coach. He wanted only to please her, and she was overjoyed that he was willing to marry her despite the difficulties. Neither of them under estimated those.

"Was it the portrait?" she asked when more urgent problems had been settled. "I did not think it a particularly good likeness."

"Not of your face," he answered. "He did not catch the light in your eyes nor your strength of character, but he showed your fine broad forehead and rendered faithfully that wisp of hair that will not stay in place."

He laughed and tucked it neatly behind her ear. It did not remain there.

"That I recognised at once."

It rained hard the following day, but Andrela did not care. She had things to do.

She looked through her extensive wardrobe and selected necessities. They did not quite fill the small bag that she packed and she was glad. There was room for her personal jewellery. There were some good pieces, and they, with the inheritance from her grandfather, would be a reasonable dowry. Not that Caston had mentioned money, but it was important. She was confident that he would take care of her, but accidents did occur and by definition could not be predicted. Means of her own were desirable, if not precisely necessary.

Her preoccupation was not noticed by her family. They discussed the weather and the races – and the effect of one upon the other and upon the chances of the various runners and the odds that were offered. The High Princess did try to engage her daughter in discussion of fashion, but was unsuccessful. Andrela advised her mother to wear waterproof boots and an oilskin coat and cap, it being positively dangerous to step on damp grass in high heeled slippers and ridiculous to venture out with no protection for one's head other than a frothy confection that would flop in the rain. She was sincere, however, in her hope that the rain would cease on Friday. She did not want the meeting to be cancelled.

It was not, though the rain was exceptionally heavy for the time of year and did not cease until late on Thursday evening. Andrela rejoiced with her brother when the sky cleared and the wet leaves glistened in the last rays of the watery sun.

"They will race tomorrow," she said. "You will see that bay you call your lucky horse win the Cup."

Fidel shook his head.

"Blue Blaze will not run tomorrow. The ground will still be too wet. I shall put my money on Fielden's Fan."

He talked of horses and their chances for a while before asking his sister what she planned to do.

Fidel had always known when she lied, so she had a standard answer for when she did not want to tell. She gave it then.

"I shall sit at home and read an improving book."

And he laughed and gave his usual response, "One page or two?"

They parted amicably.

The following morning Andrela dutifully read a page of *"The Lives of the High Princes of Eland"* which she kept by her bed. It was informative, but dreadfully dull. She laid it back in its place for she would not need it again, and she joyously packed the last few items that she planned to take.

The bag was heavy and she was not used to carrying heavy bags, but she would not be carrying it far. Caston would take it at the moment they met and they were meeting in the park only a short way from her hidden exit.

There were no problems. The palace staff did not fret about the Princess. She was not demanding but would call if she needed anything. Once the Royal Party had departed, all were free to watch the races on the visi-screen, or to sleep, if that was their choice.

Most of them were gazing at the screen as presenters interviewed jockeys and trainers and assessed chances. No one noticed Andrela as she dropped her bag out of a convenient window, nor when she placed a letter in Hal's room. It contained a bank draft. He would need money when her absence was discovered. The letter to her parents she left in her own quarters. They would be searched first and it would be found before anyone became unduly anxious.

She informed an underling that she was going to walk in the gardens and left boldly through one of the main doors. She wandered for a few minutes in familiar places before she collected her bag and went through her secret gate.

"The last time," she thought.

Caston was waiting as she was sure that he would be. He took her bag, but asked her sombrely if she was sure, before he moved.

"Yes, I am sure," she replied. "I love you. I want to be with you always. The pomp and the title and all the other things that go with it, are not important. You are."

He smiled and turned towards the carriage he had hired.

"I am glad of that; for once I have you I will not easily let you go."

She leant her head against his arm as they walked. It did not matter now if anyone noticed. They would be in Malport before the races were over and in Shyran for dinner. She did not know what arrangements he had made, but it was possible that they would be wed that very evening. She hoped so. She could wait if she must, but she did not want to wait for long.

They did not stop until they reached Angel Heights. The horses were tired after the long haul uphill and there were several good inns there, most with splendid views to admire whilst you ate.

He had booked a private room in one of them, with a view to the south.

"We will look forward, not back," he said.

She smiled and commented that he was looking towards his home.

"I am returning," he agreed, "but Shyran with you will be different, and my home will contain a treasure that I had not thought to possess."

They lingered over lunch, and when he went to pay the bill, she noticed the clock. "The races will just have started," she thought and wondered idly if he were interested in them. They had never discussed the subject. She stood up and stared at the view as she waited.

The moment he returned, she knew that there was something wrong. He looked so grim that she scarcely recognised him, but he walked straight to her and wrapped his arms around her. There was no preamble. He spoke at once.

"There has been an accident at Measham. Your brother is dead."

"Fid!" she said, and again, "Fid! But he cannot be dead. He has not been ill."

She realised the stupidity of her denial and laid her head on his breast.

"What sort of accident?" she asked quietly.

He stroked her hair as he explained.

A stand had collapsed. It was one of the old stands by the start, where entry was cheap. Her parents were safe. They had been by the finish, in the smart enclosure. Fidel had been with them, but had gone to speak with someone about the next race and had been near the start. A shower of rain had caused a rush for cover and many, including some children, had clustered under the stand. One of its principle supports had begun to slip in the soggy ground and the stay that held it firm had pulled away from its fastening.

It was thought that Fidel had seen the slip and had realised that the whole structure could collapse; tumbling the people who were on it and burying those who were sheltering beneath it. It was known that he had run, with others, to warn of the danger and to try to prop up the wavering post until everyone was safe.

Unfortunately, they had been too late. Some had escaped, but many had fallen with the stand, and some, including Fidel and his bodyguard, had been crushed beneath it.

The numbers of the dead and injured were not yet known, but the races had been cancelled and all transport was being commandeered to take the wounded to hospital.

"He would do that," she said. "He would help anyone. They were his people," and she buried her head in his chest and cried.

After a while she raised her head and regarded him soberly.

"It is true, that," she told him. "Fidel *cared*. There were some I know who thought him feeble. They thought that he would be a weak and ineffectual ruler, but they were wrong. He would have been upright, firm and true. He would have been as fine a High Prince as any we have had."

She was sincere in her praise of her brother, but she stopped abruptly, realising suddenly that she had been using the past tense. Fidel was dead and she was now heir to the throne of Eland.

She did not flinch, nor did she turn away.

"I must go back," she said, and her voice was as heavy as his heart.

"I know. I have called the carriage."

The return journey was fast. It was downhill and the coachman did not feel that either of his passengers was in a mood to admire the passing scenery. The lady had been very pale and the gentleman grim. He himself had heard the relay reports of the accident at Measham and such happenings were depressing, even if there was no reason to suppose that anyone you knew had been hurt. It would be good to get home and see his wife and their three boys.

He stopped as directed by the park. A light rain had begun to fall, but both his passengers alighted and he was bidden to wait. The gentleman began to say something else, but he interrupted.

"I drive the horses. I ask no more than a fair price, and I say nothing."

"Thank you," said the lady.

The gentleman followed her into the park carrying a bag, but he did not watch them. He had spoken truthfully. Intrigues, elopements, drunken young men and foolish young women, he had seen them all and had spoken of none.

Andrela walked along the familiar path towards the palace wall. They had not spoken on the journey, nor did they speak now, but she was glad of Caston's presence.

The rain had driven away the few strollers and the park was deserted, but she looked around when she neared the arm of the shrubbery that led to the hidden gate.

"We part here," she said and stretched out a hand for her bag. Their hands touched as he gave it to her and she put it down and flung both arms around him.

"I love you, Caston," she cried. "I do not want to leave you."

"I know; and I do not want to let you go," he replied softly and held her close.

They stood wrapped in one another's arms, but the moment she moved, he released her.

"I will never forget you, my love; and you, oh please, remember me," she pleaded then she gathered up her bag and moved away.

She stepped across the grass and disappeared behind a shrub. He did not see her again, although he stared at the swaying branches that indicated her passage.

"I will remember," he promised the wet path and the dripping leaves. "How could I forget you, Andrela Palynd, my Margren, my wanted one? I will remember you as long as I live."

Chapter 8

The palace garden was not deserted. Andrela heard voices as she slipped through the door. It did not matter now, she would never use that way again, but she locked it carefully behind her and waited, still and silent, until she was sure that the speakers had passed. Habit again made her cautious and she crept out from the bushes and made her way through the trees to the more formal area. She hid her bag in one of the thick hedges.

Someone would retrieve it if her absence had been noted, or she would collect it later if, as she hoped, she had returned before her parents.

She encountered Hal quite suddenly by the round summer house, and they stared at one another.

"You know," he said.

It was not a question, for he had seen her face, but she answered anyway.

"Yes. Are my parents back?"

"Not yet. They are waiting for – for." He stopped, neither willing to mention a name, nor to state crudely that they would not leave until transport for their son's body had been arranged. An oilskin sack was not an appropriate receptacle for the remains of the heir to the throne.

"For things." She finished the sentence for him. "I am glad. I would not want to be out when they return. They will need to see me; my mother especially."

He was surprised at her comment. It was well known in the Royal household that the High Princess and her daughter were frequently at odds and that the blame was normally laid on the daughter's thoughtlessness.

He answered calmly. "Yes, she will. His Royal Highness has made a statement on relay, but it is widely reported that the Princess is extremely distressed."

"Fidel was her joy," said Andrela. "I have often been a cause of tribulation."

Once she would have smiled at the acknowledgement of her own rebellious tendencies, but now it was no longer amusing. It was a problem that she must address.

"I left a letter for you, in your room," she said as they walked towards the palace. "Have you opened it?"

"No," he answered without hesitation. "I was watching the races with most of the household when the news of the accident broke. I expected that you would be 'somewhere in the garden' as you usually are on race days and I came out at once to look for you."

"You are a loyal servant, Hal," she acknowledged. "Please bring it, still unopened, to my sitting room. I must change my clothes before my parents return."

His assent was brief. Initially, he was annoyed at the phrase 'still unopened'. Did she think that he would open a letter from her if she had requested its return?

Further thought allayed his anger. She had been 'out' much more often of late and she had tested his patience as she had never done before. The letter was important, and it was not his place to question why.

Andrela had changed her clothes and was standing by the window when he took it to her sitting room. She held another letter in one hand and was tapping it nervously against the knuckles of the other. He could see that it was addressed to her parents, and knew that it, too, was, or had been, important.

He offered his own letter.

"Do you wish to destroy these papers, ma'am?" he asked.

She was slightly startled by his formality.

"Yes, I must burn them, but the ashes will be noticed. Can ashes be read?"

"Only with difficulty," he assured her, "and not at all if they are buried. In summer it is preferable to use a container, rather than the fire place, so that the ashes can be collected and disposed of safely."

He brought a heavy metal bowl with a lid, and she tore her letters into small pieces and set them alight inside it. He did not stand near, but he watched from the other side of the room. She was glad that she had not put notes in her letter to him. She was able to destroy it without him seeing the bank draft inside it. She had been generous. He would have lost his post and she had not wanted him to suffer for her happiness.

Afterwards she went with him to the garden and the ashes were buried under the branches of a low growing bush.

"Walk in the garden for a while," he advised. "The roses are beautiful just now. I will collect whatever you left."

She did not ask how he knew and he did not volunteer the information. Of necessity, a bodyguard came to know the person whom they protected.

She answered briefly. "A bag, in the great hedge; second arch on the left."

It was a good idea of Hal's, she thought, as she wandered in the rose garden. It was calm, colourful and scented. She stooped over a newly-opened bloom to inhale its sweetness.

Two gardeners appeared at one corner. The younger one moved away, but the other was not deterred by her presence. He had known her as a child and had often warned her of the thorns. Now he sought a particular bush and cut a bloom. He came towards her and held it out.

"This variety was named for him," he said. "His Highness does not like titles in flower names and there are many shrubs called Fidel. This we called 'Heir'."

She took it and gazed at the deep crimson petals, firm-textured and smooth-edged. The scent was crisp, spicy rather than sweet.

"It was well named," he said as he offered it to her, "and is well given."

She watched him as he walked away and wondered how many others knew Fidel's character so well, or her own.

Hal brought her bag to her sitting room immediately she returned, and he left without comment. She had not seen him in the garden, but he must have been there, watching; and now he would be close at hand. She must learn to bear this increased attention.

She unpacked the bag, returning the jewellery to the safe and the clothes to her closet. The dress that she had intended to wear for her marriage, she hung at the back. She could not envisage wearing it for any other occasion. Brushes, jars of cream and pots of make-up were replaced easily, but she paused over a string of beads.

She could have worn it in Shyran as Mrs Caston Ambril, but she could not wear it now. She did not even want to look at it now, but nor could she throw it away.

Her 'childhood shelf' provided an answer. There, among the worn furry toys, the battered books and boxes of treasured sea shells, she found a small silk bag. It was empty. She had kept it because she had loved the smoothness of the silk and the vibrant blue and red of the pattern. It was just large enough for the beads.

She put them in, drew the string tight and left them in the care of the mountain lion that had kept her company so often at night. His whiskers had long since been pulled off and he had lost an eye, but his expression remained benevolent and uncritical. She stroked his fur. It was still soft, but no longer reassuring.

She shut the cupboard door. She was no longer a child.

The rose she put in a vase on the table so that she could smell its perfume. She was now 'Heir'.

The High Prince found his journey back from Measham more difficult than he had anticipated. His wife was still weeping, sometimes noisily, and he and Lady Campenden had already offered, several times, what words of comfort they could find. He was glad of the company and the endless supply of handkerchiefs that Lady Campenden was providing, but her scarlet dress and the bright feathers on her elegant hat seemed a mockery.

Margren's hat, gloves and bag lay beside him in a jumbled heap. She had tossed them aside when she had first heard the news and had not considered them since. It was fortunate that some official had ensured that they were in a private room when told of their son's death. Her cries of anguish had not been caught on relay.

He waved his hand once again at the crowds lining the road. People were waving black flags and some were weeping, but their grief would soon give way to speculation and discussion. Margren would grieve for the rest of her life and he, though he would do the same, would be involved in much of the discussion.

He thought of his daughter, light-hearted, impish and with scant regard for convention. He knew that she sometimes ventured beyond the palace without proper escort though he was not quite sure how. He had not tried to find out – he had not considered it important enough. She was an intelligent adult and could take care of herself. Now he wondered.

Had she heard the news, and where had she been when she heard? How would she react? She and Fidel had been close. He had been solitary, an only child with no close companion. He did not feel able to understand the loss that Andrela would surely feel.

He gave a last acknowledgement to the crowd as they turned into the palace gates. Lady Campenden looked up and gave an almost inaudible sigh of relief.

Her exclamation, when she saw Andrela coming down the steps to meet the carriage, was louder and her relief was so evident that she turned to Prince Roddori with an embarrassed explanation.

"Annia was worried, so I am pleased to see her."

He understood.

"I too," he said simply.

He was more than pleased to see her, he was proud of her. Whatever her feelings, she controlled them firmly and her first words were for her mother.

Princess Margren wept anew at the sight of her daughter. She was tenderly embraced, but she was also mildly admonished.

"Come, Mama. Do not make yourself ill with weeping. You must be strong; for Papa and for me."

"For you?"

"For me. He was my brother, and I loved him dearly."

Andrela thanked Lady Campenden briefly, touched her father's hand and led her mother up the steps. She did not look at the carriage that bore Fidel's body. She would make her farewells in her own time and in her own way.

Prince Roddori, having also thanked the lady, found that arrangements had already been made for transport home for her, and for any other person who might have accompanied them on their sad journey. He followed his wife and daughter into the palace.

Andrela took charge. That did not annoy him. He was sure that his wife preferred to remain in her own suite and to dine there alone. He was content with the simple meal that was served; he had no appetite for the usual elaborate four course dinner. He was disconcerted, however, by his daughter's questions. They concerned the lying in state and the provision of books of condolence.

"Such things will be dealt with by the Council," he told her. "You do not need to worry. I conferred with Berrondol at Measham. We will meet tomorrow morning."

That satisfied her. She nodded approval and promised to attend. He attempted to dissuade her, noting among other things that no woman had ever sat on Council.

She smiled sadly. She knew that.

She also knew the history of her country. Lord Parandour had been the first Great Lord, and his granddaughter had married one of King Cendara's sons, and Eland had become a Princedom. When his line died out, there was a fight for the throne and the winner had taken the title High Prince. Since then there had always been a male heir, though the Palynds, for the last few generations, had only had one son.

"Now I am your heir, am I not?" she asked.

"Yes, yes," he assured her. "That was decided soon after you were born, for there are a dozen men with fragile claims and no one is stronger than another."

"So," she said, "I will take Fidel's place."

Her voice did not waver, but she looked down as she spoke his name.

She raised her head when she spoke again and her expression was uncompromising.

"I did not expect that honour, nor do I want it, but it is mine and I will take it."

Prince Roddori murmured acquiescence. His Council must accept her presence sometime and, for the present, he thought it best to let her do things in her own way.

He discovered later that she did many things in her own way.

Chapter 9

Andrela woke early on the day she had determined to speak at the Council meeting. It was six months since Fidel had been killed, and she was well aware that the Lords, and her mother, were becoming impatient.

As soon as the funeral was over, she had been courted with determination. Prince Darmon, who had represented his family at the burial, had been the most tactful, but then he had engagements in Westland that prevented him staying more than a day or two after the solemnity.

She had liked him, as much as anyone can like a man after such a short acquaintance. He had seemed gentle and tolerant. If one was obliged to marry without love, and her love had already been given, such qualities were important. Nor was he ill-favoured, and though ugliness was not a bar to being loved, if one did not love, a husband (or a wife, she conceded to herself) on whom one could look without repulsion, was to be preferred.

Mama pressed her at breakfast. It was not only the Council, the whole of Eland awaited her decision on whom she would marry; and Jared, Lord Darnford's son, was extremely handsome and obviously taken with her.

"He was not so attentive before Fidel's death," Andrela commented drily, "and I am not disposed to decide quickly. I may not marry at all. Despite the undoubted advantages of being Royal, I feel that there is much to be said for living in a republic. I may devote my life's work towards that end."

Having temporarily silenced both parents, she laid down her knife and fork and excused herself. She wanted a clear mind before the meeting.

Her father remained silent. There were some who thought a republic preferable to a monarchy, and when he was especially weary of his subjects, he agreed with them, but usually he did not. Most, who fancied that a republic would be an improvement, were either idealists with little idea of the burden of responsibility, or those who considered that such a system would give them more power or influence; and possibly greater wealth.

His wife was less restrained.

"You must speak more severely to her," she complained. "A republic indeed! And she a Palynd! She has no sense of duty."

"No, my dear, that is not so," replied the Prince gently. "She was not brought up to take the throne and she has told me that she does not want it, but she has accepted the situation and has come to every Council meeting since Fidel died. The first one, certainly, was hard for her."

"I will admit that she has behaved well recently," owned the Princess, "but I wish that she would choose a husband. The country is in need of cheer, and the prospect of a wedding would carry everyone through the colder months."

"Perhaps."

The Prince did not challenge the argument, but he did not consider the cheering of his subjects a sufficient reason for encouraging his daughter to embark upon marriage. He was sure that she would not either. He was relieved that she had not heard the remark.

That feeling was reinforced when he heard her speech to the Council.

She spoke first of her grief at her brother's death and her appreciation of the period of mourning. Some family occasions, such as Naming Ceremonies and marriages, could not be postponed, nor could the coming festival of Namier's Moons, but she asked that it be marked soberly this year.

It commemorated the triumph of Namier over the scaly giants of Hadron who had demolished the homes of Erion's people, and it was thus appropriate to donate, at this time, to charities for the homeless. Fidel had been patron of one such charity, but there were others, equally worthy.

The time for celebration would come at the Festival of the Flower, the time when new growth sprung from bare soil, the time when Prince Darmon of Westland had suggested that the Royal Family of Eland visit his country.

She paused at that point to allow the dreamers to awaken and the listeners to make their exclamations.

"You will remember that he attended my brother's burial, but you will not know that he and I have exchanged letters since that time. His intentions are plain, but all he is able to offer at present is the position of his Chosen Woman. He is well aware that I will not accept that.

"A Royal visit from Eland could, however, help his father to persuade his people to change their law and render obsolete the concept of their prince choosing a woman and marrying only when she is with child. If that is done, a marriage between Prince Darmon and I may be possible.

"On a personal level there would be few problems. We both know that heirs to thrones are rarely free to marry for love. A union between us would be for the unity of Salima and for the benefit of our respective countries. Unity is desirable, but certain decisions must be made.

"Which city will be the capital? Which the seat of power? What will be the currency? It is true that our island will not be ruled by one Prince until both he and I are dead, but the decisions must be made long before that time.

"I do not think that Prince Darmon will make an offer unless these things are agreed, and I will certainly not accept. Rather I will remain unwed and will work with you to ensure a smooth transition to a new rule; either by another Royal dynasty or as a republic.

"I ask you to think on these things so that, when we discuss the matter in greater detail, all arguments are prepared, well presented and unemotional."

She thanked them and sat down.

There were many protesting murmurs, but no one indicated that they wished to speak. Prince Roddori, almost as stunned as his lords, closed the meeting and left with his daughter.

"I knew that you were writing to Prince Darmon," he admitted carefully, "but I have not mentioned it to your mother. She wants to see you married, but she also wants you to stay in Bosron. If you did marry Darmon, you would be obliged to move to Kaldor."

"Yes." Her answer was almost disinterested. "Westland will want the capital. They feel that their country is of greater importance because it is bigger in area; but, if they want union, then they must accept me – and the krown and the fen."

71

She smiled suddenly, wickedly, with a hint of her former delight in mischief.

"And *we* will decide the rate of exchange."

"Perhaps," he allowed, "but they will drive a hard bargain."

She smiled again. "Yes, Papa, they will certainly try; but I am not in love with their Prince. He is not in love with me, but he does have to find a wife or a Chosen Woman, and I am not under such pressure.

"According to Lord Pandour, who accompanied the Prince, Westland still adheres to old ways. He thought that good, I thought it old-fashioned and restricting for women, but either way it means that the country is not yet ready for a republic. Eland is, or will be, by the time I die. I hold the better hand."

There was no triumph in her voice. There was not a trace of emotion that he could find either. She was stating facts as drily as if they had been multiplication tables. She continued in the same manner.

"The capital is important, but it is a status symbol. The currency affects the economy; and that has a greater effect on the general population than does status."

"The capital is a focus point," he protested. "People need a focus. Yes, it is emotional, but emotions are important too. You do have a heart."

She fell silent and did not speak again until they reached the door of his study. He stopped and looked at her. She returned his gaze steadily.

"No Papa, I do not have a heart," she said. "It was given and I cannot call it back. You would not have approved and nor would Council, for he was from Shyran and a business man; not a suitable husband for an Eland Princess. We planned to marry in his country and were on our way there when we heard that Fidel had been killed."

She shrugged as she turned to walk away.

"So I came back."

He did not stop her. He remembered his own youth and the sweet fair-haired girl whom he had loved, but could not marry. She had wed another and had moved to Guorl, and after a time his heart had healed.

He did not refer to the conversation again, nor did he discuss it with Margren. With her, he promoted the idea of a visit to

Westland. Later, he would attempt the more difficult task of preparing her for the long term absence of her daughter.

Both she and his Council welcomed the idea of a State visit to Kaldor. The Royal family toured Eland every few years and had once crossed the border to New Stannul in the north and passed through one of the larger mountain tunnels to a resort in the south, but the tours had never included the capital of Westland. Despite the new road to the great dam in the south, the journey from Bosron to Kaldor was easier by sea.

The Prince suggested that they sail up river to Tarkbridge and ride south to Siburn to take ship there. They rarely went to either town and this would be an opportunity to do so. His wife had no objection. The location of public appearances was less important to her than the type of occasion, for she needed to plan her wardrobe and she was meticulous in that.

Andrela was more aware. The proposed journey avoided rounding the peninsula of Bellue and traversing the straits between Eland and Shyran. Also Siburn was a naval port, larger and further west than Malport. There was a wide straight road linking it with Tarkbridge, very different from the pretty winding way to Angel Heights. Nothing would remind her of her abandoned journey to Shyran. They might not even catch sight of that island.

She was not sure whether to be annoyed or grateful for her father's consideration so she did not discuss it with him. Instead she discussed clothes and fashion with her mother, which pleased that lady greatly.

"Andrela is happier," she declared to her husband. "She is looking forward to this trip. I know that she has seen little of Prince Darmon, but I believe that she has become fond of him. I did not fall in love at first sight, but she is more impulsive. Perhaps she has. Do you think so?"

Prince Roddori disliked lying, especially to his wife. He gave a non-committal reply and allowed that Andrela respected the Prince, and that love between them might grow. If Andrela was set upon the match, he hoped that it would, for he realised that marriage to any of her suitors from Eland could cause envy and resentment.

Fidel could have married almost where he chose, for a woman did not expect power; but a man marrying the heir to the throne might seek greater influence than his peers would tolerate. His daughter had his sympathy.

As he had planned, the initial stage of the journey to Westland avoided Shyran. The naval force at Siburn was delighted to receive its Supreme Commander in person and put on a splendid display of sailing and battle skills. It lasted until sunset and was followed by a ball. There was little time to stare out to sea and Andrela showed no sign of wishing to do so.

They left the following day before the morning mist had cleared. Shore and escort ships were visible only because they were lit and the dampness did not encourage anyone to remain on deck. The sun broke through in due course, but by then Shyran was far behind them.

The journey was uneventful unless one counted the curiosity of the Westlanders in Ostara where they docked. Ostarians were not noted for restraint and rumours were rife. Everyone was familiar with photographs and visi-screen pictures of the Princess Andrela and they knew her reputation. Everyone wanted to see her in the flesh.

She obliged. Her parents considered a short tour of the town quite sufficient, but Andrela wanted to see the naval dockyard, the hospital and the charity school in addition to the main square where long ago Prince Nikkor had announced that Kaiealestria, his Chosen Woman, was expecting his child. Her guides were impressed with her knowledge of that era of their history and presumed, rightly, that she admired the Eland mountain girl who had caught the eye of their Prince.

As for this Princess, they found her easy. She waved to the crowds, posed for photographs and accepted bunches of flowers from small children. Later, she went to the burial ground and laid the flowers on the graves of those who had been killed at Ostara Bay.

She was aware of its importance. It was the last battle fought in Salima waters and had decimated the pirates who had roamed the coast for centuries. She was not the silly sensation-seeker that the onlookers had feared. One bold man ventured to hope that they would meet her again and she thanked him gravely.

In fact, his remark amused her greatly, as had her whole day, but she did not laugh, not until she had reached the privacy of her cabin. Ostara was a fascinating port with lively inhabitants, but it would not do to upset them by making fun of their interest in her. She must practice tact; it was a desirable quality for a Princess.

She found many opportunities to practice that virtue when they arrived in Kaldor and encountered the Princess Indola.

Kaldor's welcome was enthusiastic. Each individual may have been more restrained than each inhabitant of Ostara, but there were so many more of them that the effect was similar.

Prince Darmon stood beside her on the palace balcony and explained the system of 'one-way viewing'. She watched with interest as the crowds proceeded through the palace gates, passed close enough to obtain an excellent view of the Royal family and their guests and disappeared around the corner of the enormous building. He also explained the security system, but she had never felt in danger and was in no need of his reassurance.

"I went close to many in Ostara," she told him. "Is Kaldor more dangerous?"

"Not really, but it is different. In Ostara, they celebrate by making a noise: horns and drums and sometimes even cannon. It can be deafening. In Kaldor, they drink. Drunken men are unpredictable and often belligerent; and drunken women, I am told, are worse, but that is perhaps because the guards will readily fell a man, but do not like to strike a woman."

"How very gallant," she remarked and suggested employing women guards. "They will have no compunction about hitting another woman if it is necessary."

Princess Indola overheard.

"In this country, we encourage women to develop the feminine virtues," she announced repressively. "Guards are trained to apply force and I doubt that many women would find such training to their taste."

"Eland's security forces have employed women for years without problem. The Princess Kaiealestria was one, and she was reputed to enjoy unarmed combat."

Andrela answered with exaggerated sweetness and her father promptly asked some trivial question of his hostess. At almost the same time Prince Darmon engaged Andrela's attention, pointing out a building of no great beauty or importance.

The incident passed unnoticed by the general populace. Even the watchful men behind the visi-screen cameras failed to associate the brief expressions on the faces of the Princess Indola and her young visitor with a possible dispute.

"We dine together tonight," murmured Prince Maldon to his guest. "There will be a reception beforehand, but the meal will be private."

Prince Roddori had seen and approved the scheduled events that they were to attend, but he had forgotten the details. He was grateful for the information and relayed it to his wife. There would be no problem in keeping Andrela and her hostess apart at a reception and other company might lessen the tension between them.

He thought it unfortunate that the seating at dinner was formal, with Prince Maldon at one end of a table that was rather too long for six people, and the Princess Indola at the other. He sat beside her, opposite his daughter, and whilst he had no objection to being at a distance from his wife, he did feel that the young people might have been happier had they been closer together.

He listened with growing apprehension as Princess Indola talked of their tour of Kaldor, planned for the following morning. She did not hide her opinion that the streets and squares, the buildings and museums were far superior to anything in Eland.

Andrela asked if they were to visit the Charity School as she was extremely interested in the era of Nikkor the Third and understood that the wing of the school named after his eldest son was a fine example of the architecture of that time.

The Princess agreed that it was so noted, but they would not be viewing it. She herself had never seen it as it was in an area of the town that she did not frequent.

"No, the Charity School in Bosron is not in one of the best areas," replied Andrela, cheerfully, "but I have been there. It is now supported in part by the State, but alas it does not attract the best teachers."

"It is difficult, my dear," said her father, "for the State to equal the salaries that are paid to teachers in the private schools."

"In Westland, the schools are filled with the offspring of tradesmen," noted the Princess. "The aristocracy prefer to educate their children at home."

"I enjoyed school," pronounced Andrela robustly. "My friends were mostly from the aristocracy it is true, but we were taught to appreciate our good fortune. When we were old enough, we were taken to the nearby state schools to help teach the younger children. They were generally more respectful to their teachers than we were, but some were very poor; without shoes and often with fleas or lice."

The Princess remarked that in Westland young girls preferred to avoid fleas and lice, and Andrela commented, with equal acidity, that nonetheless they seemed willing, if not eager, to become the mistress of the heir to the throne.

The retort was sharp.

"If you are referring to the position of Chosen Woman, it is an honour."

Andrela smiled sweetly.

"Practices are different," she said with every appearance of tolerance. "I, and most of Eland, would consider it an insult."

"If you were offered that *honour*, you would need to learn the manners expected of a Princess."

"My daughter *is* a Princess," noted Prince Roddori mildly. "She is my heir and will be High Prince of Eland when I die. It is not a position that she expected, nor one for which she was prepared, but she has shouldered the burden with exceptional courage. I am proud of her."

Andrela coloured and applied herself to her plate. Princess Indola was also silent. At that end of table the meal continued quietly.

Prince Darmon, whose sharp young ears had managed to follow two conversations at the same time, interrupted the silence.

"Princess Andrela," he began, with only the slightest stress on her title, "I know that your morning is occupied, but I do hope that you will let me show you the palace gardens after lunch. The Children's garden, created by Nikkor and Kaiealestria, is very interesting."

"The Children's garden?" Andrela looked up with interest and edged her chair nearer to the centre of the table. "I have heard of it, but thought it only for children – and gardeners. Are we allowed in it?"

"I am allowed," he replied, "and I may invite whomsoever I choose, unless they have children of their own. Parents are banned."

"How delightful! I should love to see it." Andrela returned his impish grin. "Who then shows the children the garden, if parents are banned?"

"Their grandfather may, or a special friend is nominated; usually one who has shared its joys with their father. My grandfather was too ill, so Lord Narethan led me around it when I was three or four. I played there with his son, but he was not one of my special friends. Lord Pandour and Esquire Jonal Tesher have that honour." He paused and grinned. "Or pleasure, if it is such. I have asked them for tomorrow, but I can send them away if you prefer."

Andrela declared that unnecessary and they duly made arrangements for the following afternoon, informal dress being recommended.

Andrela noticed that Princess Indola disapproved of the invitation, but she did not let that spoil her joyful anticipation. If agreement was reached and she married Darmon, she must get used to disapproval, for she certainly had no intention of changing her views to suit a mother-in-law.

The tour of Kaldor was interesting. It was a splendid city built on a grander scale than Bosron and in a different style. It would have been easy to praise its beauties had its Princess been less prejudiced. Andrela remained silent whilst her parents made the required exclamations, but she did glance at Darmon from time to time and felt sure that he appreciated the antagonism between her and his mother.

He said as much that afternoon. First he introduced Esquire Tesher. Lord Pandour she had already met, for he had accompanied his Prince to Eland for Fidel's funeral. He made polite reference to that, gently and briefly. It was not an occasion to be dwelt upon.

Master Tesher was equally formal until they had passed Seabee's bush.

"We are now hidden from all prying eyes," said Prince Darmon. "There may be gardeners about, but they never report anything that they see or hear. They would be banned from this area if they did. I know," he added, "for Mama once tried to bribe one."

"Did she?" Jon was surprised. "How very stupid of her! I had credited her with more sense than that."

"My mother does not have that kind of sense. The poor man was very indignant that she thought that he *could* be bribed, and she did not understand why; just as this morning she did not understand why Andrela was silent."

"And why were you silent, ma'am?" asked Lord Pandour.

"The High Princess described everything in such great detail that there was little left to say, Lord Pandour," replied Andrela tactfully.

"We are not formal here, no titles. We are Ped, Jon and Dee," noted Darmon.

She smiled at him delightedly.

"Then I shall be Drey. That is what my close friends call me in private."

"A splendid name," exclaimed Jon and eyed her long elegant gown. "I would challenge you to a race, Drey, if you were more suitably dressed. I might beat you. Ped and Dee are so impossibly tall and thin that I never win."

"Dee! Tall and thin!" objected Ped. "He is becoming quite paunchy due to sitting in Assembly meetings."

Dee promptly thumped his friend and Andrela turned to Jon.

"I *am* suitably dressed underneath," she told him and began to unbutton her dress. "Darm–er–Dee said informal, but I did not think that my parents or his would approve of my walking through the palace like this!"

She slipped out of the dress and flung her arms wide to display tight-fitting trousers worn with a short-sleeved top that reached to mid-thigh. Its length was the only feature that made any pretence of hiding her figure and it did not appear to restrict her freedom of movement in the slightest.

She laughed at his expression and folded the long dress carefully before laying it on a nearby bench.

"Where do we start, and where do we finish?"

The mock fight between Dee and Ped was abandoned in order to provide a starter and a judge, and the race was run.

Jon won, but only just. He had, he declared, intended to allow the lady to beat him, but as that gallantry proved much easier than he had anticipated he had decided to make a greater effort, and now they both needed a drink.

"Ped's turn, I think," said Dee and suggested a bench rather than their usual place.

Andrela, having enquired about their usual place, declined to sit tamely on a bench. She could not manage to jump the necessary distance, but she climbed the rope without much difficulty.

"I am out of practice," she explained as they helped her up. "We learnt at school. The mistress in charge of our physical wellbeing taught us much more than the dancing that was written into the prospectus. She told us that the ability to climb a rope might well be useful one day, and it was as well to be prepared. I don't think, though, that she envisaged this."

She kicked her legs in delight and was promptly seized by Dee and Jon who were on either side of her. They apologised when she looked at them in surprise. They were not used to females, especially ones who climbed ropes, and they were thus inclined to be over-protective.

"Did you never invite girls into the garden?" she asked.

"Some, but only Vee – Lady Vealla Marishen – did more than jump the stream and pick flowers; and she was banned by her mother after she scratched her face falling out of a tree."

"She would not have *said* that she fell out of a tree," Jon defended his friend fiercely, "but the fear of a blemish on her face was enough to send Lady M into hysterics. Such a thing would have severely limited her marriage prospects – according to her mother."

"As it is," noted Ped lazily as he opened a bottle of Air Gold that he had brought from Eland for just such an occasion, "it is her character that limits her suitors. She is too bold."

"She certainly has spirit," allowed Jon, and added to Drey in explanation that Western Lords in general were poor things and felt intimidated by any woman of character.

The present company he excluded from that generalisation. Ped and Dee were sturdy enough, for neither had chosen a partner and both had been under great pressure to do so.

"And you?" she asked, sipping from a wooden cup and thinking that the wine lost neither flavour nor sparkle in its humble container.

"I am not a lord," said Jon grandly. "I am the third son, and I trade. I have only money to my credit; no power or influence. No one cares whether I marry or not, and no ambitious mothers try to pair me with their daughters.

"Dee, of course, has suffered greatly from mothers and so has Ped. He is top of Lady M's list of desirable husbands for Vee, despite the fact that they do not like one another."

"I do not dislike her," murmured Ped. "I merely find her dull. She knows the latest gossip and the latest fashion, and very little else."

"Is that due to lack of interest, or lack of opportunity?" challenged Drey.

"You were fortunate in your schooling, Drey," interrupted Dee. "I would wager that you know the place where this excellent wine is made and how it was discovered. We do not have anything quite so effervescent."

"You might wager, Dee, but we will not take your bet," said Jon. "Ped rarely gambles and I would not bet against a lady. It goes against my principles."

Dee noted that 'rarely' did not mean 'never' and Ped made an unflattering remark about Jon's principles and declined the wager. He gave his reason.

"For although we travelled to Bosron for a sad occasion, my host there entertained me lavishly. He introduced me to Air Gold and mentioned that it was much favoured by the Princess Andrela and that she had visited the vineyards and caves in the foothills of the Kevaine Mountains where it originated."

Drey laughed at their banter.

"I do like it very much," she told them, "though I do not usually drink it in the middle of the afternoon."

The remark reminded Dee of the time. They had seen only a small part of the garden and there would not be another opportunity. They descended from the branch rather more quickly than they had mounted it.

Ped volunteered to wash the cups in the stream. It was not, he remarked, particularly hygienic, but none of them had died so far.

"Ped has made a joke," exclaimed Jon, exaggerating his surprise. "You must be a good influence, Drey."

She doubted it, but whether it was so or not, she enjoyed the afternoon. It could, she reflected later, have been the effects of Air Gold drunk well before six o'clock, but the company, the informality and the garden had pleased her and though she knew that her time in the garden would be severely limited, it did make the prospect of marrying Prince Darmon a little less of a sacrifice to duty.

Chapter 10

They were married in Bosron cathedral some ten months later.

The negotiations had been hard. Some of Eland Lords considered that a distant capital would increase their power, but the people had not wanted their city to lose its status. They did, however, want to see their Princess married, and the more politically aware realised the problems that might ensue if she chose a home grown husband.

Westland had reluctantly abandoned its tradition of Chosen Woman in the interests of uniting the island. It expected, being larger in area though of similar population, to merely assimilate the east without any great change and it certainly had no intention of losing Kaldor as capital city, but Eland was obstinate.

So too was their own Prince. He declared publicly that he would marry no one but the Princess Andrela. The more romantic news sheets made much of his supposed love for the lady, but he confessed to his parents and close friends that his criterion was suitability. He admired and respected the Princess, but he did not love her. He might easily have chosen a Westland lady. The problem was that he was too closely related to all who were of sufficiently ancient lineage to be considered worthy, and he had no desire to father a weak-minded or deformed child. Such offspring were becoming increasingly common amongst the aristocracy although they did tend to keep them safely confined on their country estates.

He was surprised to find that both his father and Lord Pandour understood. His father told him that he had chosen Indola as the furthest blood relative of sufficient standing and Ped had smiled.

"I have the same problem," he had owned. "Look at our family trees. Yours and mine are decidedly intermingled and we are related to almost every other family of note. It is not the principle reason for my single state, but it is one of them."

He also supported Prince Darmon in his desire for a separate dwelling. He strongly suspected that it was Andrela who insisted. Having met her and knowing the Princess Indola, he felt that they would be for ever at odds and Darmon, and possibly his father, would suffer because of it.

Eventually compromise was reached. New currency was minted, prices in Westland began to be displayed in krowns and fen and building work was started to convert one wing of the palace into quarters for the Prince and his new wife.

Eland had no immediate adjustments to make. It would remain independent until both Prince Roddori and Princess Andrela were dead and that, it was hoped, would be many years hence.

Bosron welcomed all the visitors from Westland who came to take part in, or simply to see, the wedding. The rich were bombarded with offers of luxury goods and tickets to plays and concerts and the poor were relieved of what monies they had brought with them, but all was done in an amicable way. The city decked its streets and squares, the gardeners tended its parks with competitive zeal and all its inhabitants prepared to celebrate the Royal Wedding.

The Westlanders did not disappoint. The Royal visitors rode out in style, the Lords who accompanied them showed their fine clothes at public and private occasions. The aristocracy became acquainted with their equals from Eland and all sought the company of the bride and groom.

There were many 'unimportant' people too. They had come to watch, because they realised the importance of the occasion, but they were welcomed and they spent their money.

Andrela conducted herself in such an exemplary manner that her father began to wonder if she had forgotten her previous love and had fallen for Prince Darmon. He did not like to think of his daughter as fickle, but he did not dare to ask and he allowed his wife to believe in the romance of their marriage.

Princess Margren was so happy that she was well disposed to everyone and did not notice the superior air of the Princess Indola. Others did, but no one remarked upon it and all assumed, as all the news sheets declared, that both Royal families were delighted with the match.

Caston Ambril ignored it as far as that was possible, but even he went to the Central Square in Lorton, the small town in the centre of Shyran, where the Lord had organised a great battery and a visi-screen so that all his people might watch the wedding and his small part in it.

The square was crowded, so too were the houses and shops that surrounded it. Enterprising owners had rented out seats in their upper rooms and were selling drinks, cakes and mementoes of the occasion. It was important. Every adult knew that Eland had been seeking to incorporate Shyran into its princedom, and a united Salima would surely do the same and be more difficult to resist.

The show was brief. There was just enough power to show the arrival of the most important personages and the ceremony itself. Caston saw the Prince arrive, splendid in a uniform of some Westland regiment of which he was titular commander. He watched more carefully when Andrela appeared and listened to the report on her dress. He knew that she was beautiful and that she preferred simple styles, but he smiled when told that the cream linen and the lace which adorned it were from the mountains. She had expressed a love of the mountains.

The skirt trailed behind her, but there was no train. As a small child she had been an attendant at several weddings and had once stepped on the bride's train. Inadvertently, it was said, but Caston wondered, and he quite understood that she did not trust small children to behave as instructed. The four small attendants carried posies and were kept in order by Lady Vealla Marishen, a cousin of the Prince and Lady Annia Campenden, a close friend of the Princess.

His face was sombre as he listened to her make her vows. *She* would keep them, he was sure, but he doubted that the Prince would do so. He did not know the man, but he was careful in all his dealings with the aristocracy, especially those from Westland. He recognised his prejudice and realised that it had now grown greater.

The sound came clearly over the relay, but the power was fading, and the screen flickered and went black as the Padros spoke the final words.

A great sigh arose from the crowd. The show was over.

"How annoying!" exclaimed the young girl who was standing nearby, "I wanted to see *all* the ladies, for they are sure to be dressed in the latest fashion."

"We saw the Princess," said her friend soothingly, "and fashion here is not of great importance. It changes very slowly."

"Everything changes slowly here," came the disconsolate answer. "It is ridiculous that we do not have electricity. We might have come by electric coach instead of on foot, and you would not have hurt your ankle. As it is, I do not know *how* we are to get home."

Her complaint was answered with a laugh.

"No one is going far just now. We must wait until the crowds thin a little. I shall sit on a wall or a bench somewhere and perhaps buy a drink later. You need not wait. You go with Shane when you please. He will not want to walk slowly. My father is meeting me at the crossroads, so if you see him, tell him what has happened and perhaps he will drive further into to town to meet me. There is no problem."

Caston had no option but to hear the exchange. He was standing still, as were the young ladies, for the crowd was milling around aimlessly, and anyone wanting to progress in a particular direction was finding it difficult.

The sharp-voiced girl moved away, but despite her determination she was obliged to move first one way and then another. Her companion waved to her departing back and was jostled by a large man who was shouting and trying to attract attention by waving his stick. She apologised, stumbled as she moved out of his way, fell against Caston and apologised again, more profusely.

He steadied her and thought it ironic that on this day of all days, he was once again coming to the assistance of an unknown young female.

She did not look in the least like Andrela. She was shorter, plumper and fair-haired, and she was, as he discovered as he helped her to a bench, a farmer's daughter. When the crowd thinned, he brought her a drink and a pastry and fetched his cart to take her to the crossroads where her father waited. She accepted the assistance with gratitude, but insisted on paying for the refreshments.

On the journey he learnt a great deal about her life and her family. It was a simple life and hard. She worked on the farm, feeding and herding the sheep and washing the wool. Most of the fleeces were sold at the market, but some were kept to make into rugs in the traditional manner. She and her mother also spun and wove and knitted garments for the men of the household, but she preferred making rugs. She liked gathering the lichen and petals and berries for colouring the yarn. She sometimes experimented and made new colours, and she loved to vary the old patterns by working in her new shades.

Caston was intrigued. There was always a market for well-made traditional rugs and there were few who still made them by hand, usually on the more isolated farms. He made sure that he knew the exact location of her parent's farm before they parted, and he resolved to investigate further.

Shyran's view of the Royal wedding might have been cut short, but Salima's was not. Cameras recorded the newly married couple as they left the cathedral. The Shower of Fortune was faithfully described as were the coats, dresses and hats of guests. Even the most dedicated followers of fashion were satisfied.

Some of the remote parts of the country were unable to receive the visi-screen pictures, but everywhere else they were watched with avidity. People had grouped together and food had been cooked in advance so that communities could enjoy their lunch and discuss the great event whilst the wedding party were at the ceremonial Breakfast in the State Dining Room at the Palace. During that time, only pictures of Bosron's parks, parties and lavish decorations appeared on the screens, occasionally interspersed with images of an ornate invitation and a glittering menu card.

Andrela and her new husband were at the forefront of the procession from cathedral to palace. Thus they arrived first, as was proper, and having accepted the good wishes of the staff gathered in the entrance hall, they stood with their parents to receive their guests. There were a great many and Andrela was glad when all were happily drinking wine and sampling savouries and she was able to escape to her own rooms. Her attendants accompanied her.

Lady Vealla looked around with undisguised curiosity, but she did offer to help remove the bride's gown, "For you probably do not want company in the closet, and that dress will not be easy to manage alone."

"Grizzie will help me," responded Andrela. "We are used to one another and it took an age to fasten all the buttons."

Before she disappeared with Lady Annia, she waved a hand towards a table and requested that Vealla pour drinks.

It was some time before they reappeared which was fortunate because Vealla was not used to opening bottles of Air Gold.

"Excellent timing!" exclaimed the returning Andrela as the cork finally flew out of the bottle with a satisfactory 'pop'. "We need this. All that waving and smiling has made my jaw ache and we are due to 'walk the boundary' this afternoon."

She tucked a large white napkin around her neck to protect her dress and helped herself to a large savoury pastry as well as accepting the brimming glass that Vealla held out to her.

"Does 'we' include us?"

"It certainly does. Only the parents will be allowed to rest." Andrela sounded almost scornful of the older generation, but that might have been because her mouth was full of pastry, "but you are my attendants and must be around me today.

"In fact, you may be expected to be around me for years. Grizzie has accepted the position of my First Lady of the Bedchamber and will be coming to Westland with me, but Darmon has asked that I also appoint a Second Lady, one from Westland. You are the obvious choice, but I am not sure that you want it."

Andrela selected another pastry and blessed the cook who knew that these were her particular favourites. She turned to study Vealla.

"Do you?" she asked, sure that the girl did not. "You need not speak, just shake your head. I shall not be in the least offended, and you may say truthfully that the position has not been offered."

"But it has," said Vealla, turning away to hide her face. "Princess Indola has already asked my parents, and they have accepted on my behalf."

She took a deep breath and added, unable to conceal her anger and bitterness, "It seems that as Second Lady of your

Bedchamber I shall meet a great many eligible gentleman; Lord Pandour being the particular attraction."

Andrela set down her glass carefully.

"Princess Indola is *not* in charge of my bedchamber," she said quietly, "nor is she in charge of my household, my finances, or my friends. I will make my own decisions."

"I am sorry, I did not mean –"

Vealla stopped short. She was not often at a loss for words, but she had put her annoyance and distress firmly behind her, at least for this day, and now it had been recalled unexpectedly.

"There is no need to apologise," said Andrela. "Certainly not for my mother-in-law and your parents."

She laughed suddenly and turned to Lady Annia.

"Grizzie we need another drink; and do you think I can squeeze in another pastry? We have a huge feast before us, but buffalo steaks are my father's favourite and are sure to be sadly overcooked for he likes them hard, the fish is in an overpowering sauce that my mother insisted upon and the sweet is a heavy pudding that was apparently much praised by Darmon when he came for Fid's funeral. All I chose was the carrot mousse. Mama was most put out. She hates carrot mousse."

"I thought you made your own decisions," observed Lady Annia drily as she filled their glasses and held out the plate of pastries.

"Important ones," answered Andrela loftily. "After the discussions about the currency exchange and the costs of minting and printing it, food at the wedding seemed not to matter in the least."

Her grand tones were somewhat diminished by the accompanying grand gesture which resulted in spilt wine and scattered crumbs.

"Shades and Skies!" she exclaimed and handed her glass to Annia with a brief warning that it was not funny. Her gown would one day be put on display somewhere, and she did *not* want it to have stains down the front.

Vealla envied their easy relationship, but as she did not share it she hastily gave assistance. Fortunately the large napkin had saved the dress from harm and she said so with great relief. She also drew discreet attention to the time. They ought to be re-joining the guests.

"Shades!" said Andrela again, "We must go. We must not waste the AG," – she seized her glass and drained it swiftly – "but we cannot keep two High Princes and their wives and assorted nobles waiting.

"Do not concern yourself about Lord Pandour, Vee," she continued as she led them down the stairs. "He is too closely related to all Westland's aristocracy, including you, to want to marry any of them."

Vealla laughed and agreed. Pandour was far too intelligent and educated to risk a marriage that might produce an idiot child. He ought to emulate the Prince and marry an Elander.

She saw the Princess smile and turned to include Annia in the joke, but only a tight little smile was on *her* lips and the trace of a blush coloured her cheek. Vealla continued down the stairs in contemplative silence.

Andrela interrupted her serious thoughts with a whispered apology. She had done her best, but Lord Cumbler, Vealla's neighbour at table, was dreadfully dull and would talk of his ancient lineage through several courses.

"But do enjoy the carrot mousse," she finished.

Vealla's mystification was changed to amusement when she saw Lord Cumbler. He was a sturdy man of about thirty, dressed in clothes of good quality, but so out-dated that she wondered if they had belonged to his father. His hair was thick and curly and reddish-orange.

Being sure that she had not encountered anyone with that shade of hair, she remarked as she took her seat that she did not believe that they had met.

"No," he replied ponderously. "I do not come often to Bosron. My country place has all that I need. I arrived yester eve, however; for an occasion such as this merits my presence."

Vealla swallowed. He spoke as if he were doing the Royal family a favour. She soon learned, that in his opinion, he was.

Chapter 11

Lord Cumbler's country place was near Winisham, and his family had been Lords there when the town was called Winnis hamlet and before Lord Parandour had conquered the north.

Vealla knew little about Eland's history and was foolish enough to admit to the fact. He queried her schooling, read her name from the place card and concluded that she was from Westland. He had not heard of her or her parents, he declared, but did not apologise for his ignorance. Westland aristocracy was new compared to Eland's great names and he was well acquainted with *their* history. He proceeded to enlighten her.

She listened in wonder. How could he talk so and eat at the same time? There was hardly a second where she might have interposed a comment, had she thought of one, and yet he managed to eat half-a-dozen of the delicate savouries – smaller, she noted, than the ones that Andrela had consumed, – a generous plateful of the fish in its spicy sauce and to down several glasses of both the excellent wines that accompanied them.

"That is a very brief history of our ruling class," he concluded, "but I have covered all the most important events. It will be useful for you to know these things for you will undoubtedly meet some members of the families that I have mentioned."

"There was certainly a great deal of information," began Vealla. She intended to make some polite remark about its usefulness, but a plate was set before her. On it was a small glass dish filled with reddish-orange froth topped with a feathery green leaf.

"This must be the carrot mousse," she thought, and turned towards Andrela.

The bride was in conversation with Prince Maldon, but she looked up. Vealla had a fleeting impression of laughing eyes and curving lips, but a second later Andrela turned to the Prince with an earnest expression on her face. She was clearly making a contribution to a serious discussion.

Vealla did not have the Princess's control. Her lips remained obstinately set in a broad smile. She picked up her spoon and turned determinedly to the gentleman on her other side.

"This, I suppose, must be the carrot mousse," she announced.

"A favourite 'tween courses' of Princess Andrela," he agreed with an answering smile.

She wondered if he had noticed their exchange of glances, but decided that he could not have done. She thought him too old to catch such brief communications. He *was* old, older than her father, but he proved to be livelier and much more interesting than Lord Cumbler.

Unfortunately he excused himself when the speeches finally came to an end. He was quite open; he needed a nap and would join other friends in a room specially set aside for elderly gentlemen. Elderly ladies, he declared, talked in the afternoons and did not need to sleep.

Vealla was not required to comment on the statement, for Lord Cumbler promised the elderly gentleman to take care of her and proceeded, much to her disgust, to do so in his most assiduous manner. She could not even escape by pleading the need for privacy. He escorted her almost to the door of the ladies' room and promised to await her return.

The procession along the path by the side of the railings would not start for another hour, at least, he assured her. There was plenty of time. She need not worry about the procession either. There was no danger. The 'walks round the boundary' as they were sometimes inaccurately called, were made on all great occasions and were entirely safe. The common folk could see through the railings, but an electrified mesh prevented any person or object from penetrating the fence.

"Really!" exclaimed Vealla. "I own that I had not given a thought to security. I suppose that it is necessary."

She shrugged her shoulders in dismissal of the subject and left him.

Unfortunately, though she spent a long time in the closet, combing her hair and exchanging comments with other ladies, he was waiting for her when she emerged.

She tried another ploy and invented some spurious reason for seeking her parents, but Lord Cumbler was immune to hints. He not only professed his great desire to meet her parents, but he also remembered that her mother's hat was crowned with crimson feathers. It was thus easy to find in a crowd and he did so without difficulty.

As an invited guest at a wedding in another country, she did not feel able to resort to rudeness and she followed him in apparent acquiescence, but with gritted teeth. So tightly was she clenching them that she could not smile at the tall gentleman who was approaching. She had met him and had liked him, but she could not remember his name. Only his nickname came to mind, and one could not greet a gentleman as 'Colly', especially through gritted teeth.

He came up and greeted her escort cheerfully.

"Ah, Lord Crumbler," he said. "I trust that you are enjoying your visit to Bosron, but I fear that I have been sent to take away your lovely companion. The Princess Margren desires to see her."

Vealla was amused at the mispronunciation, surprised at the message and startled by her escort's reply. He sounded angry.

"My name is *Cumbler*, Lord Collingwade, as you very well know."

"I cannot imagine why Princess Margren wants me," she said quickly, removing her hand from Lord Cumbler's arm and placing it on the one stretched out towards her. "Something to do with the Walk I suppose, so I must answer the summons."

Lord Collingwade smiled and drew her gently from Lord Cumbler's side.

"Indeed, you must," he said, "and Lord Clumber must forgive my slip of the tongue, for it is sadly embarrassing when one mistakes a person's name."

Vealla willingly followed her new escort, but she could not speak for fear of laughing and he waited until Lord Cumbler's sharp corrections were lost in the general chatter.

"I *was* sent, Lady Vealla," he assured her. "Princess Andrela asked me to rescue you and suggested that her mother's wish to meet you again could be used as an excuse. She knows that I do not like to lie and that Cumbler is only impressed by the great and good. *I* know that he is quite capable of supplanting me in a way that is difficult to refuse and leading you to the Princess himself, so I made him angry. It is the most effective way of disconcerting him."

"How kind of Princess Andrela," answered Vealla. "I could not get away from him without being very impolite." She smiled up at him suddenly. "I do hope that *you* will not be disconcerted to learn that I have forgotten your name and remember only the nickname 'Colly'."

"Everyone calls me Colly," returned the gentleman. "I inherited the title at about nine years old and was sometimes mocked for it at school. I thumped any boy who dared to bow and call me 'lord'. Fortunately I was tall for my age and could land a good punch. They soon stopped calling me 'lord', but I accepted 'Colly'.

"I am still tall for my age," he noted, "and that makes it difficult for me to lose myself in a crowd. I will, therefore, lead you to the back of the group that surrounds Princess Margren. You will be hidden from Cumbler's sight and there will be other company for you. I shall walk out on to the terrace. They are now opening the doors."

Vealla was happy to be hidden from Lord Cumbler, but a little disappointed to be abandoned by her present companion. He did, however, invite her to join him on the terrace if she did not find other and more congenial company.

She felt it unlikely that she would find any more congenial company than his and therefore accepted the invitation with grateful thanks.

She was right about the company, and he was right about Lord Cumbler. That gentleman was not in sight but neither were any of the Elanders whom she had met and liked and neither was Jonal Tesher. The two young Westlanders whom she saw were pleasant enough, but both were on her mother's list. She made her way to the terrace and joined Lord Collingwade.

"Being so tall, you are easy to find," she said. "Is that an advantage or a disadvantage?"

"It depends entirely on who is looking for me," he answered.

Jonal, she thought, would have taken that opportunity to pay an extravagant compliment, but his compliments were always extravagant, and not to be taken seriously. She saw that he too was on the terrace with a group of Elanders and appeared to be enjoying himself. She also knew that he had not wanted to come to the wedding.

"The grand lords of two countries will be there, vying for favour," he had told her. "The social gatherings will not be to my taste, even if I am invited to any, but I have been invited to the wedding and I will be there. His Highness Prince Darmon will have to make do with Pandour's support at other times."

She tried to catch his eye, but could not.

"A friend," she said to Lord Collingwade. "He is a good friend, but not one with 'Influence'. He is the third son of Lord Barre, and third sons, even of the great lords, are not considered important; but I like him."

There was a touch of defiance in her last words and she continued quickly in the hope that it would be unnoticed.

"I did not see him before. He is not much taller than I am and thus not easy to see in a crowd."

"Jonal Tesher?" enquired Lord Collingwade and smiled when she nodded. "We have met. Bosron harbour is very crowded just now and his yacht is close to mine. Shall we join him, or would you prefer to walk in the garden?"

Vealla chose to walk in the garden. She wanted to see as much of Eland as possible in the short time that was left.

It was a most enjoyable interlude. Her companion was amusing and informative. He listened to her opinions and appeared to value them. They discussed trees and flowers, friends and families, modes of transport and history. Quite how they arrived at the past rulers of their respective countries, Vealla could not remember, but it was not important.

What was important and occurred to her suddenly, was the time.

"The Boundary Walk!" she exclaimed suddenly. "I am supposed to be there, and I have no idea of the time."

"Do not fret," replied Lord Collingwade lazily. "It is not due to start for at least ten minutes and we are now approaching the start."

They walked through an archway and she saw that the hedge ended and the high railings bordering the garden were visible. A broad path ran alongside them and guests were standing in groups at its start. Crowds were also gathering outside, already pressing against the wooden barrier that protected them from the electrified fence. Lady Annia was there with the small attendants, but Andrela and her new husband were not in sight.

"Thank you!" breathed Vealla with heartfelt gratitude. "I had completely forgotten about it and I would *not* have been popular had I been late."

They walked up to Lady Annia who greeted them cheerfully.

"Vealla, I am in desperate need of help with these children. Thank you, Colly, for returning her in good time. Two of us will manage better than one, and I am not fond of small children."

She was in need of help; one child was kicking dirt over her shoes and another, whose arm she was holding in a fierce grip, was struggling to pick up pebbles from the path.

Colly grinned.

"I know. You prefer books. I am surprised that you did not bring one and read them a story."

He looked down at the girl who was pulling petals from the flowers in her posy.

"Do you know the story of the ugly princess and the beautiful witch?" he asked.

The child frowned at him. "Princesses are never ugly," she contradicted, but he had her interest. A moment later he was sitting on the ground with two children on each leg telling a story.

Lady Annia moved gratefully away, but Vealla stayed and listened. He finished the story just as the bride and groom arrived.

"Your trousers will be ruined, Colly," said Andrela. "The ground is still damp from the shower last evening."

"But the girls' dresses will be relatively unsoiled," he returned with a smile; and they were.

"It was an interesting story," Vealla told Lady Annia as they took up their positions, "and he timed it perfectly. He finished just as the Prince and Princess came up."

"Colly always times things perfectly," replied Lady Annia. "It is one of his talents. He rescues people, too. I have cause to be grateful to him, as does most of the young aristocracy in Bosron. Andrela is included in that, and probably many others of whom I know nothing."

Vealla assumed correctly that some of the 'others' were not aristocratic, but she did not think any the less of Lord Collingwade for that. She liked him and wanted to accept the invitation he had given for the following day, but she had postponed her decision. She asked Lady Annia's advice.

"He has offered to take me for a ride in his electric car and to show me how to drive it! I would not do so in Kaldor, but is it acceptable here? I do not mind shocking my parents, I have done that often, but shocking foreigners is a different matter."

The reply was positive. It was quite acceptable to go out with a gentleman in public and driving was not frowned upon either. Annia added a sympathetic comment on the difficulty of adjusting to the habits of foreign countries.

Vealla was too happy with the answer to dwell for long on the restrictions placed upon her in Westland.

"Perhaps you and the Princess will change things," she said cheerfully. "I do hope so."

She went on to discuss yachts, friends and Jonal and was delighted to find that Annia understood exactly. Annia, Drey and Colly had been friends for years, with no complications.

The question of why Colly had a yacht, a coach and an electric car in Bosron at the same time, was not so plainly answered. Vealla could not see why it had anything to do with the Princess, and she did not understand the story of two paths. Why would it be easier to take a difficult path simply because another path was there?

She did not press the point. She followed Annia's example and smiled and waved, and she resolved to find Colly as soon as the Walk was over. She would accept his offer, but insist on an early start. She would not tell him that that was in order to avoid her parents, she would lie and say that she adored early mornings. Perhaps they might have lunch together. She must remember to take some money.

Chapter 12

Andrela enjoyed her wedding day in many ways. The Lords and Ladies seemed happy to meet their fellows and the commoners rejoiced. They turned out to see her and her groom, they decorated the streets and houses, and they organised parties of their own.

She would have liked to have seen one, but it was not possible and the evening party at the palace was some compensation. The band was excellent, and Darmon proved to be a more than adequate dancer. She also found much to amuse her.

She had expected that Lord Pandour would partner Grizzie at least once, he was so very correct, but he did so four times which was not necessary. She laughed to herself at the frowns on the faces of some Westerner matrons.

The fact that Colly danced with Vealla several times was also noticed. Eland ladies smiled indulgently for many had reason to thank him, and Western ladies raised their eyebrows and looked with pity on Lady Marishen. Her daughter seemed addicted to the lesser aristocracy. All had noted that Lord Collingwade had rated no higher a place at table than Esquire Tesher.

Colly disappeared from the ballroom at about ten o'clock. So too did Vealla. Princess Indola noticed and felt it her duty to inform Andrela, for the conduct of her Ladies of the Bedchamber must be beyond reproach.

Andrela smiled sweetly and agreed. She would choose as her Second Lady a person of impeccable reputation. That disconcerted her new mother-in-law in a very satisfactory manner.

She resolved to meet more of the younger westerners and promptly joined a group of youngsters from both countries. Most of them were barely out of school. Lord Brey's daughter was amongst them, and Andrela discovered the reason for Colly's absence.

After a breathless compliment on the bride's appearance and on her handsome bridegroom, the girl told her that Colly was caring for her brother, *again*. Her exasperation was plain as she recounted that Geral had been *warned* that the bubbles in Air Gold made the alcohol go to the head very quickly, but had *still* become drunk and this time sick.

Colly had noticed, and he and his partner had come over. He had taken Geral outside and the lady had taken care of Mara.

Mara, it seemed, was a young western girl who had also succumbed to the delights of Air Gold and become 'unsteady'.

"She was drunk," declared a young man emphatically. "She was as drunk as I am."

He smiled happily at Andrela and tried to bow. It was not an elegant bow; he came near to falling over. A western girl took charge.

She saved him from tumbling, bade two companions to take him away and dunk his head in cold water, apologised to Andrela for his state and excused it on the basis that Air Gold was a wonderful wine, and the hospitality being so generous, it was to be expected that some of the inexperienced would over indulge.

Colly arrived at that moment. He praised the girl for her good sense and reported that Geral was walking in the garden in the care of a footman and that Mara was being transported to her hotel in his carriage and in the company of Lady Vealla, who would return.

He led Andrela away. Such unsophisticated company was only interesting up to a point. That point, he declared, had now been reached and the group might now take more note of Miss Ashton's excellent advice and steer clear of trouble.

"That sensible child is Miss Ashton?" asked Andrela and was answered with a nod.

"I do not remember her, or anyone else of that name. And I made such an effort to set the westerners in my mind!"

"Do not castigate yourself," said Colly. "She is here as companion to Lord Narethan's grand-daughter, and though she is distantly related, she is of no importance whatsoever."

"Good!" exclaimed Andrela. "I find people of no importance whatsoever *so* much nicer than those with lots of it." She gave a satisfied smile.

He too smiled, but did not speak. He recalled some words of Vealla's and wondered if the Princess had found her Second Lady of the Bedchamber.

Andrela was in no doubt. She had.

The wedding night was spent at Senby. Lord Berrondol had offered the freedom of his house and the service of his staff.

He and his wife would remain in Bosron so that the young couple would have the place to themselves and, as an added incentive, he pointed out that the State Rooms had a balcony with an eastern aspect and, if the weather were clement, they might view the sunrise across the Bay.

Darmon had thought that strange. Did the man really think that a newly married couple would want to rise before sun-up to stare at the view?

Andrela had too many memories of Senby and sunrise to wish to spend her wedding night there, but it was difficult to refuse. She therefore accepted and told Darmon that the Berrondols were an old family, renowned for their love of their home. It was a great compliment to be offered hospitality.

Less seriously, she also mentioned that though son had succeeded father for many generations now, all the Lords of Berrondol had been married for several years before said son had made his appearance. The sunrise was obviously a considerable distraction.

Darmon made jokes about it on their way there, but he was impressed with the house and the State Rooms. They were large and richly furnished and there was a superb view of Bosron Bay from the window. It was not easily seen at such a late hour, but the moon was bright enough to show the long garden and the great expanse of water beyond.

They returned to Bosron late the following morning for a formal lunch given by the merchants of the city. It was, to Darmon's surprise, held in the palace.

"They pay for its upkeep," Andrela commented drily. "They are entitled to see inside it sometimes; and they are providing the food and the wine. Both will be good."

They were; and the wedding gifts presented by the various groups were also impressive. Darmon had witnessed the grief displayed at Fidel's funeral, but such emotion could be stirred by the fear of change. He felt that most of the sentiments expressed for their future happiness were genuine; a tribute to the Royal family of Eland. He happily reported this to his fellow countrymen at the various social gatherings that occupied their afternoon.

Later, they travelled to Measham. There was a ball that evening in their honour.

"I refused the dinner that was offered," Andrela told him, "for we have eaten far too much already, but I could not refuse to visit the town. Fidel died there and the people need something to cheer them. I have never blamed anyone for Fidel's death, but many have and the town has suffered because of it. Our stay will help."

Darmon was happy to stay in Measham and to dance as many dances as Andrela felt was appropriate. It was her country and she seemed to know it well.

He was less happy when she told him casually that she asked Miss Elizabeth Ashton to be her Second Lady of the Bedchamber.

"Miss Ashton?" he queried, not immediately recognising the name.

When she explained and he realised whom she had chosen, he objected.

"But she is a nobody! And she is far too young! What possessed you to ask her? My mother will certainly not approve. She wanted Lady Vealla, who is a much more appropriate choice and was your attendant. I thought you liked her."

"I do," answered Andrela. "I like her far too much to offer her a position which she does not want and will find difficult to refuse."

"It is an *honour*, so it is certainly not lightly refused," declared Darmon indignantly, "but I cannot imagine why she would want to refuse."

"According to your Mama," pronounced Andrela sweetly, "the position ensures contact with a great many eligible gentlemen, Lord Pandour being one of them."

"I suppose that it might," he answered doubtfully and asked if she had discussed it with his mother.

"Certainly not! It is none of her business," she replied forcefully and she drew his attention to the view from the carriage windows. They were approaching Measham and from one point it was possible to see the town.

Darmon stared out of the window. He had always tried to avoid confrontation with his mother. He had gone his own way where possible or, he thought regretfully, he had done as she wished.

His wife did not know her well, he thought, and when she did, she too might take the easier route and comply. On the other hand, she might not. Was it Eland or its Princess that had proved so obdurate in the negotiations that had preceded their marriage?

Their stay at Measham was sweet, but short. They left mid-morning the following day for Corbay. There, Andrela promised her husband, they would stay in one of the hotels famous for their views of the sunrise. It was necessary to wake early to see the spectacle, but not to rise, for all the best rooms – and they would assuredly have the very best – had beds that faced the window and shutters that were operated by a switch conveniently placed by the alarm clock.

Corbay welcomed them as enthusiastically as Measham had done. They toured the town and every road on their route was lined with people waving and throwing petals. Darmon kept a few, for they smelt sweet and they were going to see a newly discovered fishing boat. It was, however, an ancient boat that had been buried for years in the sand and all trace of fish had long since been washed away. The petals were not needed.

Fish was served for dinner, but that smelt as delicious as it tasted. Corbay prided itself on its many ways of cooking fish, and on the quantity and variety that was landed onto its quays. The town was also proud of its traditional cake, a spicy mix of dried fruits and nuts. It was offered as one of a selection of sweets and Darmon, finding it to his taste, had a large piece. He noticed many approving smiles.

Andrela explained later. The women of Corbay made it for their men when they returned to shore. Its various ingredients were reputed to restore vitality and ensure that the men were potent and vigorous in bed.

That did not please him. He felt that he ought to have been told before the dinner. Her laughing response did not please him either. She thought it encouraging that everyone hoped that they would have a child, for their two countries would not unite without one. He thought it tactless of her to remind him of the sole reason for her consent to their marriage.

He had forgotten his annoyance by morning and they lay in bed to watch the sunrise. The sea mist lifted slowly and Andrela felt the prickle of tears. She pulled on a wrap and went to stand by the window. She did not want him to see her cry.

The sun had appeared and turned the sky to gold before he joined her.

"What is it?" he asked gently.

She brushed her tears away and answered briefly, "A memory. Eland is sunrise and I shall be leaving soon."

"Not forever. We will come back to visit."

"Yes, but it will not be the same. Nothing is ever the same. Each new morning is a fresh beginning and the previous days must be left behind."

"Mistakes as well as triumphs are left behind," he said trying to comfort her.

He put his arm around her, and they stood in silence and watched the sun rise clear of the horizon.

She moved against him. He was not the man she wanted, but he was the one she had married. It was he who suggested that they return to bed, but it was she who pressed the switch to close the shutters and she who offered the first kiss.

The day went well. She pushed her regrets aside and concentrated on enjoying the seaside. Corbay had two faces; the old fishing port and the smart new hotels, shops and clean swept beaches. She preferred the old town, but she liked the contrast.

They had no engagements. The Mayor had decided that one dinner was enough, and the local gentry had returned to their country homes, satisfied with a single evening with the Princess and her foreign husband. There was no timetable. Dinner was to be served in their suite and on the morrow, they would depart for Pittern and a restful week by Lake Warne.

On that morrow, a relay message for Prince Darmon interrupted their breakfast. He craved her pardon and left to read it alone, but he returned almost immediately, a deep frown creasing his forehead.

"It is from my parents," he began then corrected himself. "Well, from my mother. She is concerned about Lady Vealla. It seems that she has disappeared."

Andrela set down her cup.

"What exactly does your mother mean by 'disappeared'?" she asked.

"She seems to have left the hotel last evening after dinner and now cannot be found."

Darmon referred to the extremely long – and therefore expensive – relay in his hand.

"Also, a Lord Collingwade has disappeared. So has his yacht. My mother says that you may be able to help as you knew him well."

"I *know* him well," answered Andrela. "I doubt that he is dead or that he has disappeared, but he may have left Bosron on his yacht. That seems a far more reasonable assumption."

"Do not make fun, Andrela," he reproved. "Both have left Bosron unexpectedly and Vealla's parents are naturally worried. They fear that they are together and wish to find her as soon as possible. Do you know where he is likely to have gone?"

"I know no more than any other." Andrela shrugged her shoulders. "His yacht is usually moored at Malport. His home is between there and Angel Heights, but he did not tell me where he intended to go after the wedding.

"If Vealla is with Colly, however, there is no cause for concern. He will look after her. Colly looks after everyone."

Darmon looked in exasperation from his wife to the paper in his hand. His mother had not been brief, nor had she spared her criticism of Vealla, Andrela or Eland's aristocracy and their lax habits.

Andrela had spread preserve over her slice of bread, but she paused with it half way to her mouth.

"Does your Mama say whether Vealla took spare clothes with her?" she asked before taking a bite.

"Yes, she took clothes and she left a note declaring her intention of getting married." Darmon's answer was impatient. "Does that tell you where she has gone?"

"Yes. She will have gone to find a Padri. Does she say who she is going to marry? I do *hope* it is Colly. I sent him to rescue her from Lord Cumbler who is a dreadful bore, and I did think that they were getting on rather well together."

Andrela smiled and reached out a hand for the relay message. "May I?" she asked.

"No," he said shortly and placed his hand on the paper. "This Collingwade, is he the tall one who danced far too often with Vealla at the wedding?"

She decided not to challenge the number of dances that was allowable. She answered 'yes' and asked if his mother had been very rude about her.

He frowned and stumbled over his reply. Phrases emerged: could be forthright, strong opinions and not always diplomatic.

Andrela grinned. "Like me," she said.

"More rigid than you," he answered. "Now do you have any ideas about where Collingwade might be heading in his yacht? It is difficult to stop vessels on the sea, and Lady Marishen is extremely anxious."

"I expect that the yacht is returning to Malport. The berths in Bosron are very expensive. But they may not be on the yacht. Colly has an electric car and a carriage. They could have left in either of those; or they might have hired a small river boat and gone up river. The Bos and the Tark are navigable and there are several towns along their banks. Or they may have taken a public coach and travelled no further than North Beach. Lots of couples get married there because it is cheap and everyone can get there by public coach."

Darmon sighed. The answer was unhelpful and he knew that it was intended to be so. If Andrela knew anything, which he doubted, she was not going to say.

He pushed away his unfinished breakfast and left to compose a tactful answer to the relay.

It was not easy. His mother was convinced that his wife had planned the whole thing in order to discredit Westland morals so that she would be free to do as she pleased. *He* had been annoyed by the acid comments on what Andrela might choose to do if she were not restrained. He knew that she would be even more annoyed and so had not dared to show it to her.

He was glad that the alterations to the palace in Kaldor were almost complete. They would have their own quarters, and he would try to ensure that any contact between wife and mother would take place at social gatherings where the two ladies could remain at different ends of a crowded room. His wife was not a meek compliant woman.

He had never had a mistress. Mama's moral strictures and the difficulties of finding a woman who would not become too demanding or too expensive had been sufficient deterrent. He had had a few casual encounters, all of which had been too brief to become the subject of gossip that might reach his mother's ears.

Marriage had its compensations. He did not love Andrela, he had never loved anyone, but it had been pleasant to wake in the morning with her beside him.

Chapter 13

Darmon did not tell his wife how he had replied to his mother and she did not ask. They had a pleasant journey to Pittern and were warmly welcomed by the town and the palace staff.

"There has been a Royal home here for almost as many years as Eland has had a Prince," Andrela told him. "It was the chief town in the north. Why they chose this place I cannot imagine. Lake Warne was then a marsh that stretched from the Felt to the Aishe. Marshes are home to many birds, but they are damp and dismal and unhealthy."

"Perhaps the Witch of Bellue settled upon it. She was reputed to have the ability to see into the future, was she not?"

Andrela laughed, "There is very little other than folk tales to show that she actually existed," she said, but she was delighted that he had taken the trouble to read something of Eland's history. History was her favourite subject.

If he were interested, she suggested, they might hire a boat and travel to Guorl and visit the sights. There were many associated with the Witch, though none had more than tradition to support their claims. He *was* interested and they made their plans.

The news sheets informed them of Lady Vealla's whereabouts. She and Lord Collingwade had married in Senby and had spent their wedding night in one of the hotels with a view of the Bay and the sunrise, before departing for his home.

"Senby!" exclaimed Andrela. "How clever of Colly! Not even *I* considered that!" and Darmon smiled.

"Where ever they married, I trust that they will be happy," he said and they set off on their expedition.

Two weeks later they went to Feltenare. Its history was better documented. The West Gate and some of the walls remained, but the gate was too narrow for modern traffic and another broader route had been made through the walls to the south. On their way, they passed Giverren Bridge, now built of stone and lined with market stalls, and they walked around the nearby battle site.

"The landscape has changed," Andrela told her husband. "There is no longer a gully, but the women fought there, and their efforts turned the tide of the battle. Your mother would not have approved, but they saved Eland from invasion."

"My mother does not wield a sword, but she fights in her own way," he replied. "She frequently wins, so it is usually better to avoid confrontation."

He spoke mildly, but Andrela made her position clear. She had no quarrel with Princess Indola, but she would not be ruled by her. She softened her reply with a smile and a reminder that as she was *his* wife she would do her best to please *him*.

He assured her that she had done so and they proceeded to the town in good accord.

Two days later they sailed from Feltenare to Westland. Andrela had persuaded Darmon to take the northern route and to call in at some of the most important towns and cities on their way to Kaldor. It was little longer than the southern route, but she would learn something of Westland, and his people would have the opportunity to see their new Princess.

New Stannul was their first stop, then Alden, Garbay and Testeril and thence to Kaldor. The journey to her new home took her nowhere near Shyran.

They were warmly welcomed in New Stannul. It was far from both capitals and, as a trading port a short ferry ride from Eland, its people were aware of the benefits of a shared currency. They looked forward to a united island.

The crowds in the west coast ports were thin, driven more by curiosity than by any affection, and Darmon became anxious. How would Kaldor receive his bride?

Andrela had no concerns. In Eland, her marriage had been accepted and the change of capital city was far in the future. Some realised what that change might mean, but none had raised any great objections. The currency change, however, had already been implemented and she expected that Westland's populace would be annoyed, and possibly frustrated and confused by it. She did not feel diminished or insulted by the few boats that sailed downriver to escort their yacht into the city, or by the small size of the crowd that awaited them at the quayside. Acclaim and interest was for their own. She was a foreigner and expected to be treated as such.

She was a little disconcerted, however, when she discovered that they were not to dine alone in their own home that evening. They had been invited to dine with the High Prince and Princess; and Darmon, knowing his mother better than he knew his wife, had accepted.

"They *are* my parents," he replied when she complained. "It is natural that they wish to see us after we have been so long away."

"Very well. You have said that we will go, so we will, but I would have preferred a restful evening in our own home. The interest of the people is flattering, but it is tiring."

She sighed. "I feel that I have been on show for months, and, though your father is easy, I do not think that an evening spent with your mother will be restful."

Despite all Darmon's efforts to direct conversation to non-controversial topics such as their trip round Eland, he was forced to admit that she was right. It was not a restful evening.

His mother expressed her pleasure that they had not been obliged to stand on the balcony whilst one way viewing was in progress. She remembered well how tiring it had been on her own wedding day when the crowds had filled the square to overflowing.

Prince Maldon had reminded her gently that the crowds in Bosron had been dense and many had waited to see the bridal party 'Walk the Boundary', but Princess Indola did not attach great importance to Eland crowds.

She did, however, attach great importance to Lady Vealla's introduction to Lord Collingwade. He *might* have been presented to her at some official function where everyone was presented, even those with no claim to ancient lineage, but she would not have remembered him or encountered him again, had not Andrela despatched him to the lady's side at her wedding.

Andrela requested another spoon of carrots and smiled sweetly at the minion who served her.

"Colly is not a great lord," she told her mother-in-law, "nor is his Command very large, but he can trace his ancestry back for around two hundred years. The title came later."

Princess Indola interrupted. "Westland titles are *all* more than *three* hundred years old," she declared, "and there have been lords of Pandour for near a thousand years."

"Many Eland *titles* have existed for a thousand years," countered Andrela, "but they have not always been held by the same family. Lords have had only daughters, or their sons have died young, as did Fidel."

Darmon attempted to interrupt, but he was stopped by his wife. She raised her hand imperiously and continued.

"I have studied some of Westland's aristocracy and their antecedents and found, as one would expect, similar happenings. Did not a Lord Pandour die without issue in the reign of one of the Cendara Princes?"

"Cendara the Second," declared Prince Maldon firmly.

His wife did not like to be corrected, especially when she was wrong, and his daughter-in-law was beginning to remind him of a particularly tenacious breed of hunting dog. He redirected the conversation.

"I take a great interest in the history of my country, but I do not meet many who remember such details. I congratulate you on your preparation for your new position."

Andrela curbed her annoyance with the Princess and smiled at the Prince. She had no desire to antagonise him. She liked him.

"I have always been interested in the past and find it surprising that the history of Eland and Westland has been so different. We have a common language and yet we have developed separately. The mountains were a formidable barrier – indeed they still are – but the valleys on either side were only settled because of an invader and west and east have the same tales, and the same hero, Braied."

Prince Maldon smiled in his turn. The prospect of a chat about history with his daughter-in-law appealed to him. He had not expected the subject to arise.

"The early settlements here were all around the west coast," he began. "Even though it is thought that the first people here came from the south, Ostara and Osira were not inhabited until much later than Kaldor, Testeriel and Alden."

He continued, explaining his belief that the Kellains, coming from the south, had never reached the Westland coast. Elanders escaping from the invaders had fled to the mountains and found their way either over the peaks or through the tunnels to the uninhabited valleys on the west.

Darmon, who had heard his father's 'history lecture' several times before, gazed anxiously at Andrela and was relieved to see that she appeared to be interested. Even if such interest was feigned, it was preferable to a confrontation with his mother.

The Princess, however, was set upon putting her daughter-in-law in her place; that place being one which owed deference to her mother-in-law. She awaited a suitable opening. A mention of the relative sizes of the two countries provided her with one.

"Ah, yes; the distances between towns in Eland are short. Bosron is close to the south coast. I have wondered why Lord Collingwade brought his yacht into the harbour there when his home is scarce a half day's journey from the city. He must have *had* a reason," she pronounced nastily, "for I heard that the mooring fees were extortionate."

"They were similar to the fees in Kaldor, my dear," said Prince Maldon. "If you heard complaints from some of our friends, it was possibly because they expected Bosron to be cheaper, and it was not."

Andrela swallowed her last mouthful of pudding and laid down her spoon. She was immediately offered more, but declined.

"That was delicious," she told the minion with a smile, "just as were the previous dishes."

She did not send praise to the cooks. She was sure that all details of this dinner would be faithfully reported in the palace kitchen. She turned to Princess Indola.

"Bosron is the capital of Eland, and space is tight in capital cities."

She looked kindly upon her adversary. "You, as High Princess, may not notice such things, but on my first visit here I compared the price of houses in Ostara with those in Kaldor, and Kaldor is much more expensive.

"As for Lord Collingwade," she continued before the Princess could speak, "his income is large enough for him to do much as he pleases. His ancestors were merchants. They invested their profits wisely and devoted their spare time to the care of others. One was ennobled for that."

"Descended from a merchant!" exclaimed Princess Indola. "Poor Lady Marishen. She will be devastated. *She* can trace her ancestry back to Prince Pedan the Third."

"And he could no doubt trace his ancestry back to the first settlers here," said Andrela comfortably. "They, I believe, were from Eland; or possibly fishermen from Irrok, who were caught in a storm."

Prince Maldon intervened swiftly. He suggested that they retire to the drawing room for coffee. He had hoped for a brandy and a quiet talk with his son after the meal, but he sacrificed both. Family arguments were never pleasant and the current animosity between his wife and daughter-in-law seemed likely to develop into a full-scale battle. He did not wish to leave them alone together.

He was rewarded with a rueful grimace from his son and they all rose from the table and moved into the drawing room.

Andrela was tired and cross. She realised that her comments had been provoking and as such childish, but she had not wanted to come. The coffee and the privacy of the drawing room when the servant had departed, revived her. She did not tell her new family then that Colly's yacht was in Bosron for her reassurance, but she did relate the story of his title.

The first Lord Collingwade was fond of walking and made a point of visiting a lake on the boundary of his estate each day. The further bank was a favourite place for the local boys to play. They fished and sometimes swam, though the weeds made that dangerous. One day he had seen someone in difficulties in the water. He had dived in, at considerable risk to himself and had swum across to help.

He saved the boy who was dragged from the water with help from his friends on the bank, but they had not the strength to pull a man from the tangle of weeds. He remained in the water for some time before other help arrived. Later, he discovered that the boy was the illegitimate, but much loved, son of the Prince. He refused all monetary rewards, but his grateful sovereign created him a Lord and he took as his standard an outstretched hand and the motto 'Be There'.

Andrela freely admitted that the early lords may not have been true to their motto, such things were not recorded in history books, but she did know that the present lord and his predecessor had helped innumerable people. They went, as the first lord had done, to places where help might be needed, and took such things as might be useful.

"That was why his carriage was standing near the palace during our wedding breakfast and it proved useful to take a young Westland girl by the name of Mara back to her hotel. Lady Vealla went with her whilst Colly was caring for Lord Brey's son, who was also drunk."

Andrela smiled and decided to tease a little. "I believe that alert ladies noticed that both Colly and Vealla were absent at the same time, but I doubt that any thought of the real reason."

"The wine at the wedding breakfast was very fine and flowed freely. It is not surprising that some of the young ones over indulged," said Prince Maldon tolerantly, but his gentle comment did not distract his wife.

"Mara was an exception. Westland mothers take care of their daughters and guard their reputations," she declared, somehow managing to imply that Eland mothers were sadly lacking in that virtue.

Andrela ignored her remark and answered the Prince.

Yes, she agreed, her parents had wanted to show the best that Eland produced, as befitted a High Prince celebrating the marriage of his only daughter who was his heir.

The food and wine they had enjoyed that evening was also worthy of the occasion, her first dinner with her husband's parents. She included the Princess in her thanks and turned to her husband to ask if he was ready to leave. She pleaded tiredness, but omitted any mention of a delightful evening.

"You do look strained," observed Princess Indola, "though the crowds were too thin to be exhausting. Eland is different, I suppose," she added and included the inadequacies of the country and its people in her next comment.

"I cannot see why anyone with a house in Bosron, would need a yacht there also."

Darmon had already risen and now he took his wife's arm.

"They can be useful," he murmured accommodatingly and he thanked his parents for their hospitality, bade them goodnight and led Andrela towards the door.

She turned when she reached it. She was tired, but Indola's last remark had angered her. She abandoned her good intentions.

"Colly may have considered that some accident might damage a visitor's yacht, and true to his family motto, he would wish to be there."

She began gently, but she continued defiantly. "I am sure, however, that it was there for me – as an escape route, had I changed my mind. *We* are now family and do not need to pretend. Darmon and I married for political reasons, not for love. He may have a lover, I do not know, but Colly knows that I have loved. He does not know whom, nor does he know that, had Fidel lived, I would be married. I would be plain Mrs, but I would have been with my love and perhaps by now we might have had a child."

She regarded her mother-in-law with something akin to pity.

"As heir to the throne of Eland, I could not marry him. So I have done what I thought was best for *my* country. I will not shame it, nor will I shame yours. In Eland we take duty seriously. I bid you goodnight."

She pulled the door open and walked out.

Darmon caught his father's eye before he followed her, and in that brief glance they agreed. Battle lines had been drawn, but the first honours belonged to Andrela.

Chapter 14

When Andrela reached her own room, she discovered that her maid awaited her with Miss Ashton. The two women seemed happy together and all was blissfully peaceful.

Her preferred bedtime drink was prepared and several of her favourite things had been unpacked. Clothes had been hung in closets, but their precise disposition awaited her instructions and the arrival of her First Lady of the Bedchamber, Lady Annia.

"Wren!" exclaimed Andrela. "How glad I am to see you! I ought to have insisted that you stayed with me. Maids in hotels, even the very best hotels, are not the same. Someone else could have supervised my trunks."

"Indeed, they could not, ma'am," declared Wren. "You would not believe how often one or other went astray. I was very glad of Miss Ashton's help in keeping track of them. She is staying in *our* wing of the palace and will take care of your jewellery."

Andrela smiled; at Miss Ashton, at Wren's emphatic pronunciation of 'our' and at her beautifully organised bedroom.

That remained the only pleasant memory of her first night in her new home. Darmon did not come to her. She did not blame him; she did not want him; but she, they, ought not to have parted company in such disaccord.

Darmon was also unhappy. Once he had left Andrela, he returned to the main palace to talk to his father. They sat together with a bottle of brandy and the conversation was cautious until they were on their second glass.

"I knew she did not love me," he said suddenly. "She married me because she wants our countries united, and *I* wanted a woman who was not so closely related that I would fear for our children. I did not know that she had contemplated marrying another. It was –," he paused and shrugged his shoulders, "– disappointing."

Prince Maldon learnt what he had always suspected; that his son had had casual relationships, but he had not loved, nor had a long term mistress. He also saw the question in his son's eyes, but it remained unasked and he did not volunteer the information.

They were pleasantly drunk when they said goodnight.

"You smell of brandy," said his father. "Best leave her alone tonight."

Darmon nodded.

"She will be asleep," he answered, but he smiled sadly and added that he did not think that she would mind his being drunk. She minded his mother, and that problem would not be solved as easily as the headache he might well have in the morning.

He did have a headache in the morning, but his man had anticipated the eventuality and he was left to sleep late as there was nothing in his diary for that day.

Andrela had woken early, breakfasted alone and begun to unpack her various trunks and explore her new home. She discovered a music room and immediately sent for the trunk which she was certain held her music and her flute. Miss Ashton and Grizzie were called to assist. Darmon discovered them there.

He was surprised. He was merely seeking a quiet room free from the bright rays of the morning sun, where he might sit and attempt to read the day's news sheets. He winced at Andrela's voice.

"Where is Wren?" she was demanding in an exasperated tone, and a shawl was pulled from the trunk and flung onto the pile of garments in the arms of an already over-burdened Miss Ashton. "She agreed with me that this was the trunk! Oh, it is! Here is my flute."

She hauled the instrument in its case from the bottom of the trunk, scattering sheets of music as she did so, and waved it triumphantly.

She saw him mid-wave and stood up slowly.

"Good morning," she said quietly.

He returned her greeting and looked about uncertainly.

Lady Annia omitted the formalities completely. She informed him in a gentle voice that the small adjoining room faced west and contained two or three chairs. She set down her burden of clothes and opened the door for him.

He walked through it. It seemed easier than thinking.

Andrela followed and shut the door with great care. She indicated one of the chairs and sat on the one beside it without speaking. The papers rustled in his hand as he sat down and she took them from him and laid them gently on the floor.

"Did you drink alone last night, or with your father?" she asked.

"With my father," he answered ruefully. "A mistake. He has a better head for brandy than I do."

"I am sorry," she said, and he agreed. He was sorry too.

"I meant for my behaviour last night," she corrected, "not for your sore head – though I am sorry for that too. Oh, I am not doing this well!"

"Do not fret," he answered. "I should have known that my mother would rile you on your first day here. I ought to have refused her invitation." He sighed. "But she was persistent. She is always persistent."

"Next time, *I* shall refuse," declared Andrela. "I shall plead sickness or whatever, but I will not dine solely with your parents again."

She too sighed and she began again.

"It was true, what I said last night, but I ought not to have said it. It would be better if you did not know."

He agreed, but she sounded so contrite that he did not even nod his head.

"It is no matter. We will do well enough together I daresay," and he pleaded as an afterthought, "but do not play the flute just yet."

"I will not," she answered. "I seem to have brought more clothes than I knew I possessed, and I left closetsful at home. I shall go and find some place to put them."

She rose and retrieved the news sheets, placing them carefully on his lap.

"We are on the front page," she noted. "Several pictures of our arrival. Will that please your Mama, or offend her, do you think?"

117

She did not wait for his answer, but slipped quietly out of the room. She still regretted her angry words, but she had now apologised and felt easier.

Darmon had recovered his appetite by lunch time and had also discovered that his diary was not as clear as he had hoped. He attended one engagement, fortunately brief, but had postponed consideration of the mound of papers that awaited his attention.

Andrela sympathised. She had more mail than she had anticipated, but she had requested that summaries of Council discussions be sent to her.

"I expect that the largest packet is that," she said without noticeable enthusiasm. "They will have met since our marriage, and before it most items of business were probably shelved for later. Later has now arrived and I must catch up on what is happening."

"Must you?" he asked.

"Do you not feel obliged to keep up with what is happening in your Assembly?"

"Skies, yes!" he answered. "Half of that pile of paper on my desk will be Assembly business, but I am heir to the throne."

He realised his error immediately and was glad that she did not seem annoyed. She merely gave him a pitying look and said, "Precisely."

"But you will never be there," he burst out as he contemplated the difficulties.

"I will visit Eland at least once a year, for perhaps a month at a time," she answered calmly. "I have already decided that. When my father dies I will need to do so more often and stay for longer, but I daresay that that will not be for some time. We must hope that by then our children will be grown and that our eldest son can accompany me. He will need to know both countries equally well."

"It may be one country by then," he objected diffidently. He had not considered the implications of their marriage as carefully as she, quite clearly, had.

"Not until we, and our respective fathers, are dead," she said in a matter-of-fact manner, "and even if that is not for many years and we have prepared our people for the change, it will not be easy. The capital ought to be near the centre of the country, not at one end of it."

He decided to concentrate on his food. These topics were far too complicated to be discussed at meal times.

That afternoon was free of appointments and he had invited Lord Pandour to join him in the garden. He would ask Ped. Ped's advice was always considered and usually good.

He hoped that his friend would come early. So many things had happened in the last few weeks that they would need all the afternoon to talk them over. He made a mental note to take at least two bottles of wine and resolved to drink only water at dinner.

Lord Pandour arrived at exactly the right moment, but he came alone. Tesher, he said, was not intending to return to Kaldor for some time. He was planning a sea tour of Erion, including southern Irrok, the Snow Islands, Andea and a circuit of North Lound.

"That will take years!" exclaimed Darmon, distracted from his primary purpose by the unexpected news, "and it will cost. Will his captain and crew go with him?"

"For part of the journey, but I believe that they will leave him in Irrok."

They passed Seabee's bush, and Ped became informal.

"You know Jon," he continued. "He is a talker and a trader. He was entirely at home in Bosron harbour and met all manner of people. One was a Regan sailor, experienced, if age is anything to go by. He was delighted to leave his ship and sail in a much smaller vessel, but with the prospect of becoming its captain."

"A Regan?" Dee was shocked.

"They are fine seamen and travel everywhere. The north of their island is often ice-bound so they are accustomed to cold, but they cross the hot seas too, and do not fear the windless ocean. 'We row', he said when I asked."

"You met him?" asked Dee surprised that his friend would condescend to talk to a Regan sailor.

"He was clean and well-mannered and educated in his fashion. He spoke several languages, whereas I know only my own and the ancient tongue. Besides, I wanted to make sure that Jon was not being duped by a charlatan."

119

Dee nodded, though he would have backed Jon's judgement on the matter of charlatans, rather than Ped's.

He said truthfully that he would miss Jon, and Ped reminded him that he now had a wife.

"I need friends even more now," he said ruefully.

They settled themselves in the tree and had opened the first bottle of wine before Ped prompted gently.

"You did not bring her this afternoon. Are you tired of her already? Or have you quarrelled?"

"She is working this afternoon. Council papers from Eland. I had not expected that."

"She is a dutiful lady. That is why she married you. You know that?" Ped raised his eyebrows in query.

"Yes, but I didn't anticipate having it stated quite so plainly last night. She did apologise this morning, but what has been said cannot be unsaid." He shrugged. "She was riled by my mother."

Ped enquired as to the circumstances and was unimpressed by the answer.

"By the Shades of Hadron, why did you dine with them!?" and he called his Prince by several unflattering names. "Are you mad? Surely, you know that your mother thinks your wife responsible for Vealla's marriage? She is as close to Lady Marishen as ivy is to a wall and both of them consider that it was planned!"

"She told me that in a relay, and I answered that it was not so." Dee defended himself indignantly. "I don't think that it was, but I must admit that Andrela was not at all helpful about where they might have gone and seemed very pleased when we heard that they were married. Also, if she had asked Vealla to be her Second Lady, instead of that unknown child Miss Ashton, she might never have bothered with this Collingwade fellow."

"Second Lady of the Bedchamber is certainly an honour, but I doubt that it prevents the honoured one from falling in love," observed Ped in a contemplative tone. He became more definite. "Besides, Vealla did not want the position. She feared that it would bring her into regular contact with me. Lady Annia told me."

"I suppose that it might, but does it matter?"

"I had no intention of offering for her, but she felt under pressure to marry, and as your friend I think it possible that I will meet your wife's ladies frequently."

Ped smiled. "I rather hope that I do. Lady Annia is an interesting woman. She is intelligent, resourceful, better educated than most Westland ladies of quality and she is attractive."

"How do you know she is resourceful?" Dee asked reaching for the second bottle.

Ped's smile widened. "Her assistance in the matter of Vealla's elopement," he said.

Dee dropped the bottle and stared at him.

"Namier's moons! Were you involved in that!" he exclaimed.

"Unintentionally," Ped reassured him, "and only on the periphery, so to speak. When your Mama asked if I knew where she might have gone, I was able to say with perfect truth that I had no idea.

"I do hope that that cork will hold," he added peering downwards. "I can't even see the bottle from here."

"I have it." Andrela appeared beneath them with it in her hand. "I saw it fall into the long grass and that kept it upright. Only a little has spilt."

She looked anxiously at her husband. "I hope I am not intruding. Am I allowed here without an invitation?"

He climbed down and took the bottle from her hand. "You are and you are welcome, but I thought you had Council papers to read."

"They were unimportant. The noble lords talked of nothing but our wedding, how smoothly it went and how clever they all were in ensuring that happy outcome. There was no mention of my mother who organised the palace and the food, or of my father who paid the bills." She sounded scornful.

Dee concentrated on the immediate future and she elected to join them in the tree. Her ascent was inelegant. She swore mildly at her skirt and tore her stockings.

"It does not matter," she said as she settled herself on the branch. "I was given a hundred pairs as a wedding gift from a manufacturer. I cannot imagine why. Not even the most intrusive of fashion reporters knows whose stockings I wear."

She accepted a mug of wine, but remarked that she did not usually drink wine in the afternoon.

The look that accompanied the words prompted Dee to declare that they would dine simply that evening and drink only water.

"We were talking of Vealla's marriage," said Ped, "but you will by now have heard the details from Lady Annia."

"Grizzie!" exclaimed Andrela. "What does she know? She has not mentioned it. How mean! But then we have not spoken much alone. How was she involved?"

"She was with us on Jon's yacht when Vealla arrived. Her friend, a dark haired girl whose name escapes me, was also there and various crew members were around. It was mid-afternoon and we were drinking coffee on the deck."

Andrela nodded gravely and Dee grinned into his cup. Propriety was important to Ped. That gentleman hardly noticed their reactions. He continued with his story.

Vealla, it appeared, had spent the previous morning, and possibly most of the day, with Colly. He had taught her to drive his electric car and they had visited various places in and around Bosron. In the evening, they had met again at a ball, and Colly had proposed.

Vealla had warned him that her parents would not think him an acceptable suitor, but nonetheless he had visited Lord Marishen the following morning to ask for his daughter's hand.

It had been refused. Lord Collingwade's income was adequate, ("Adequate!" exclaimed Andrela. "He can buy half of Eland,") but his ancestry was not.

It was her parent's view of his ancestry that had sent Vealla, in a highly emotional state, to Jon. They had, it seemed, been scathing and had not had the sense to keep their opinions from their daughter.

Ped did not trouble to hide his scorn at their foolishness. He praised Lady Annia for her swift assessment of the situation and her speedy removal of Vealla from curious glances. It was very plain that he admired the lady's practicality.

It was she who had suggested seeking Lord Collingwade on his yacht, which was moored close by. Having found him, she sent him to Vealla to talk, having first mentioned that the lady, being of age, was able to marry whom she chose without her parents' consent.

When Colly and Vee emerged, continued Ped, slipping into informal mode, it was obvious that they had decided on that course, and Jon had cut short their blushing explanations. He had sent Colly off alone to organise a plain, unrecognisable coach and suggested that Vee and Grizzie return to her hotel to collect some clothes; for even the most ardent of brides would need a change of garments.

"I was despatched with them," continued Ped, "possibly to take care of Lady Annia's friend; but she tactfully discovered some urgent purchases and left us, assuring Vealla that she had a shockingly bad memory and had already forgotten her name. We halted again, briefly, to buy an inconspicuous bag – Lady Annia's idea – and I delivered the ladies to the hotel."

Ped had played no further part in the elopement, nor, other than helping Vealla to pack the newly purchased bag, had Lady Annia. Neither of them had had any information as to where Lady Vealla had gone. In fact, they knew nothing more until they met Jon after the marriage had been announced in the news sheets.

Jon told them that a chambermaid had been persuaded to deliver the bag to the very tall gentleman waiting by the park gate, and that he had collected Vee and taken her for a walk. He had also travelled with them to Senby, escorted the lady down the aisle and joined them for a celebration dinner at the hotel where they intended to stay the night.

"I never considered Senby," commented Andrela. "I didn't think that Colly rated the hotels there very highly."

"Apparently he did not," commented Ped lazily. "Lady Annia visited them a few days after their marriage and Vee told her that a new bed had been delivered to their room and it was made up with new linen. She had no idea whether he had bought it or insisted upon it, but she did find it comfortable."

"How typical of Colly," said Andrela with mingled admiration and exasperation. "One would expect an elopement to involve rush and discomfort, but he organises a new bed! He will look after her well, I am sure. Did she have a choice of ring, do you know?"

Ped smiled at the question. According to Lady Annia, she had had a choice of five and had liked them all. Her husband had selected the plainest as a wedding ring and given her the others to wear as she chose.

He expressed a hope that, if he ever married, his wife would not expect such indulgence and he handed his empty cup to Dee.

"I shall leave you to finish the bottle between you, and to wash the cups."

He reached for the rope and gave it to Andrela. "Hold tight now," he warned and jumped down from his perch.

Andrela gave a startled exclamation as the branch swayed, but Dee steadied her. He had put cup and bottle safely in the hollow the moment that the word 'leave' was pronounced. He knew his friend.

"He expects me to look after you," he said before she made any criticism, "and he respects your abilities. You have good balance."

"Perhaps I do," she answered, "but I would prefer to practice it a little nearer to the ground."

She maintained a firm grip on the rope as she sipped her wine and stared up into the leaves. She recalled climbing trees as a child, but she could not remember simply sitting on a branch and looking at the sky.

"This is very pleasant," she said.

"Yes. I love this garden," answered Dee. "It has always been a haven; a refuge from whatever troubled me; a special place. I shall miss it if we have a child."

"Yes," said Andrela, and her tone prompted him to look at her sharply.

"Already!" he exclaimed. "We have scarce been married a month."

"It is action, not time, that produces a child," she answered and sighed. "Oh, it is too early to be certain yet. In theory I know the signs, but as I do not have any previous experience, I am not sure."

"Are you not glad?" he asked gently, and worried when she took a long time to answer.

"I want children," she said at last. "That is after all why we married; but I had hoped for a little longer to become accustomed to your country before I was burdened with another responsibility." She gave a rueful laugh. "Everyone else will be delighted."

"They will indeed; your parents and mine and the general populace of both countries; but the responsibility belongs to both of us, and we will share it."

He was firm on that point, but spoke less confidently when he added that he knew nothing about babies. They would have a nurse.

"I hope so," she answered sincerely. "I remember very little about Fid until he could walk. He was more interesting then, but I was usually in trouble for leading him into dangerous situations."

"You will need advice from your mother," he began, and corrected himself at once. "At least, she will think so and you need not take it, but you mentioned wanting to return to Eland every year. Whether there is a child yet or not, we will plan to go in about six months.

"If we stay for a month, there will be time for you to attend at least one Council meeting and for us to visit some of your friends. Do you want to stay at the palace or do you think better to rent a house, or to stay in hotels?"

Andrela had not considered that issue. She had decided that regular visits to Eland were necessary, but had not thought about the details.

Her anger of the previous evening disappeared, and she remembered Darmon's kindness when he had come for Fidel's funeral. Had he not been so considerate at that time, she would not have entertained his suit.

She admitted that she had no detailed plans and they discussed the various options amicably over the last of the wine. Later they strolled through the garden together and returned to their own home in harmony.

Chapter 15

Darmon kept his promise. His mother objected, as she objected to almost everything that Andrela wanted to do, but the very frequency of her objections made them easier to resist, and his father helped.

Prince Maldon pointed out that the child, a possible heir to both thrones, could only be born in one country, but both had an interest. Also, as Darmon and his bride had come to Westland via the northern route, they had not visited many of the southern ports. That could be remedied. The matter was settled.

The Prince also encouraged them to make good use of the children's garden whilst they still could. It was tradition alone that kept parents out, but tradition was important. As the Princess Indola frequently used tradition in her arguments, she could not protest.

Andrela and Darmon used the garden often. Sometimes they went alone, but Pandour was invited after Assembly meetings as he had been for years, and they were usually joined by Andrela's Ladies of the Bedchamber.

Lady Annia was accepted from the start, Miss Ashton soon afterwards. She did not climb trees or ropes nor did she drink wine in the afternoons, but she was uncensorious. She brought fruit juice for herself and as she charmed someone in the palace kitchen better than anyone else had ever managed, she also provided an excellent selection of eatables.

She approved of the purpose of the garden and, as she was knowledgeable about horticulture, she drew attention to aging shrubs and suggested replacements. She was, Dee and Ped agreed, an asset. They missed Jon. No one could replace him, but the ladies were good company.

One item that occurred often on Assembly agenda was the cleanliness, or lack of it, of Kaldor's roads. The city was busy and its population had grown. More carts were needed to carry goods and people, and horse droppings were becoming a major problem. Houses had been built on open land where once the dung had been piled. Parks and private gardens did not want large quantities of fresh manure because of the smell; so now it was carried to the outskirts of the city; on horse-drawn carts.

Andrela was interested. In her opinion, none of the suggested solutions would be effective. Certainly, taking poor children from school and paying them a pittance to shovel horse dung, was not an answer.

She did not find her marriage fulfilling, despite the coming child, and could not help but wonder if she would have found life similarly tedious had she married Caston. It was a depressing thought. Her noble intention of uniting Salima was still there, but the problems were becoming more obvious.

Now she had lived in Westland she understood why it had taken that country so long to become united. Its towns and cities were so very far from one another and land links between them were not good. Even the great road from Kaldor to Malda in the north east was only well surfaced as far as Grenton.

Westland was also, in her opinion, backward compared to Eland.

She resolved to devote herself to modernising it; specifically by promoting the increased use of electricity for transport. She favoured investment in public charging points so that electric carts and cars would become common, as they had been for years in her own country.

It was true that public coaches in Eland were still, for the most part, horse-drawn. It was too expensive to build rail tracks over short distances and large electric vehicles as yet required too much power, but the problem was being addressed.

In Kaldor, the powerful members of society preferred horses to electric cars, but they were looking forward to the new rail track to Blau. That would certainly be modern, but would be of use only to the rich who had holiday homes on the beach there, and the terminal was in the affluent north of the city.

She did not approve. She felt that a rail track for electric cars going from the south-east of Kaldor to Ostara would be a more useful line, though it would certainly be longer. It would, however, be able to transport goods and passengers, increase

Ostara's importance as a trading port and rejuvenate one of the poorer areas of the capital city.

She argued strenuously, but gained few supporters. Lady Annia warned her gently that her proposal to extend such a line to the mountains was impractical at present and was regarded by some as an indication that she was mad. Such talk might threaten the throne.

"You may not be aware," explained Lady Annia, "but many of the aristocratic families have accepted you as Princess only because they consider that the Eland Royal line is free from inherited illness, both physical and mental.

"*We* know that that is true, but do not give others cause to doubt."

Andrela respected her friend's opinions and she modified her comments, but not her ambitions.

Lady Annia accompanied her mistress six months later, when Darmon and Andrela visited Eland, but she stayed with her family. Miss Ashton had a holiday.

Andrela not only freed the girl from her duties, but arranged for her to stay with one of the less important Westland families in their home near Osira. Many young gentlemen went to Osira to sail, and several had shown an interest in Miss Ashton.

Lord Pandour persuaded several of his friends to accompany him to Bosron at the same time as the Royal couple. It was, he assured them, a civilised country that offered modern comfort, interesting places to visit, different foods and excellent wines. Andrela thought it amusing that he desired male company, but she still felt proud of her match-making skills.

The Royal yacht called in at all the major ports along the south coast of Salima and Andrela showed no sign of emotion at the sight of Shyran or when they landed at Malport. She thought of Caston, but only when she was entirely alone. He was now part of her past. The people who turned out to greet her were the present.

There were many of them, keen to see their Princess again, especially now that she was carrying the next generation of the Royal line.

Her parents were equally pleased to see her though her mother found her visit less enjoyable than she had anticipated. She had looked forward to womanly chats, and Andrela soon tired of 'baby talk' as she termed it. She wanted to discuss electric cars and rail tracks. Princess Margren had no interest in such things and could not understand why her daughter found them fascinating.

Prince Roddori did understand and arranged for her to see maps showing charging stations in Eland and to talk to an engineer about the problems of transmission, but he also noticed that Darmon did not share her enthusiasm.

He understood that too. Political marriages had difficulties enough without one partner becoming dedicated to a cause that had political connotations. He feared that his daughter, once so light-hearted, had become so serious that even the coming child did not seem to fulfil her notion of duty.

In fact, Darmon was puzzled. He had thought that Andrela wanted to visit her parents and would enjoy the break from her duties in Westland. He had not found it easy to arrange – his mother and many other influential members of the Assembly had been against it – but he had insisted. She needed to see her mother, he had argued, and indeed had believed. Now she was here, she thought of nothing but electric transport!

Her father tried to explain her interest, but he failed. Darmon found her mother more sympathetic and wondered if it was usual for people to find in-laws of the opposite sex more congenial than those of the same sex. He readily invited Princess Margren to Westland for the birth of her first grandchild, but Prince Roddori was asked almost as an afterthought.

In the event, the child came earlier than anticipated and the Eland grandparents arrived in Kaldor a few hours after the birth. The first fires were blazing on the hilltops surrounding the city and the bells were ringing in celebration. They were told long before they reached the palace that the child was a boy. It was on the relay, and everyone who was able had been watching for the latest news, but it was the sequence of the bells that announced a new male heir. The fires told of the birth, but the bells distinguished between boy and girl; and both would reach the remoter parts of Westland, where there was no electricity, long before any messenger did.

Somewhat surprised to find that there were still large parts of Westland so backward as to be without electric power, the Eland Royals made their way to the palace.

Nothing there was backward, though the great building was as old as their palace in Bosron. They found Andrela comfortably ensconced in a large bedroom which boasted every modern amenity. To their great delight, she was also happy.

She had borne a son, an heir to both princedoms, which was important to her, but she was also much taken with her new role as a mother. She spoke only of her joy in her son and her interest in rail roads and electric transport went unmentioned.

It was Darmon who brought up that topic.

He had, he told them, a beautiful necklace of kaiealestrons. He had bought it some time ago, anticipating the birth of their child and knowing that Andrela admired the Princess Kaiealestria.

Now he knew his wife better. She did not only admire, she wanted to emulate; and he knew that the Prince Lanchir wing of the Charity School at Ostara had not been built by that Prince. It had been Nikkor's gift to Kaiealestria when his son was born.

Darmon confessed that he was now loath to offer Andrela a necklace. He felt that a charging station in some poor area of Kaldor would please her better, but he considered such a thing useless; a waste of money. He asked their advice.

Unsurprisingly, Princess Margren thought that the necklace was an admirable gift for the occasion. Prince Roddori questioned gently.

The discussion confirmed his view. Prince Darmon was a kind considerate man, and as such a good husband for any girl, but he was not clever. He was obliging, but rather dull. Andrela was more intelligent and better educated.

Her father sympathised with her. He had learned from experience that physical attraction and a common love for, and interest in, one's children, did not compensate for a disparity of intellect. Compatible minds were a definite advantage.

"First thoughts are often the best," he advised. "She will use a necklace and may never see a charging station, however useful."

As he had anticipated, Andrela agreed.

"How could he think that a charging station *there* would please me?" she exclaimed, when he told her of their discussion.

"He means well, but he does lack understanding. Kaldor and its environs need more charging stations to encourage the use of electric cars, but the people in the poorer areas make their living from clearing the main streets in the city centre and shifting the horse dung. They do not aspire to owning an electric car; and those who do own them would be afraid to visit such areas."

She enlarged upon the problems of the poor and the conflicting need to reduce the number of horse-drawn carts in the city.

Education for the workers, especially girls, she concluded, had helped. Most of the poor were at least able to read, write and count, and there were women from the middle classes earning their living in all walks of life. They were prosperous enough, but Kaiealestria had failed in her efforts to promote the education of gentlewomen. For the most part, the female aristocracy remained ignorant, though they could not all be unintelligent.

Prince Roddori found the conversation with his daughter very interesting and satisfying in that he was now able to advise his son-in-law. He was a little surprised to find his newly born grandson sleeping in a cradle beside Andrela's bed, but soon discovered that it was not the custom in Westland. It was Andrela's choice.

She had bargained for the privilege of caring for her own child. The nurse would assist her, but would not be in charge of the baby; and for that she had accepted that he be named Maldon, for his paternal grandfather, and not Fidel as she had wanted.

She had also decided that she would show her son to the people from the balcony as soon as she felt strong enough.

"It will not," she declared, "be today."

She would not attempt to match Princess Kaiealestria on that, for Kaiealestria had been mountain, and mountain women were extraordinarily strong.

Her father was happy to agree with her. He kissed her gently, stroked the baby's cheek and left them both to sleep.

Two days later, he experienced the 'one way viewing' that marked great Royal occasions in Kaldor. He stood for near two hours on the balcony as the population streamed past, keen to see the baby, the second in line to the throne. The ladies had chairs and did most of the waving to the crowd, but all were tired when they returned to the warmth and comfort inside the palace.

"A very satisfactory number of viewers," said Princess Indola contentedly, but she spoiled the happy comment by adding that there might not be as many for the next child, even if it too were a boy.

Darmon was about to protest that it was too early to think of a second child, Andrela was ready to declare that if she bore another boy, it would be called Fidel, and the elder Princes were still trying to find a suitable response, when Princess Margren spoke.

"There may be," she corrected gently. "It will be unusual, will it not? No Prince of Westland, or indeed of Eland, has had two sons for several generations."

"That is true," agreed Prince Maldon, "and should Andrela and Darmon be fortunate enough to break that sad record, I am sure that both countries will rejoice."

Andrela smiled at him and capped his comment.

"I hope that Darmon and I will have another child, and I see no reason why we should not. I would like another son, and will call him Fidel for my brother, but perhaps we may have a daughter."

She admitted that she had no name in mind for a girl. Kaiealestria was her idol, but the name was unwieldy. She would not wish that on any child. What did they suggest?

The ensuing discussion was wide-ranging and amicable. Andrela left for bed long before it was over, but the favoured name was never needed.

Over the next few years she bore two more sons, but no daughters.

Chapter 16

Lady Collingwade stretched out luxuriously. The bed was not new, but it was of sufficient length to accommodate her husband in comfort. He slept beside her, but he was not snoring so she did not disturb him.

She sipped the tea that had been brought by the chambermaid. She had grown accustomed to tea in the mornings. It was a pleasant drink, thirst-quenching, but not so invigorating as to prevent further sleep. In Eland watching the sunrise was considered among the wealthier population to be a delight, and she agreed that it could be beautiful, but she preferred to watch the spectacle from her bed and, when the sun had safely risen, to shut out its light and return to sleep.

She had never been one for early mornings and had always been extremely grateful to Colly's nurse, who had been with the family for years. No one seemed to know her age and no one dared to ask. As Colly said, what did it matter? She was good with children.

She had also been good with mothers. As an expectant mother and a newly delivered one, Vealla had been encouraged to rest whenever she felt tired. Activity and exercise were good if the mother felt able, but rest was essential. She had gladly accepted that advice.

Now Nurse was caring for her four children. She and Colly had celebrated their ninth wedding anniversary with a splendid dinner last night and planned to watch the sunrise as they had done on their first day as a married couple.

He was still asleep. She shook him gently, reminded him of that intention and complained that he used to wake early without prompting.

"I did wake early, but you did not and I fell asleep again waiting for break of dawn tea."

"It arrived," she said handing him a cup, "hours ago," but she modified her estimate to fifteen minutes when he pointed out that the tea was still warm.

They watched the sunrise together, closed the shutters, praised again the inspired man who had arranged that they closed at the touch of switch by the bed, and went back to sleep.

After breakfast they made their way home without hurry, for neither had any fear for the children.

"We are lucky," declared Vealla contentedly. "Nurse is wonderful and none of the children fret when we are away for a few days. Annia's youngest clings to her like curlweed when they return from even a short absence. She will not come to Eland with Andrela again.

"Mind," she said and sighed as she considered the events of the past few months, "Andrela might not come this year, not now she is High Princess."

"She has no more responsibility in that role than she had as wife to the heir," replied Colly, "but it may be difficult for Darmon to come. He will miss his few weeks here, I think. Westland, or perhaps it is only Kaldor, has so many rules."

"It is Westland," said Vealla with some bitterness, "but Kaldor is worse than anywhere else."

Colly was silent. Their one visit to Kaldor, to see her parents, had not been a success. Vealla had hoped that Jared, at two, and the six month old Linneath, would charm her parents and lead to greater contact if not to reconciliation; but it had not.

Her parents had been lavish in their praise of her brother's children. They were older, but had been properly reared and had never cried at awkward times; but then their ancestry was impeccable.

Vealla had swept up her offspring and walked out, declaring that she would rather sleep on the street with her children than in a house where they were not welcome.

Her husband had bowed politely. He had said that their journey had been tiring and had told his parents-in-law that he did not like to see his wife upset. They would not come again unless they were invited.

There had been no invitation and they had never been again.

The coach – for Colly had decided to travel in style and the car, though convenient, lacked style – turned into the drive that led to their country home.

Vealla peered out of the window to catch a sight of the house and was immediately alarmed.

"Linnie is at the top of the steps," she said. "She is waving! What can have happened?"

"All manner of things," replied Colly with a calm that he did not truly feel. "We will find out in a few moments."

They found out before they had had time to descend from the coach. Linnie ran down the steps to greet them, but she was excited, not alarmed.

"Aunt Drela is here!" she called out.

"Do not shout," responded Vealla automatically, but she did understand the excitement.

"Aunt Drela is here," repeated the child in a more controlled manner, "and she has brought – Our Grandparents."

Her mother acknowledged the information faintly and Linnie repeated the news.

Andrela had brought their grandparents from Westland; not Papa's parents who were dead, but Mama's parents from Westland, whom they had never seen.

Colly led his stunned wife up the steps to the open door. Andrela was waiting in the hall. She despatched Linnie on some insignificant errand and turned to Vealla.

"Your parents are here," she stated. "I am sorry to spring this upon you without warning. We intended to go to Bosron, but your mother has been ill, and she became upset on the voyage. I thought it best to leave the yacht at Malport and come straight here. I know that you have a good doctor nearby."

"Is Lady Marishen in need of a doctor immediately?" asked Colly.

"No." Andrela's answer was crisp. "But she was very ill and Lord Marishen was anxious. He did not trust the ship's doctor. We were past Ostara by then, and I thought it best to come here."

She took a deep breath, glanced round to check that the children were out of earshot, and said plainly, "Prince Maldon's death came as a shock to many. It was not entirely unexpected, but it frightened people. It brought to mind their own mortality. Darmon was too busy to leave Westland, so I approached your parents and asked if they would like to come to Eland with me. They came."

"They are welcome," said Colly.

A questioning eyebrow to his butler and a door was opened. He led his wife into the room to meet her parents.

The reunion was not at first emotional. The children prevented that. Jared was carefully pouring tea, Linnie had returned with a plate of biscuits and cakes, Jonal was shifting his weight excitedly from foot to foot and repeating 'We have grandparents' with great satisfaction, and Aura, not yet able to talk, was standing by her grandfather playing with his watch chain.

Vealla stood still, unable to say a word, and Colly apologised for being out when they arrived, but trusted that the children had made them welcome.

Andrela reassured him. "They have made us very welcome," she declared, "but I am going to steal them away, for I would like to see the garden. Jared will show me all that is new, Linnie will pick some roses for the spare room and Jonal needs to run."

She collected them in a sweep of an arm and murmured in Colly's ear as she took them out. He acted at once. He did not even glance at Lady Marishen before picking up a small table and placing it by her chair.

If Andrela thought her near to tears, then she was so. She was also encumbered with a cup in one hand and a plate in the other and could not reach her handkerchief.

She thanked him without looking up, found her handkerchief and blew her nose, wiping a stray tear as she did so. She addressed her daughter.

"You know of Gerharst's death, I believe. A dreadful accident. It has affected Tabbel greatly. We do not see her. She has returned to Grenton with the two girls."

"Andrela sent a relay."

Colly filled out his wife's brief reply. They had not been able to come to the funeral, but Vealla had gathered petals from the garden and sent them to Andrela. She had arranged for someone to throw them and had told them whom to look for on the visi-screen. That had been a great comfort.

Lord Marishen transferred his attention from the child to the father.

"That cannot have been easy to arrange," he commented. "Was the funeral screened in Eland?"

"No, it was not. The deaths of Lord Marishen's son and grandson were mentioned, but the funerals were not screened."

Vealla's voice shook as she spoke to her father, but it became firm, almost defiant, when she turned to her mother.

"Colly takes great care of me. He organised a private screening, because he knew that I wanted to see it. We would have come, but Aura was due at any time."

Lady Marishen glanced at the child, still standing, supporting herself by holding her grandfather's knee.

"We did not know of that," she said, "or of Gery's concerns about his son's illness. We might have been able to help."

"No, my dear." Lord Marishen was definite. "There is nothing to be done for Shaking Sickness. The symptoms can be alleviated for a little while, but is that kind? I watched my brother die slowly. He suffered bruises, cuts and broken limbs and had been bed-ridden for years before the dreadful tremor that killed him."

"You never told me that," said Vealla, dropping to her knees beside her father. "I knew the disease was in the family, but thought the last instance was generations ago. Did Gery know?"

"Yes. I watched him when he reached the age when it first strikes, and I told him to watch Fiordan." Lord Marishen touched his daughter's hand and commented sadly, "He must have watched very carefully. The boy had not reached his tenth birthday."

"It was an accident!" Lady Marishen was vehement. "He cannot have meant to drive over the cliff."

Her husband agreed gently. It was an accident, but Gery and Tabbel knew that their son had the sickness.

"How old is Jared?" he asked.

"Jared will be eight next month," Colly answered. "He is as prone to sickness and accident as is any other child of that age, but there are no hereditary illnesses in the Fairlea family. We have a tendency to grow taller than average, have large ears and suffer from indigestion, but no serious illness. Vealla knows that. She asked before she agreed to marry me, and she told me why she had asked."

"Good," said Lord Marishen. "We have worried."

The butler chose that moment to inform them that the baggage had been taken to the guest suite which was now ready for occupation. It was a welcome interruption.

Vealla spoke lightly as she took her parents upstairs. Jonal would want to draw them. He had started at the local school and all the children had drawn pictures of their family members. Grandparents had featured, and he had felt it strange that he had none. Two that lived in another country and whom he had never seen, did not rate very highly with anyone, especially when one child boasted six.

"Six grandparents?" queried her mother, fearing her grandson's contact with strange and scandalous practices.

"'Four normal ones'," quoted Vealla solemnly, "'and two big ones'. I think that means 'great'."

"They are plainly long-lived in this area," commented her father, but his words did not conceal Lady Marishen's relief.

Vealla agreed and showed them into the guest suite. She did not expect criticism because her home was luxurious, but she was pleased by her mother's praise.

She left them to themselves for a while. Her father had the day's news sheets and her mother had the view to admire, when she had finished inspecting the bathroom and the closet space and had decided where her maid should place the various items she had brought with her.

"I am glad to see you here," she said as she left them, and she meant it.

When she returned to the drawing room the children were nowhere to be seen and Andrela was talking to Colly. She was apologising for arriving without warning, but the original plan had been to travel by sea to Bosron and arrange for Vealla to meet her parents there, without obligation on either part.

Lady Marishen, however, had become ill. She attributed her sickness to the sea, but both Andrela and Lord Marishen considered it due to anxiety.

"She was afraid that you would not want to see her," said Andrela, "and your father was also uncertain and so of little comfort. *I* knew that they would be welcome and decided to bring them straight here so as to minimise the waiting.

"The journey from Malport was *very* wearing, but," and she smiled broadly, "our arrival could not have been better timed.

The children were waiting for you, but they greeted me with delight and when I told them that their grandparents were with me, they went wild.

"Jonal leapt about shouting 'grandparents, hurrah!', Jared bowed beautifully and welcomed them formally, Linnie asked if they were going to stay, for the guest room might need dusting and Aura tripped over and cried – until she saw your father's watch chain.

"I own that I had forgotten that it was your anniversary yesterday, but you could not have made them feel more welcome had you been here."

"I am not sure that I would have welcomed them," replied Vealla, "not immediately. I needed a little time. To forget, and to forgive. Colly does not bear grudges."

She looked admiringly at her husband.

"No," Andrela agreed, "but they are not his parents. Somehow one feels responsible for one's own parents, whereas nothing can be done about one's in-laws."

"Is the Princess Indola very aggravating?" Colly was sympathetic. He had caught the hint of bitterness in her voice.

Andrela sighed and agreed. "I am sorry to bother you with my troubles, but the last few months have been very trying. Darmon has few problems with the affairs of State, but family affairs are different."

She sighed again before she continued. "I may as well tell you. Your parents know, Vealla, and so do some others, but the news sheets do not have it yet.

"Maldon had a mistress; a long-standing affair with an undemanding woman, but he kept it secret and did not make provision for her. *She* has requested a reasonable sum and does not seem to want the matter made public, but the Princess was very upset and confided in several 'friends'. She also made known her willingness to pay whatever was asked in order to keep it secret.

"Not surprisingly, someone talked, and now we have no fewer than six females claiming intimacy with Maldon and demanding money. We do not have that much money.

"Contrary to common belief, Princes are not necessarily rich. Much of our life is funded by the State, but it cannot be asked to pay for any prince's extramarital adventures, and I do not see why my children's inheritance should be spent in order to keep their grandfather's reputation spotless and their grandmother's pride intact. Only one of the women has any credibility. The others have no substantial claim, so *I* would tell them to publish, but warn them *and* the more sensational new sheets, that they will be sued for defamation of character.

"Indola will not do that; so we have quarrelled bitterly and poor Darmon is in the middle."

There was little that Colly or Vealla could say in consolation. Both were grateful, as they had always been, that they were not Royalty, but that could not be said. They were glad when Andrela took her leave. She wanted to be in Bosron that afternoon so that she could contact Darmon on the palace to palace line, to tell of her safe arrival.

That line, she informed them, was funded by her parents, so that they could speak to their grandchildren without fear of the conversation being overheard and reported. The Dowager Princess Indola, having her grandchildren close at hand, thought it a shocking extravagance.

Colly did not, and as they watched Andrela's carriage depart, he made a suggestion.

"A private line is a good idea. Perhaps we should have one, to your parents. They might like that if their visit goes well, and it would please the children."

"And you?" queried Vealla.

"I have no quarrel with your parents," Colly assured her. "I wish to please them. I am grateful to them. They provided me with you."

Andrela did not quarrel with her parents, but she was not easy with them. They understood that her husband was unable to leave his country, but not why she had left her children behind. They had looked forward to seeing them.

She tried to explain her dilemma. Maldon was the heir and now had two body-guards and did not go anywhere without them. Fidel had only one guard, but he idolised his brother. The only place that he went without him was the children's garden, and he could be very awkward when he chose. Darmon worried and his mother fussed. That combination was unbearable.

She agreed that she would not be there to suffer from their anxiety, but she would be here and the private relay would never be silent. Either her husband or her mother-in-law would be calling to check on him. She had not wanted to burden her parents with the trouble or the expense.

She had not brought her youngest son because poor little Lanchir was so often ill. It was not fair to bring him on a long voyage.

Her parents made polite enquiries as to his health. They thought that she worried unduly and she did not wish to explain her concerns.

She was ready to concede that these might be unfounded. She knew little about diseases, but she had read the history of her adopted land. There were many instances of sickly children who suffered from breathing difficulties. As was usual, most were amongst the poor, but there were some amongst the aristocracy and the Royal family. They had all died young. Their symptoms seemed similar to those that plagued Lanchir, so she worried.

She felt that her youngest son would benefit from a sojourn in the mountains, but it was not easy to reach the mountains from Kaldor. She had made a tentative suggestion to Darmon, but he had responded with a laugh and a comment about her love of the mountains, especially when she had been young and free from the burden of 'heirdom' as he called it. All she really desired was an excuse to promote her ideas of transport by electric rail car. As this was partly true, she had had no answer.

Her stay in Bosron was not a holiday. She attended two Council meetings, opened a new hospital, distributed prizes at her old school and visited the Defence of the Realm establishment to learn about their newest devices.

She strongly suspected that she was left in ignorance of their very newest inventions, for she was not yet High Prince and she had married a foreigner. She did not object. Secrecy and suspicion were a part of life to everyone who worked in Defence. It was an essential element of their work.

She was also invited to several social occasions and organised some meetings with electrical engineers and designers of rail tracks. They were interesting, but tiring, for she had studied history and literature rather than science and her understanding of technical terms was limited. Nevertheless, she returned to Kaldor with her head full of ideas.

Chapter 17

The return journey to Westland was easier for everyone. Lady Marishen was more convivial than Andrela had thought possible and her husband sat contentedly on the deck and enjoyed the view. He was superbly relaxed. The crew sensed the easier atmosphere and found their duties less onerous.

Andrela also enjoyed being on deck but, somewhat to her surprise, she was happy to sit below sometimes and chat with Lady Marishen.

"I did not want Vealla to marry an Elander," confessed the lady one day. "I wanted her to marry Lord Pandour; but perhaps it is better this way. Lord Pandour's family has had recurrent health problems, as we have had.

"Sadly, Gerharst and Fiordan are dead and we have no heir, but we do have some grandchildren who are healthy. That is a great comfort."

"I am pleased that you are now reconciled," responded Andrela. "Lord Collingwade has been a great friend of mine for many years. He was a friend; a good friend. He did not flirt with me. I doubt that he flirted with anyone. I never saw him look at a girl in the way that he looked at Vealla, so I was glad when they married."

She softened her last words with a smile and added that though their disapproval had been a disappointment, she understood it now that she knew Westland so much better.

"Yes. There, great importance is placed on birth." Lady Marishen sighed and admitted that it had led to a continuation of certain health problems.

"Your children may be well, but they may find it difficult to find a girl who is free from inherited disease and whose family is of sufficient standing for them to marry. For generations, the

Royal family in Westland have selected their Chosen Women for political reasons. It will not change because they marry first."

"Nikkor chose Kaiealestria," noted Andrela. "He may have *asked* those members of his Assembly who were with him in Eland for their opinions, but it was not a political decision."

"That was different." Lady Marishen knew her history. "Everyone, including Nikkor himself, thought him incapable of fathering a child."

"Yes," Andrela nodded as she considered, "that is true and must have made a difference. He was free to choose; and as it happened, he chose well."

A trace of envy in the reply made Lady Marishen look up in surprise. She had thought that Andrela and Darmon were well suited and very happy.

She agreed that Nikkor had been fortunate in his lady and mentioned some other Westland Royals whom historians had considered to be fond couples, but commented that it was not always easy to tell whether people were happy or not.

As Andrela seemed unperturbed by her remark, she dared to mention the rumours that she had heard in Kaldor.

"It seems that Prince Maldon was not as content as we all assumed," she concluded. "He made his own choice of lady as far as I remember. There were several other girls he could have married and some of them were more acceptable politically than Indola; but I have heard that he had other interests, and I doubt that Princess Indola knew of them."

Andrela did not answer at once. She had never regarded Lady Marishen as an ally. She was a friend of Indola's, but now that might be an advantage. Also the death of her son and her visit to Eland had changed her attitude, at least towards her daughter.

"Maldon was content," said Andrela at last. "His Choice of Woman was unopposed, she bore him a son and he was faithful for many years. They had been married for more than twenty years, before he took a mistress. *One* mistress," she stressed.

"I had heard of several," murmured Lady Marishen faintly. She had not expected such a direct confirmation of the rumours

"There are several *making* such claims, but none have any evidence," replied Andrela robustly. "My mother-in-law was greatly affected by her husband's unexpected death and shocked by the revelation of his infidelity. It is perhaps not surprising that she confided in friends. Not you, for you had your own grief at that time, but in some. Not all kept the news to themselves."

She smiled as she continued, remembering the woman she had met.

"The lady whom he kept in Kaldor is a most unassuming woman and approached the family only because she could not afford the rent of her house. Maldon had paid it. He wanted her in Kaldor, so she said, and I believe it. He could not have visited her often in Blau where she lived. She wants to go back, for her sister is there, and she did not ask for money, only for some assistance with moving her furniture and possessions."

"Perhaps the possessions are worth money," observed Lady Marishen cynically.

"No, they are not. I have seen them. I went to the house."

Andrela smiled again. Maldon had chosen carefully. It was an unpretentious house with a tree-lined garden and was easily accessible from the palace. She had been surprised at the short time it had taken her to walk there from Maldon's study. He had had a key to one of the little-used garden gates. That had brought back memories of her own.

She hauled herself back to the present.

"She took nothing that was new," she explained, "Her most treasured possessions were her wedding ring, for she was a widow, a large pan, a book of recipes written by her grandmother and some framed photographs of various members of her family. She was a very *easy* lady."

Lady Marishen pointed out that she had been a lady of easy virtue and expressed her surprise that Andrela had visited her.

"Indola would not, Darmon did not care to and he could not decide which of his trusted Assembly members to send. I offered and he accepted in the hope that the matter would be kept within the family."

Having started on her tale, Andrela decided to tell almost everything.

Mrs B, for the lady's name was not pronounced in full even in the palace, had run a store in Blau with her sister. They made soups and stews, pies and savouries, cakes and sweetmeats. They were patronised by the residents, but they made most of their money selling to the servants of the aristocratic visitors who arrived hungry, but at short notice.

Maldon had enjoyed one of their cakes, enquired as to its provenance and had thus heard about the shop. He had visited it one day and met Mrs B.

"I don't think it was a passionate relationship," commented Andrela. "He seems to have been more interested in her kitchen and her cakes, particularly a concoction of fruit, nuts, egg whites and honey. She told me that they often sat in the kitchen and he talked of his problems whilst she cooked."

She grinned suddenly and added, "She never mentioned the bedroom, though that featured heavily in the later claims. So much so, that after we had seen the first claimant, Darmon interviewed them alone."

"Was Indola present at the first interview?" Lady Marishen sounded anxious.

"No. It would have upset her greatly; and in truth she would have been a hindrance rather than a help. She was already talking of selling her jewellery in order to pay them off."

"Did Darmon believe them? Will he bargain with them?"

Andrela smiled and shook her head.

"He did not believe half of what they said. Their stories varied a great deal, but none gave dates or times, only details of their activities. Some he mentioned to me, others disgusted him and I felt that he considered his father incapable of such things. He will not want them published."

Suddenly she became angry and did not trouble to hide it.

"*He* will not tell those vile creatures to take themselves to Hadron where they belong. *I* would do so. *I* would tell them to publish what they wished, but to be sure that they could provide confirmation of their allegations. *I* would threaten them with the courts and damages – very large damages – if anything was printed that they could not prove. I would also warn all the news sheet proprietors of my intentions.

"I doubt," she added more calmly, "that any of the women can prove that they had even *met* the High Prince other than in public, let alone that they had spent passionate hours in bed with him."

"I knew Maldon quite well when we were young," commented Lady Marishen in a contemplative tone. "Not intimately, naturally, but quite well, and we have been guests at the palace on many occasions. I was not unduly surprised to hear rumours of a mistress, many men take mistresses, but kitchen and cake does seem more in character than passionate hours in bed."

Andrela sighed. "That is exactly what Darmon said; but I am so afraid that he will not fight, and if one is paid off, all must be paid off, and more will come! And the very act of paying them will encourage belief in their silly stories."

"That is certainly true."

Lady Marishen pondered for a moment before she continued in a matter-of-fact tone, "If Darmon does not challenge them, perhaps *you* could do so."

Andrela stared at her. She was a pillar of Westland society and here she was, recommending a course that that society would find shocking. Wives were subject to their husbands; they did not usurp their roles.

"No. I have thought of that," she shook her head sadly, "but Darmon would feel belittled, and I cannot treat him so."

"He might," agreed the other. "He might also be grateful. He has a gentle nature and will be a fair ruler, but it is fortunate that the country is peaceful just now, for he is not a fighting man. You are tougher."

Lady Marishen picked up her embroidery with a determined air and bade Andrela to take a walk on deck and think about the problem. The sea breeze, she declared, would blow away her doubts.

Andrela walked and thought and the sea breeze blew strongly, but still she doubted.

Darmon had been gentle and considerate towards her always. She did not love him and Caston was now a distant memory, but her husband deserved her respect and she did not want to hurt him.

Lord Marishen, sitting in a sheltered spot, watched her pace the deck for some while before he called her to come and sit by him. She was pleased to oblige, thinking to sit and view the distant coast with a quiet companion. Alas, he did not prove as quiet as she had anticipated.

"You are troubled," he said after only a few moments of silence. "We are continually reminded by the good Padri that

Namier may cut off our lives at any time, but we are still surprised by death. His Highness Prince Maldon was, I am sure, and though he left his country in good order, he was not as careful in his private life. It is hard on the widow.

"Collingwade is a wealthy man and has made proper provision for Vealla and the children, but they have been married for less than ten years. Who knows what may happen in the future."

Andrela gave him a startled look and turned away. She had never considered that Colly would be unfaithful, but it was possible. It was possible for any man or woman to tire of the one they had once loved. She could not imagine doing so herself, but she had lost her love almost as soon as she had found him.

She wondered about those whom she knew who had been married for twenty years or more. She dismissed most of Westland's noble couples as unimportant in the context. They had not married for love, but the parents of her Eland friends, what of them? What of her own parents? How did one tell?

"No one knows the future," she said at last. "Darmon did not know. He may have wondered, but he did not know."

"A pity," observed her companion. "Death comes and family grieve. That is normal. Unpleasant discoveries are not wanted. Your husband has my sympathy. He has enough new responsibilities to occupy his mind without having to arrange his father's unfinished business."

"I agree with that," replied Andrela wholeheartedly. "Your wife suggested that I might confront them."

"Did she indeed?"

Lord Marishen looked speculatively at the woman beside him. She was not afraid of confrontation.

"I have always considered that troublesome females are better dealt with by other females," he ventured, and when the only response was an eyebrow raised almost in amusement, he continued.

"If you did approach them," he said, choosing his words carefully, "you might find a threat, a deterrent of some sort that would not occur to your husband. He is a fine man and will make a good ruler, but he does not understand women. Few men do."

Andrela smiled at his tact.

"I might, but I might make things worse."

"I doubt it," he answered. "Talk to your Ladies of the Bed-chamber about the matter. Both are sensible and discreet." He smiled. "I was not happy at the time, but you made a good choice. Even the Princess owns that the Ashton girl is efficient and undemanding, and that husband of hers, whose name I can never remember, is there at every occasion to support her, but always in the background."

As he spoke, he nodded to emphasise his approval, but he did not wait for her to answer. It was becoming cooler and he needed a drink.

Chapter 18

Andrela took his advice. She found when she arrived in Kaldor that she had more worries than she had anticipated.

Darmon greeted her abstractedly, and his problems had obviously not been solved. Maldon was polite but unaffectionate. He had spent more time with his grandmother than with his tutors and Fidel had accompanied him for the first weeks. The conversations had upset the younger boy, however, and he had made his own decision to return to his books. He was subdued and Lanchir was ill again.

Andrela cursed her stupidity. She ought not to have left her children for so long.

Her ladies were supportive. She had left her children, but that was done. In future, if she were obliged to leave them, she would make more precise arrangements. Lanchir ought not to be confined to his bedroom for every little cough. Fresh clean air was better for him.

Annia suggested that Fidel and Lanchir accompany her husband and their two elder children to Osira for some sailing. Fidel and Leon were of a similar age and would be company for one another, and if Lanchir did not care to sail, Annia was sure that her daughter would stay on shore with him. The sea air would do him good.

Andrela rejoiced at such a solution, but Darmon's agreement was a necessity.

First Andrela approached Fidel's body guard, a highly skilled young man with a cheerful disposition. He was, he assured her, happy to take care of Lanchir in addition to his usual charge and was perfectly capable of minding them both. The sea would be the greatest danger and he had once rescued two men – he just stopped short of calling them fools – whose dingy had capsized. Neither could swim, but they had not thought to provide themselves with floating aids. He further endeared himself to Andrela by remarking that Prince Lanchir needed a bit of fun.

Andrela did not use quite the same words when she asked Darmon's permission, but she did remind him of the enjoyment he had had as a boy in the company of Ped and Jon. Jon was unavailable – Namier alone knew where he was – but Ped would care for their youngsters as if they were his own.

For a moment, Darmon's cares had seemed to disappear. He smiled and gave his consent.

Andrela needed nothing more. Within an hour she had packed her younger sons off to Lord Pandour's Kaldor home and he left that afternoon for the Osira and the sea, with four excited children bouncing up and down in the coach.

Having solved two of her small problems, at least temporarily, Andrela turned her attention to the greater one.

She was furious to discover that Princess Indola had responded to a threatening letter by complying with the writer's demands, and she came near to quarrelling with her husband about his attitude.

"How can you have allowed your mother to give a valuable piece of her jewellery to a slut!" she stormed. "Did you not think, in the circumstances, that it might be sensible to monitor her incoming post? Those wicked lying women have troubled you enough; did you not think that one or another might contact your mother directly?

"Now one has, and her fool of a secretary gave the wretched letter to her. What in Hadron was he thinking of? She is grieving for her husband still, and though their great love for one another may be a figment of her imagination, it is real enough to her. It was her pretence and her pride."

She gazed at her husband in exasperation. He had agonised over the problem and had discussed it with one or two of the most trusted members of his Assembly, but they had come to no firm conclusions.

"I am doing what I can to minimise the publicity," he assured her. "I do not want my mother publicly shamed. She has been hurt enough, and I doubt that it would help her pride if I insisted on reading her letters before giving them to her."

"Nor will it if her necklace is pictured in the news sheets around the neck of some cheap tart!" retorted Andrela. "Namier's Moons, can you not see that the action, having succeeded, will be copied by others?"

She drew a deep breath. Darmon's frown had deepened. She had not intended to worry him further; she had wanted to stir him into action, but he did not know what to do.

"You have the country's agents at your call. Can they not retrieve it?" she asked in a softer tone, but he did not think that feasible. The Special Service was for the protection and defence of the country. He could not ask any member of it to burgle a private house simply because it suited him.

"Very well, if you cannot, then you cannot."

Andrela shrugged her shoulders in disgust as she walked away and she muttered under her breath, "I will retrieve it myself."

She had spoken in anger and without thinking, but later she considered her words more carefully. Darmon had mentioned burglary, but that was not the only way of retrieving the necklace and his words had implied that the address was known. She must find out.

First she visited Princess Indola. She was not welcomed. The Princess was convinced that she come to 'turn her out of the palace', as she phrased it, and after several unsuccessful attempts to reassure her, Andrela gave up and asked bluntly about the letter.

To her surprise, Princess Indola had kept it and also two others which had arrived more recently and to which she had not as yet responded.

Andrela scanned the ill-written missives swiftly. They all gave an address and were, she thought, rather similar, but that did not prove that the senders knew one another. All the uneducated, whether male or female, might use the same words for the same message. They had, she presumed, only a basic vocabulary. It was very basic in one context.

"Has Darmon seen these latest ones?" she asked.

He had not. The Princess was too ashamed to show them to him, but she fully intended to comply with their demands.

"I must send my bracelet tomorrow," she said tearfully, "for I cannot have such things about my dear Maldon published in a news sheet."

"Do not send the bracelet," responded Andrela firmly. "Send a note, on plain paper, not on a sheet emblazoned with the Royal crest. In fact," she added, suddenly recalling that the Royal paper was specially made and had a distinctive paper mark, "have your secretary buy some as cheap as this," and she waved the letters.

"Tell this person that your bracelet is in the bank vault and cannot be obtained for a few days. That will give us some time."

"But it is not," objected the Princess. "It is in the palace safe as is all my jewellery; and yours too."

"And who knows that?" demanded Andrela. "But if you do believe that this scum of a woman knows where their Royal Highnesses keep their valuables, then tell her that it is being cleaned or repaired. Play for time. I will keep these letters and discuss the matter with Darmon."

It was not a lie. She fully intended to discuss the matter with Darmon, though not necessarily immediately.

She looked at her mother-in-law with more sympathy than she usually displayed towards her.

"Try not to worry about these lies. You have been within doors too much. Take a walk in the garden and enjoy the flowers. The weather is pleasant just now."

She did discuss the letters with her ladies. Both agreed that they were most probably a tissue of lies, but Annia's advice was to leave the matter to the High Prince.

"You are a grown woman, Andrela," she said severely, "not a wild young thing to go adventuring alone."

The argument that a woman might have better success in confronting the presumably female writers did not sway her. She had grown away from Eland and its relative freedom and closer to her husband and her new country.

It was inevitable, thought Andrela sadly. Pedan had become a little less rigid and Annia had become more so.

Elizabeth was also cautious. She knew Kaldor better than either Annia or Andrela. The addresses were unrecognised by them because they were in an area where ladies of quality did not go. She found a map of the city and pointed out that the three streets all connected with the Brank Road. Women of virtue did not frequent that road if they could possibly avoid it. It was a haunt of prostitutes. It would not be sensible to go there, certainly not alone.

Andrela did not go alone; she went with Hal and another.

As a Westland Princess, she had two bodyguards, one of whom had been employed and approved by the Palace before her marriage. He probably knew Kaldor better than Hal, but she trusted Hal. He had come with her to Westland.

She had not asked him to come with her, but he had offered.

"I know you," he had said, "your new guard will not, and I will learn the dangers of a new country faster than a stranger will learn about you."

She had been grateful. He had undergone retraining to obtain Westland credentials that would satisfy any who might question his competence. He had also married and had made friends.

One who had advised him in his first months in Westland had remained a friend. It was he who was with them now.

He was older than Hal and past his prime, but he had been Prince Maldon's bodyguard for many years. A faithful and trusted servant, he knew much about his master, but said little. Rather, Andrela suspected with a twinge of guilt, as Hal did about her.

Hal had arranged a meeting and she had thought a great deal about what to say. It was fortunate, for the Westerner volunteered nothing. She had asked specific questions and had been given very short answers. They were helpful answers, however, and when she finished he had asked a question of his own. Did she propose to take action?

She had replied with a single word and he had offered his assistance. Hal had smiled as she accepted and she was inordinately pleased at their approval.

Now Hal was strolling down the street ostensibly inspecting the numbers on the doors, but they knew the house and all three were watching.

She wore a shabby dress, with a torn shawl covering her hair and she sat in a cart pulled by a bedraggled donkey. They proceeded slowly, the driver hunched over the reins.

She caught her breath when a man emerged from the door and felt ashamed of her lack of control.

"A client? At this hour in the morning?" she breathed, scarcely moving her lips.

"All hours," came the muttered answer, and the driver hoped that the visitor had not been a debt collector.

Andrela could now see Hal more clearly. He had lengthened his stride and had almost reached the door. Her heart beat faster and she took a long slow breath. There were people about and no one must have reason to look twice at her.

Someone spoke to Hal as he pulled on the bell. They could not hear the words, but they heard Hal's laugh and the passer-by continued on his way.

The door opened, Hal disappeared inside and the cart continued without change of pace. It reached the end of the street before it stopped.

"He will be waiting. I saw the signal," muttered the driver and Andrela scrambled down.

It was an ungainly descent as she was not accustomed to carts, but it was in keeping with the old woman's clothes that she was wearing.

She swore, for the benefit of any within hearing and she also cursed the driver for taking her too far. The words were not ones that any would expect a princess to use, but they were not uncommon in that street. She continued muttering crossly as she stumbled along.

Hal was lolling in the open doorway when she reached it, and she slipped inside. He grinned at her as he led her down a dark passage and into an untidy room.

A large bed, partially hidden by a screen, occupied the further end. Two sagging dining chairs and a table stood in the centre of the other end and a half-open door showed the kitchen area. A woman sat in a worn armchair by the fire, nursing a glass half-filled with cheap brandy. Her hair was dyed a vivid red and hung unfettered around her pale face. Watery blue eyes stared in surprise at her visitor.

"I have told her that you are my mistress," explained Hal pulling out the better chair and offering it to Andrela, "but that you are inexperienced and I want her to teach you some of her more interesting techniques."

Andrela curbed the temptation to giggle. That part had not been in the plan.

"The first part is true enough," she said, with only the slightest tremor in her voice. "As High Princess, it could be said that I am everyone's mistress."

She put back the shawl that had covered her hair and half her face and she addressed her 'hostess'.

"I did not wish to advertise my presence, for both our sakes, but now we are alone there is no need for concealment."

The woman almost dropped her glass. She said nothing, but she stared at her visitor in disbelief.

"I have come about this," continued Andrela. She removed the worn woollen gloves that she was wearing and held out a letter. She used her left hand with its well-known ring adorning the third finger.

"You are Issie Tarren, who wrote this letter, are you not?"

"Yes, er–no. Er–" The woman stopped. She was Issie Tarren, but did not want to admit to writing the letter.

"So sad when one cannot remember one's name," observed Andrela. "Have you also forgotten Prince Maldon? You claim to have known him quite well."

Issie had recovered from her initial shock and said that, yes, she had known the late Prince very well indeed. It seemed that many women had, and none of them had been paid enough. That was why she had sent the letter. She wanted her money that was all. She could get it from the news sheets, if the palace didn't pay. Some of them loved to have some good scandal to publish, and Royal scandal was better than anything.

"Yes, but it needs to have some basis in truth," replied Andrela easily. "They will not risk printing lies. Can you substantiate your statements?"

Issie looked blank, so Andrela asked specific questions.

Where and when did she first meet the Prince? How many times had they met? Did the Prince come here, or did they meet elsewhere? In a hotel perhaps; which hotel? Would the staff recognise her? How had he contacted her to arrange the meeting?

Any question that Issie answered was followed by another, more searching until she was totally confused.

"You can't expect me to remember all those sorts of things," she said angrily. "He was a client like any other man."

She began to qualify that, but was interrupted.

"No. I did not expect you to remember and I do appreciate that you have many clients; but, as that is the case, I do not think that any news sheet will print a word of your story. Now, where is the Princess Indola's necklace?"

"I haven't got it. It didn't come," Issie said defiantly. "I was going to give her another day or two."

Alas, her defiance did not improve her intelligence. When Andrela produced a signed paper declaring it to be a receipt, she answered indignantly that the signature could not be hers because the man had not asked for a receipt.

The final words tailed away dismally as she realised what she had said.

"The kitchen, behind crockery or under a saucepan," said Andrela crisply to Hal, "or in her underwear drawer, if she has such a thing."

He watched her eyes, ignored her words, and went to the bed. He found the case without difficulty and the necklace was still inside.

"Under the mattress," he said laconically.

Andrela stood up.

"You have been foolish," she said to Issie. "So have many others including," and she mentioned the names on the letters from nearby streets. "They will receive nothing unless they can offer proof of their claims, and the press will be warned not to print or pay for any tales that cannot be supported by impeccable evidence."

She did not explain the meaning of 'impeccable'. She assumed that she had made the message plain.

Chapter 19

"Well done," said Hal when they regained the street and began to walk towards the waiting cart.

"Perhaps," she murmured softly, "but we must ensure that the press is warned. I am not sure that that will happen."

"It will if *you* do it. Now, whilst you are dressed for a part."

Andrela's heart beat faster. It was years since she had ventured abroad in disguise and she was finding it exciting, but she did not assent immediately.

"We have not planned," she said, and Hal took that as assent.

He spoke to his colleague and he drove them to quiet spot where they could discuss tactics. Having agreed a plan, they returned to a busier part of Kaldor, the street where the news sheets had their offices.

Hal pointed out three buildings where news sheets were produced as they passed along. One printed little but sport and sensation, another was slightly more discriminating and the third was noted more for its excellent reviews of plays and music. Andrela began with the first.

Hal was watching, she knew, but she was still a little nervous as she entered the building and sought the reception desk.

She need not have worried. The showy young lady who greeted her with a distinct lack of enthusiasm almost fell off her stool when 'Royal scandal' was mentioned. A further whisper of 'exclusive' and 'position in the Royal household' produced immediate action. The drab clothes and the stoop were forgotten – when did Royal household servants look elegant?

Andrela was escorted to the upper floors in a lift considerable faster and more modern than those in the palace.

The large office into which she was shown was also modern and boasted a visi-screen larger than any that she had ever seen. She stared at the man behind the desk. He did have the courtesy to rise to his feet and offer her a chair. She waited until the door was closed behind her before she took it.

"Thank you. You may sit," she said in her grandest manner.

The amused expression that this remark produced was swiftly replaced as she began her warning.

Yes, it was true that the late Prince had kept a mistress. That lady did not wish for publicity and her interests would be protected by the Palace Organisation. The first fact had become known and had prompted many spurious claims, some of a highly titillating nature. Imaginative women had threatened to publish their stories and had demanded money.

The Palace did not intend to pay this blackmail; it being an offence to demand money with menaces. It also planned to sue any person or organisation repeating or publishing stories that could not be proven conclusively. She stressed the last word.

"I am sure that your news sheet does not publish anything without checking its authenticity, but if you are offered a 'tell all' from one claiming to have known the Prince Maldon, I advise you to be extra careful."

She stood up, pushing the shawl from her head and rising to her full height. A lock of hair escaped and fell against her cheek.

"Officially, I am at home today, resting and recovering from my recent trip, but I suggest that you spread my message amongst your colleagues. You will not then be blamed for missing an 'exclusive'."

She bade him good day and left, shawl and stooped posture being resumed before she had reached the door.

He was still staring at the draft article on his desk when a colleague entered.

"Well," the newcomer asked. "Did your prim old visitor give you a good story?"

"She was not old, early thirties I think; and she told a tale of warning."

He sighed, picked up the draft and tore it across.

"This is just supposition. We do not have any *facts*. Wiser to wait until we have."

Andrela visited another office, but decided against a third call. She felt that she had been successful, but she had been out longer than she had originally intended; and she was becoming elated. It was dangerous to continue in such a mood.

The cart was nowhere in sight, but Hal was lolling against a lamppost further down the street. Unhurriedly he stirred as she approached and ambled idly along ahead of her. She followed him.

Half an hour later she was safely in her own rooms. There had been one or two awkward moments, in the street and in the palace gardens, but recognition had been avoided and now she stood, dressed in her own clothes and in possession of the 'spare' key to the garden gate. The case containing the necklace lay on the table.

She looked at the clock. Lunch would be served whenever she requested it and she was hungry, but was it a good time to tell Darmon?

She decided that it was and was disappointed when told that the High Prince was engrossed in business for the Assembly meeting that afternoon. He had asked for a simple meal to be served in his study.

It was the third time that he had done that since she returned and she was becoming tired of eating alone. She ordered lunch and sat and thought as the dishes were brought in.

She must see Darmon and talk with him. He was looking careworn and ill, and she had something to tell that would not wait. Lunch looked appetising, but she was too concerned to enjoy a meal. She sent the servants away and loaded a plate. She selected a few of Darmon's favourite titbits as well as making her own choice. She would have lunch with him, however busy he was.

With a jewel case under one arm, a laden plate and a full glass in her hands, she made her way from their quarters to the study door, but opening it was beyond her abilities. There were no servants about. That was unusual, but she was thankful. She kicked at the door and shouted.

It was opened after several kicks and Darmon, as angry as she ever seen him, stared at her in amazement.

"Andrela! What in Hadron's name are you doing?"

"Bringing my lunch," she answered. "I cannot open the door with my hands full. Please take the plate. Then I can come in and explain."

"We have servants for this," he told her, but he took the plate and carried it to his desk, dropping the carefully balanced cutlery as he did so.

Andrela laid the jewel case beside the plate, retrieved the cutlery and set it down with her glass. She pulled up a chair and sat down.

"You have dealt with all your paperwork, I see," she said waving a hand over the desk, "or have you simply moved it aside to make way for the food?"

"I was busy," he protested. "I like to have a clear head for meetings, especially just now."

"Well, one matter is settled. Here is your mother's necklace."

He opened the case, but did not speak, so she continued.

"You had better return it to her, but do not tell her that I retrieved it. She would not approve. Tell her that Security rescued it. That is true in a way, for Hal accompanied me, and also one of the men who used to guard your father."

Once she had started her tale, she found it easy to continue. Darmon asked a great many questions and she answered them truthfully. He was relieved, but he was not pleased with her actions. They worried him. So too did her remark that she had forgotten what fun it was to escape from princess-hood for a while.

She did not, therefore, tell him that she had retained the key.

It was not until they had finished their discussion and their lunch that she asked why he was avoiding her.

His denial was half-hearted and unconvincing and the worry lines deepened on his face.

"There is something I must tell you," he said at last, "and I have been putting it off."

He stood up and paced about the room. There were two things that troubled him, but he only intended to tell her one.

"It is Lanchir. A doctor from Alden was here. He specialises in treating chest problems and I summoned him."

He looked sadly at Andrela and spoke quickly, as if bad news were less distressing if given in a single breath. "He was not hopeful. Lanchir's lungs have not developed properly. He will never be well and may die before he reaches twenty."

Andrela stood up and held him close.

"Oh, my dearest," she said. "Did you think I did not know? I am his mother. I held him so often when he was tiny and listened to him struggle to breathe. He could not feed easily, nor sleep, nor lie still.

"I have looked at every book in the great library that mentions such problems and none mentioned a cure. All talked of 'alleviating the suffering of the patient' though some of the ways suggested were not gentle."

"You did not say," he protested. "Oh, neither did I! I feared that you would blame me – for not telling you of the possibility. It may be not be hereditary, though it does seem to run in families, but it is rare."

He was anxious, but his arms were around her and he did not slacken his hold.

"I know. I knew when I married you. I looked up all the hereditary problems of the Westland aristocracy before I agreed and I decided that the chances of a sick child were no worse with you than with any other man. I do not blame you."

She spoke without emotion and was gratified to see his face clear. She leant her head against his chest and sighed.

"We cannot help but worry about Lanchir, but we must not worry about one another. We have done well enough together so far."

He kissed the top of her head and agreed.

"We have, but I did have my doubts when we first arrived and you clashed with my mother. I wondered if we might have to live apart to keep the peace. And now you have rescued her from her own folly."

"Yes, she is foolish," she answered, drawing away from him, "but that is in part due to Westland ideas and her own ignorance. It is not entirely her own fault.

"Now you must go to your meeting. It will not do to be late."

He laughed. "Your manners are impeccable. In Westland it is almost necessary for the Prince to be late for Assembly in order to keep ambitious Lords in their place. I will go, but first I must tell you something. Pandour sent a message. Lanchir has been sailing and he enjoyed it. 'Liked the movement' apparently. I thought that strange. He does not like moving much when he is here."

"No, but the flies and the smell of horse dung bother him. He cannot run, but would love to propel himself on a scooter as Fidel does in the garden; but even there the air stinks of horses."

He anticipated her next words and excused himself at once. The agenda for this Assembly meeting was already set.

"Next one then. Kaldor *needs* electric cars." She was definite.

He promised nothing, but she would prevail, he knew that. She was a splendid Princess and perfectly satisfactory as a wife, but she was persistent.

His arrival at the Assembly Room was perfectly timed and the meeting went well. Expected business was dealt with easily and when the inevitable question about his father's extramarital affairs was asked, he was able to answer with confidence.

The next question surprised him. It concerned electric transport.

The company who ran the charging station on the rail track at Blau terminal had purchased a six-seater electric cart. They took passengers from the train to the town centre and also ran short round trips for anyone who cared to pay.

These had proved so popular and profitable that the company had installed another charging station at the other end of the town to enable them to travel further. Now they wished to run a similar enterprise in Kaldor. Thus, they needed permission to install another charging station in the city.

The discussion was acrimonious. Some who had seen electric vehicles in Eland or travelled in one in Blau were in favour. Others were against, fearing that objects moving by themselves would frighten the horses.

Darmon spoke last and in favour of the proposal. Lanchir's ill health was common knowledge, but he had not informed anyone of the latest diagnosis. Now he did and he repeated Andrela's words about the effect of the flies and smell of horse dung.

"Where, in our beautiful city, can you escape from either?" he asked.

The proposal was passed in principle. The siting of any charging stations would be discussed later, probably the arguments would be presented over several meetings. Darmon resolved to spend more time with his youngest son.

He kept to his resolve, taking trouble to meet both the boys when they returned from Osira. They were excitedly relating their adventures to their mother when he joined them, and he was disconcerted when they fell silent.

Andrela was equally surprised to see him, but she recovered herself quickly.

"Have you come to hear about their holiday?" she asked and, seeing the answer before he spoke, she began immediately to tell him what they had done.

She did so cleverly, interspersing her account with questions that first Fidel then Lanchir answered. Their answers grew longer as their confidence grew. They were not used to their father's presence save on formal occasions, but he said nothing to alarm them and they spent almost an hour together before Lanchir ran short of breath.

Andrela went with him and Darmon was left alone with Fidel. He learnt much in their short conversation.

Lance had been much better by the sea. He had been fun when he was feeling well. Mal wasn't fun anymore. Now he was Heir – the word was pronounced with a capital letter – he wanted to be called Maldon. Grandmother had told him that it was more dignified. Fidel sniffed in disgust.

It was an action copied from Andrela. Fidel was like his mother, but Maldon seemed to have much in common with his paternal grandmother.

Andrela returned and sent Fidel to play Pirate Treasure. It was a board game that they had played with Pandour's children and Lanchir had started to play with Maldon, but was finding it difficult to explain the rules.

Fidel made no objection, but he did remark than Mal would be cross if Lance won, and Lance had won often in Osira. He seemed stupid sometimes because he didn't have breath to speak, but there was nothing wrong with his brain.

"Does Maldon think his brother stupid?" asked Darmon when Fidel had gone.

"Perhaps. He certainly will not want to be beaten by him at anything." She smiled at her husband. "He is conscious of his place as your heir and does not accommodate easily. When you start to take him to Assembly meetings, you will have to teach him to listen; and to answer tactfully."

"He is a little young for that," answered Darmon.

"The years go quickly," commented Andrela and they talked for some time about their children.

"I have left them too much to you," owned Darmon. "I have left many things to you."

"You did not care for small babies. You will find them more interesting now they are older, and you have always had state duties."

She excused him without rancour. Once he had married, his father had handed him most of the duties that involved travelling, saying that it was an opportunity to introduce his wife to the populace. He had continued taking those duties even when said wife was unable to accompany him.

"And of late, you have been extremely busy; and worried," she continued. "Do not leave Mal in the same position that your father left you. If you have a mistress – or several – do not keep it secret. Tell me, or Mal if he is old enough. And make provision for them."

Darmon stared at her in surprise. "Tell you! Would you not be angry and offended?"

"No. We married for political reasons, not for love; and though I am fond of you and I respect you, I do not love you. I expect that you feel much the same way about me."

He agreed, mentally adding 'I admire you' to the list.

He did not tell her about the woman with the red-brown hair whom he had met at the official Naval Tribute to his father. He had desired her as he never desired any other woman. She had made his heart sing. He had struggled to keep his eyes away from her and give due attention to the proceedings, but he had no idea whether she felt the same way.

If he met her again, he would find out.

Chapter 20

Lanchir died a few months before his fourteenth birthday. It was not unexpected, but Andrela found it harder to bear than she had anticipated. For the first time, she understood her mother's lack of control at Fidel's death. She too wanted to wail aloud and tear her hair. She restrained herself. Such behaviour might help her, but would certainly not help anyone else.

Lanchir was buried in the mountain valley where he had died. Princess Indola complained bitterly. He ought to be buried in Kaldor. The mountains were too far away. She could not possibly travel that far.

Andrela's restrained response about her own parents and the travelling that they must do, did not change her mother-in-law's opinion.

Lanchir had been a Westland Prince, she countered. His Eland grandparents may have loved him, but they could never have expected that he be buried anywhere other than Kaldor.

Darmon had intervened, observing tartly that Prince Roddori and his wife had already grieved over their own son and had not expected to be alive to grieve over a grandson.

"Lanchir is *my* son," he had added with the authority usually reserved for contentious Assembly meetings, "and I and his mother will decide where he is to be buried. We will also take note of his own wishes."

The funeral was well attended. For every Westland aristocrat who declined to travel through 'the wilds', there was an Eland lord who came to support Prince Roddori and his heir, Andrela.

There were also many mountain people. All approved of Eland Princesses, but the western valley people acclaimed them. The first had brought dams and electricity and new people. There had been problems then, but there had also been opportunities.

This Princess had brought her son and had promoted the fine air of the high valleys. It had brought improved roads, other visitors with money, and the prospect of a rail link to the capital.

Besides all this, those who knew him had liked the young Prince and they too grieved for his early death.

Andrela stood beside her husband and her sons as the coffin was lowered into the ground. They were high up the valley and the grave had been carved out of the underlying rock. In the mountains, bodies were not buried for long because fertile ground, and that was any that was not rock, was scarce. After a suitable time the dead were disinterred and the bones dropped into one of the deep chasms that scarred the slopes.

Lanchir's body would remain in its place, but this special plot was not in the lower valley. The Theale had wanted a permanent reminder of the Prince who had found some respite from his sickness in their valley, and Darmon had not objected. His son had not cared where his body was laid to rest.

"Leave me here when I die," he had said. "My spirit will have fled and what is left is not important – the eggshell when the bird has hatched and flown."

When the gritty soil had been replaced and the first petals scattered over the bare ground, the Royal party began their descent. The less important mourners remained and waited their turn to say their prayers and add their petals to the colourful mound.

Andrela helped her mother down the narrow path. Princess Margren was not used to uneven ground. Fidel aided his grandfather and Maldon walked beside his father who needed no help. Darmon took his comfort from the unobtrusive woman whose red-brown hair was covered with a black lace scarf.

She did not stay for the meal that was set for all who had travelled. She had stayed the previous night in another valley and she returned there before making her own way back to Kaldor.

Prince Roddori and his wife stayed in the hotel where Lanchir had stayed. It was high in the valley and close to a tunnel that led back to Eland. Andrela had chosen it, hoping that her parents would visit their grandson there. They had done so once or twice, but recently they had found the journey too tiring.

They had come for his burial, but the strain showed in their faces.

Andrela had visited them only a few months previously, but that had been in Bosron in their own palace. She was shocked to see how tired her father looked after the journey.

"He does tire very quickly now," said her mother. "The Council meetings exhaust him. If you had stayed in Eland it would be easier. You or your husband could take over some of his duties."

As Andrela had married Darmon to avoid an Eland husband taking over Royal duties, she did not answer. She asked for the doctor's view, but her mother did not know.

"He does not tell me," she complained.

He did tell his daughter and, as she feared, the news was not good.

"They would operate," he said, "but that would necessitate months of recuperation even if it went well. It might well kill me if it did not. Either way, it does not seem worth the risk. I may live just as long without it."

He smiled at her. He could see the next question hovering on her lips and answered it before she spoke.

"I have tablets for the pain."

The Royal party returned to Kaldor swiftly. A visit from the recently installed ruler of Zorrenna was imminent and, though Westland would give its prince time to mourn his son, the same consideration could not be asked from foreigners.

Darmon apologised to his wife for the lack of time and suggested that she stay and travel to Bosron with her parents, but she declined. Her presence would not help her father and the Zorrennans were expecting to meet her also.

"They want two for the price of one," she joked with her family.

Maldon frowned. "But you are not important," he said, "not to Zorrenna."

"Your mother will be High Prince of Eland when her father dies," Darmon reminded him gently. "Zorrenna maintains diplomatic relations and trading links with Eland just as it does with Westland. You should know that."

"It is not that long since you have been to Bosron, Mal," noted Fidel. "You cannot have forgotten how busy the docks are. There are often ships from all parts of Erion."

Maldon was unconvinced, but waited until he was alone with Fidel before he commented.

"I cannot see that any will want to talk to *Mama* about trade. She is a woman. And Eland is not nearly as large and important as Westland."

Fidel had a standard answer when Mal 'went Westland' as he termed it, but he did not use on this occasion. This time, he agreed that the visitors would discuss only generalities with Mama. They would certainly not want to discuss detailed *terms* with her about anything, for Mama drove too hard a bargain.

He grinned at his brother's surprise.

"Gramps E told me," he explained. "*She* did the bargaining with Westland before she married Papa; and though she conceded that the capital would be Kaldor, she wrung the last pakor out of Westland on the currency deal.

"Zorrenna will want to maintain its contact with her. She is influential now and will be more so when she is High Prince."

"That may not be for years," answered his brother scornfully.

"It may be soon," said Fidel sadly. "Gramps looked ill."

It was not years. It was only months later that Andrela received a tearful relay from her mother. She should come home if she wished to see her father again.

She no longer thought of Bosron as home, but she did want to see her father before he died. She cancelled all engagements for the next three months, packed a few necessities in a saddle-bag and set out on horseback the following day.

"It is quicker to ride and cross through the mountains near the southern dam," she told Darmon. "It can take days to sail round Bellue if the wind does not obligingly change direction. The road to the mountains is safe now and there are so few towns along the route that I can travel fast and without ceremony. My mother will arrange for me to be met in Eland."

She agreed to a female companion. A Princess was expected to conform.

The party was larger than she had hoped because both her ladies volunteered and her two bodyguards were, she admitted, necessary. Elizabeth's husband made the numbers even.

"Three men, three ladies; a normal arrangement," he had said when he offered and Darmon, though still unhappy at the informality, had agreed.

He would not have been pleased at the pace that Andrela set once they were out of Kaldor and the public eye, but her companions were not surprised. Annia and Hal had warned the others, but they knew the Princess too and were prepared.

It was certainly quicker than the sea journey. Darmon was relieved when the relay reported his wife's safe arrival in Eland, but he did comment on the short time that it had taken. Maldon, meticulous as always, calculated the speed at which they must have ridden, given that they had stopped for proper food and rest.

Fidel commented that Mama had been close to Gramps and he was glad that she had arrived in time to see him. She would rest easier and eat better now that she was there, in her own palace.

Darmon glanced uncertainly at his younger son. It was almost twenty years since he had married Andrela and she had lived here, in his palace, for all that time. *This* was her home; except that the Princess Indola had never offered to move out of her rooms after his father's death, and he had never pressed her. Andrela had not complained and his sons had seemed happy to remain in the new wing, but the slight stress on the word 'own' told him that one son had noticed and felt that his mother had been slighted.

Perhaps, he thought, he ought to tackle the situation, but if Prince Roddori died, Andrela would be High Prince of Eland and she might choose to live there. She would certainly spend more time there. He was not sure whether he would regret that or not.

Andrela did rest when she reached the palace in Bosron, but not until she had seen her father.

He was, she was told, having a good day. That did not, she discovered, mean that he was able to rise from his bed or do very much for himself. It meant that he was awake, could speak and understand.

They talked for an hour. They talked State business because, as he said, he was dying and this might be the last opportunity to discuss what was to happen to his country.

"I love you and you love me. That is enough for us. We both love Eland, but uniting with the west will bring problems. We must discuss those."

They did and found that they agreed about most things.

"If Maldon were like Fidel, or even like Darmon," she acknowledged, "Eland would accept his rule willingly; but he is not and I am afraid that the country will resent him. He is like his grandmother and he will marry the daughter of one of the powerful southern lords. He thinks Eland unimportant compared with Westland and will not visit often, so he will not know the feelings and views of Elanders. He will, however, expect to collect taxes."

"The state must collect taxes," said her father tiredly. "Must be fair. You know that the big towns now elect a representative to Council?"

She nodded, and he continued. It had worked well enough for Bosron, Feltenare and Pittern, but other towns wanted to be recognised. Lairmouth and Winisham, even Guorl and Measham. Something must be decided. Population, perhaps, or volume of trade.

She reassured him. Yes, there must be some standard. It must be discussed and agreed in Council. Organising voting was expensive. It was good that people felt that they had a say in what was decided, but they must be aware of the cost. Many desirable things were set aside because of cost.

They discussed many of them; education, public amenities such as parks and sports fields, provision of clean water, burial of the dead and the funding of churches and charities. He was exhausted when they finished, but he was content.

He was half asleep when she kissed him and he murmured indistinctly. Something about Fidel and proud, but she heard nothing clearly.

It did not worry her. It was natural that he should think of his dead son as he was handing over the direction of his country, and that he should be proud of him. He might also have been trying to express his pride in her. She hoped so. She would do her best to be a worthy High Prince.

She did not have any further serious conversation with him though she sat beside him for many hours. She played to him on

171

a borrowed flute and she sang, old traditional country songs, simple and undemanding. Speech tired him, but he liked to listen.

She was there when he died, knowing that this was the hour; holding his hand and singing a lullaby from the mountains. It was a peaceful death.

The days after were far from peaceful and Andrela was glad that her two ladies were there. They went through her wardrobe and found clothes for her. Many were too small or too dated, but there were some in sombre colours that were wearable with a little adjustment.

She was obliged to purchase new clothes in black for public appearances, but it was not an enjoyable task and she was pleased to have a few suitable outfits for meeting the many people, friends, officials and chiefs of staff, who called on her.

Some she met alone, for there were no women on Council to offer to support her, but most she saw with her mother at her side. Princess Margren had prepared herself as best she could for the loss of her husband. In public she behaved with great dignity and composure and only her daughter and her closest friends saw her tears.

The funeral was an even more splendid occasion than Fidel's funeral had been. All of Eland was represented. Half of Westland's aristocracy accompanied their Prince and his two sons. Two Kelis came from Regan, the Lord of Shyran attended and there were representatives from Zorrenna, some parts of Irrok and some of the northern islands.

Prince Roddori had encouraged the trade that had existed for centuries and the foreign traders wanted an introduction to the new female High Prince, in the hope that the goodwill would continue. They had their introduction, talked for longer than they had expected and were encouraged. Woman she might be, but this Prince Andrela was not a fool.

She introduced them to her husband and her elder son, so that a personal contact with Westland's Royalty was made or reinforced and they were duly grateful.

Their praise of his wife was accepted by Darmon with genuine pleasure, but she was plainly regarded as his equal and that disconcerted him. Not entirely to his surprise, his elder son also felt annoyed.

Fidel laughed at his brother's discomfiture.

"Mama is cleverer than you," he said bluntly, and that irritated Maldon further.

It was Lord Pandour who noticed Jonal Tesher amongst the mourners outside the cathedral, located his yacht in the harbour and brought him to the palace. Jonal came reluctantly, declaring that he had not intended to intrude, but had wanted to honour the father of his friend's wife. He had been too far away to come to their son's funeral, but he had visited the grave.

Darmon was delighted to see him again. Eland court did not follow as strict an etiquette as did Kaldor society, but it was different and strange and Darmon did not find it easy. Jon's gentle humour and informality was a welcome relief. He also had a fund of stories about his travels. Fidel especially hung on his words and resolved to sail around Erion himself as soon as he was of age.

Whilst Andrela was occupied with state business, her husband and sons spent many hours with Esquire Tesher and Lord Pandour. They went one day to see Lord Collingwade and his family. It was an easy afternoon. There, even Maldon relaxed and joined in the youngsters' games whilst the older generation talked.

Jon had not lost his ability to charm. Annia and Vealla were showered with compliments and he showed his talent for language by using foreign words that he had learnt whilst abroad. He did, however, save his most sincere compliment for Andrela telling her that she was as lovely as ever, but now had greater dignity and was a worthy successor to a fine Prince.

She questioned his knowledge of her father and was truly pleased when he explained that Eland's ruler had been much admired in many of the lands that he had visited.

Jonal did not stay long in Bosron. He was on his way to Galtera in the far north and wanted to arrive before the first chill froze the harbours. Darmon left soon after he did and took Fidel with him, and Andrela remained in Eland with Maldon.

She wanted to introduce him to Eland's ways, but it was not a happy time. Maldon did not agree with any of her ideas for the future, and the more he argued, frequently quoting from old books that Princess Indola had advised him to read, the more she resolved to leave her country with a strong Council. One that would make its own decisions and not rely on leadership from Kaldor.

She was, therefore, inclined to grant elected representatives to towns with smaller populations than she had at first envisaged. They would hold on to their freedoms.

It was not easy to persuade Council to agree. Lord Berrondol was notoriously conservative, but Lord Geraish, who had succeeded his grandfather, was young and was susceptible to the charms that Andrela did not scorn to use. Each had their following and their more independent supporters.

She did not push her point of view too hard. She modified her proposal and it was passed with a good majority, but she did include a clause that allowed towns a representative as soon as they had maintained the required size for a year; and disallowed towns whose population had decreased. That, she thought, would encourage the town elders to care for their population.

She returned to Kaldor some months later. Now that she was High Prince, she promised that she would come to Eland more often and for longer periods than she had been used to do. Her children were now almost grown and she had few responsibilities in Westland. Here, she declared, she had great responsibility.

She was cheered. Maldon was accepted. It was hoped by all that he would grow more tolerant.

When they arrived in Kaldor, it was evident that the populace there had different ideas. The Princess was liked and accepted, but Maldon was the heir. He was cheered, and he revelled in it. He moved into the main palace with his father and Fidel stayed with his mother in the wing which had become her home.

Chapter 21

Darmon did not tackle his mother about the strange situation. They ate as a family in the main palace whenever their various commitments permitted. Maldon was happy, Fidel did not care where he lived as long as he had enough to eat and Andrela did not complain.

It might have been difficult if Darmon had wished to visit his wife at night, but he had not done so since he fell in love with the lady with red-brown hair. She loved him and had been his mistress for several years. He had brought her to Kaldor, set her up in a smart house and had made suitable provision for her as Andrela had suggested. He did not know if his wife had a lover. He would not have objected, but he did not ask.

Andrela was crowned in Bosron in the traditional manner. Elanders celebrated with enthusiasm tinged with sadness, for the next High Prince would not be one of their own. The Westland party was small, which, noted Andrela with a laugh, was fortunate, for it would have been almost impossible to accommodate all Eland and a large contingent from the West in the cathedral.

When she returned after the great event, Andrela gave Maldon most of her Westland duties. He was keen to become more involved in the running of the country. He was not entirely happy with the sponsorships that she passed on to him as he was not particularly interested in charity, but she persuaded him. As soon as Fidel had completed his studies the sponsorships could be given to him.

Fidel wanted to attend the Art and Music College in Kanmei. She suspected that her younger son would like Kanmei and would extend his studies for as long as possible, but she did not know and therefore did not mention it.

She had visited Kanmei on two occasions. Both had been official, but the usual stiff formality that most of Westland considered essential had not been in evidence. They had been welcomed, feted, wined and dined. Nothing was left to chance and everything had gone according to plan, but there had been a relaxed air about both visits and she had loved it. Fidel would too, she was sure.

Andrela spent more than half the year away from Kaldor. Not all that time was spent in Bosron for she toured her country from Dolant in the south to Gilburn in the north, from the mountains near Valke to Fort Bellue and East Point. She met all her lords, seeking out those who rarely came to Bosron and asking their opinions on a variety of issues. It was interesting, but it was hard work and she had no one in whom she could confide.

She visited Colly and Vealla when Bosron claimed several weeks of her presence and that was relaxing. They were an easy family.

Once whilst she was there, Jon Tesher called. He had sponsored Jonal at his naming ceremony and took the opportunity to visit him whenever he was passing Malport. Unfortunately, he did not stay long.

Andrela thought that a pity. He was such fun and so good with the children

"He never stays long," said Vealla. "He is always on the move."

On that occasion the older children were away at the University in Winisham and Andrela banished a dream that she had had. Maldon would never marry Linnie.

If he did meet her whilst she was staying with her grandparents in Kaldor, he would not fall in love with her. He did not approve of women studying; and Linnie would certainly not pursue him.

Andrela loved her eldest son, but there was no denying that he was fond of formality and the trappings of power. He would probably marry some well born girl without brains, whom Andrela disliked. The thought depressed her; but she had not been liked by her mother-in-law, so it was perhaps fair.

Maldon married Lord Bordilen's daughter when he was twenty-one. She was, as expected, a young woman whom Andrela disliked and despised: proud and haughty, with no interest in art or music, but addicted to fashion, gossip and the furtherance of her family's interest.

The wedding, early in the year, was vulgar in its splendour. It had been several generations since a Bordilen had married into the Royal family and Lord and Lady Bordilen did not intend anyone in Erion to miss the event. Everyone who listened to the news on relay or watched the visi-screens knew that they had cleared the market of the best vintage wines, of Alden crabs, of young lamb and of early roses. Even silk and satin were rumoured to be in short supply in Kaldor.

The bridegroom wore cloth of gold. The bride was resplendent in white satin with a train so long and heavy that it almost caused her to stoop. It was embellished with crystals and silver embroidery and was carried by ten small girls in crimson satin with cloth of gold sashes and towers of red roses on their heads.

Andrela wore a simple dress of dark blue silk which clung softly and emphasised her still-trim figure, but she did adorn it with the finest of the sapphire and diamond pieces from Eland's State Jewels. Princess Indola was wearing green, with emeralds and the kaiealestron dragonfly.

Darmon murmured to his wife that she looked almost insignificant beside the others in the bridal party, but she did not care. She was High Prince of Eland and she chose to dress in a manner that she felt her people would like.

She was gratified when Annia smiled wryly and said, "Tut, tut. You do not look at all ostentatious."

She was further pleased when greeting the many guests. Jonal Tesher was announced and whispered a compliment as he bowed to her. She did not have opportunity to speak to him, but Fidel did and later reported a part of their conversation.

"He said that the bride's lack of lustre was not mended by the excess of sparkle on her gown, that her mother could scarcely carry the weight of her jewellery and that your inner glow outshone them all."

She laughed and reminded him that Jon was a master of elaborate compliment.

Andrela had not found her son's wedding particularly pleasant, but it was the last joyful Royal occasion for almost two years.

Princess Indola died less than a year after her grandson's marriage and the Royal family was plunged into official mourning.

Andrela was in Bosron at the time, but she returned for the funeral, as did Fidel who was staying in Kanmei. Both noticed the subtle change in the palace atmosphere. Maldon and his father were at odds.

Darmon wanted to bury his mother with slightly less ceremony than he had accorded to his father. Maldon wanted the same coach and horses, similar flowers in the cathedral and a full week of mourning, just as had been given to honour the passing of their High Prince.

It was not only the funeral arrangements that caused disagreement, but matters before the Assembly, especially the increasing provision of charging stations and the simultaneous increase in popularity of electric cars.

"The Bordilens are wielding their influence. They like their grand coach," commented Andrela drily. "They would probably solve the problem of dirty streets by limiting the ownership of horses, banning public coaches and business carts and making those who collect the horse droppings carry it on their backs!"

She was being facetious, but was told that some of those ideas had been put forward. None as yet had been approved, but Darmon was worried.

"Maldon does not think that I should discuss the problems with you. He thinks you are subversive and want to 'ruin' Westland by importing Eland ways." He smiled ruefully. "And yet he listens to his wife repeating all that her father bids her say. It is natural I suppose. I listened to you."

"Not all that I advise was learned from my father. I want to increase the power of the people and decrease that of the Prince. He did not care for that."

Darmon did not either. He looked weary, and she tried to lighten the mood by bidding him take care of himself. He must keep his throne for years, to allow time for their son to mellow.

"I will not manage that," he answered sombrely. "I have been unwell of late, and the doctors – all four of them – advise me to give up Royal duties and make my will. They agree that I will not last the year. I shall try, however, to prove them wrong."

Andrela returned to Bosron with a heavy heart.

She told no one of Darmon's illness or of her own distress; not even her mother. It was too late to regret her marriage, but her eldest son was not the Prince of Unity that she had envisaged. She loved him, but she owned to herself that she did not like him very much.

She concentrated on Council business. The new representatives from the towns had been accepted and were bringing new ideas to debates. The population was growing and in time there would be as many elected members as there were Lords. That would bring problems, but every change brought problems and she would lead her people through them.

The work that this involved kept her from dwelling on her family problems. Princess Margren seemed healthy, but she was losing weight and becoming forgetful; and visits to Kaldor were dominated by Darmon's slow deterioration.

She was torn between husband and mother and the journey from one to another was long. As High Prince she could not ride and come through the mountains. She was obliged to travel with dignity and some ceremony and she worried that both might die whilst she was on a ship somewhere between the two. It was a difficult time.

Darmon lived beyond the end of the year, but there was little joy in proving his doctors wrong. He was given drugs to ease the pain, but they were not completely effective and affected his mind. He knew it and became frustrated as he struggled to maintain a conversation.

Andrela was with him for the last six weeks. She sat by his bed and sang to him, the lullabies that she had sung to their children.

Maldon wanted to have music relayed to him.

"You will hear professional singers and have a wider choice," he said.

"Too hard," answered Darmon. "Leave it to your mother. In fact," he struggled to express the thought that had just occurred to him, "leave all to her. Care, death, burial. She knows what I want."

Maldon was happy to leave care and death to his mother, but they had an argument about the burial.

Andrela had visited the lady with the red-brown hair to tell her of Darmon's death before it was made public; and she invited her to the funeral.

Maldon was furious when he heard. A cheap woman amongst the highest in land! It was appalling! It was an insult! It was –

He stopped when he ran out of words and his mother smiled at him.

"Your father and I respected one another, but he loved *her*. He asked her to Lanchir's funeral, to comfort him. She came and was so discreet that scarcely anyone noticed. I daresay that she will act in the same manner at your father's funeral. I doubt that she will come to the meal afterwards, but I will not have her barred from the burial. She loved him, she made him happy and she has a right to mourn him."

The lady with the red-brown hair behaved exactly as Andrela had expected. Tears ran down her face as she threw her petals, but others cried too, and no one noticed one more than another.

Andrela did not cry at the funeral. She grieved. She had lost the father of her children and a close and long-standing companion; and she was glad of Fidel by her side.

She did cry when the Will was read.

"To my honoured wife Andrela," read the lawyer, "for her humour, her affection, her wisdom, loyalty and support and for the happiness that she brought into my life, I leave –"

She bent her head before the details were read and wept into her hands. She had tried to be dutiful, as a wife and as a Princess, and this statement of his appreciation touched her deeply.

Chapter 22

A week later, Andrela packed all her belongings and went to live in Bosron. She gave generous parting gifts to her Ladies of the Bedchamber and warm invitations to visit her there. She offered a retirement gift to Hal, but he would not have it. She was his charge and he would follow wherever she went. He had warned his wife of the possibility before they married. She would come with him.

She came, with their youngest child. The older ones stayed with their grandparents. Andrela worried that his wife might not wish to come to Eland with him, but when she met her, she was humbled by the answer to her question.

"He has guarded you since you were a child. He will not leave you. He is loyal – loyal to you and loyal to me. How could I divide his loyalty?"

Fidel accompanied his mother, ostensibly to help her on the voyage, but in reality, he fancied living in Eland. He liked it as he had liked Kanmei and there were interesting courses at the University in Winisham. He did not have much money of his own, but he would manage. He did not expect a large house and a retinue of servants, though someone to cook and clean would be useful. He objected to the body guard.

"I have been obliged to have two for most of my life," said his mother firmly. "You may have just one, but you will have one."

He sighed, but he accepted, and she hoped that he would cause his guard rather less anxiety than she had caused Hal.

They settled easily into the palace at Bosron. It was not as large as that at Kaldor, but there were fewer servants and Hal was able to live in with his family. Andrela occupied a state guest room and Fidel took over his grandfather's rooms. They held no memories for him.

He did not stay idle for long. He decided to learn something useful and went to study engineering at Winisham, coming back from time to time to see his mother and see the latest news on the visi-screen. Study and social life occupied so much of his time at University that, when there, he did not bother to watch news items.

Andrela wrote to him every fortnight, but she called on the relay to tell him when her mother tripped on the stairs and fell heavily. He came back at once. It was not strictly necessary as Princess Margren lived for several weeks after her fall, but Andrela was glad of his company.

"These last few years we seem to have done little but bury people," remarked Andrela sadly as she planned her mother's funeral.

"One has to bury people when they die," replied Fidel practically, "and as I knew all four of my grandparents I have seen more funerals than many of my friends. Linnie did not know her father's parents nor did Tammy nor –"

There followed a long list of his contemporaries whose grandparents had died when they were very young or before they were even born, and he finished cheerfully with the observation that, as Royals, their family funerals were grand affairs that required great organisation and involved meeting numerous people whom one scarcely knew. They therefore took up more time and were more exhausting.

Andrela smiled. "When I die you may bury me quietly," she said.

He looked at her with great affection and shook his head.

"Not possible. All Eland will want to come and pay their respects."

She said only, "Perhaps," because she was no longer sure that a united Salima would benefit her country.

"What will happen to this place when you die?" asked Fidel suddenly. "Will Mal own it? I cannot see him using it. He will not come often to Eland."

"Bosron merchants pay for the upkeep," she answered. "Whether they will continue to do so when Maldon is High Prince and Bosron is no longer the capital city, I do not know. It will depend."

She did not elaborate on what it would depend, but Fidel could guess. If they liked and respected his brother then, yes, they might continue to pay, but if they did not – and he considered that more probable – then they would not.

Andrela thoughts were similar, but neither spoke.

The State might pay through taxes, and Maldon would certainly expect it to do so, but if it were used only on rare occasions, there would be resentment.

Andrela knew some of the history of the building, but she began to study it in more detail. She also went into each of its rooms, from the cellars and kitchens to the tiny attic rooms now filled with discarded bits and pieces.

It was, she concluded, far too large.

She said so before she closed the next Council meeting.

"I, and the High Princes who follow me, can live very well, with their families if they bring them to Bosron, in what was the nursery wing.

"I propose, therefore, that the State Rooms and the library remain as they are and be used by the State for grand occasions, that the nursery wing is redecorated and updated for my use and the use of my descendants, and that the family and guest rooms are allocated to Council for their use.

"This building is becoming crowded. The population is growing and more towns will have representatives in the near future. We must plan to accommodate them. The palace has space. Some of the reception rooms can be made into one that will provide sufficient seating for Council meetings, and there will be rooms available for offices and for committee meetings.

The State will maintain the palace, and this building could be given to the merchants who have for many years ensured that my home was sound and comfortable. The number of Merchant Associations has grown and the Group of Associations has outgrown the Exchange Building. They too are in need of new premises.

"Think on these proposals. Set up a committee to deal with them. Visits to see the palace and take photographs and measurements can be arranged. I will write personally to the President of MAG and if there is a positive response from him and from Council, I will arrange a meeting between us.

"I do not expect, or want, votes on this until you have thought deeply about the implications; but whilst you do," and she became almost apologetic, "consider the palace swimming pool. I would like to use it still, but will confine my use to certain times so that the excellent facilities may be opened to others. I realise, as you will, that that will present a security problem, but it is not unsurmountable. Perhaps school or college groups could make use of it.

"This meeting is now closed, but we have much to think about and to discuss."

The usual shuffle that followed formal closure of the session was noticeably delayed as the members considered her words. There was indeed much to think about.

It was not long before agreement was reached, at least in principle and work began. Andrela called on several ladies of the court to help her clear the rooms of the nursery wing, and to select items to furnish them from the guest rooms in the main palace, but she chose the colour schemes and she tackled the family rooms alone.

She began with the room that she thought would affect her most; Fidel's room.

She had not entered it since his death. It was dust free and tidy as she expected, but in its neatness nothing of him remained. She emptied cupboards and drawers quickly and without tears. He had died years ago, and she had become accustomed to his absence.

Her father's room was equally tidy and had been well aired. The smell of sickness had gone and what remained was a reminder that death could be a blessing. She was careful in her clearing, but there was nothing of significance amongst the books and papers. His secretary, now retired and living in Pittern, had been thorough.

She was less careful with her mother's room, not anticipating anything of importance or anything nostalgic; but there, at the back of a cupboard, she came across something that disturbed her – a blue swimming costume.

She remembered clearly when it had been confiscated; the day before she had met Caston. She smiled at the silly behaviour that had so upset her parents and she sighed at the realisation that the lovely garment would no longer fit her. She pushed those thoughts away easily enough, but memories of Caston kept returning as she piled up clothes and filled the waste basket with old letters, worn gloves and the contents of a make-up drawer.

She wondered what she would find in her own room. She had not used it since her marriage, staying always in one of the grand guest rooms as befitted the Princess of two countries. She went cautiously into the once familiar room.

The drawers caused few problems, though the jewellery box that she had had as a child brought back memories. She had no use for it or any of its contents now, but it could be of use to someone. She set aside some unworn stockings and gloves, but everything else was added to the waste or the 'pass on' pile.

The wardrobes still contained clothes, most of which were now too small. The 'pass on' pile grew larger. When she found at the back of one wardrobe the dress that she had intended to wear for her marriage in Shyran, she buried it deeply in the 'pass on' pile and continued sorting with determination. These things should have been thrown out or re-used years ago.

The last cupboard that she tackled was different. It contained toys and books that had been her favourites. All were now worn and battered; beyond repair, but not condemned to the waste bag without a sigh.

On one shelf, she found a bag containing a string of beads. She put it to one side and determinedly pulled the collection of sewing scraps from the shelf beneath. They were discarded with no more than a cursory glance. She had remembered what was tucked behind them; two bags, hidden years ago.

Andrela opened the white bag first and shook out the dress it contained; white, flimsy fabric, near transparent and decorated with silver-gold crescent moons. The head-dress tumbled to the floor as she drew out the gown.

She stared at it and saw again the grey misty dawn over Bosron Bay.

She did not dwell long on that, but folded the dress into its bag again. It and the beads would go to the charity shop, be used again and make some money for the poor. Lord Campenden may have ceased to host a fancy dress ball, but others had them. They were still popular.

The second bag she opened with less care. Maid's uniforms were sturdy rather than delicate. They were also generously cut.

This one would still fit her, but she could not slip out now! Not now that she was High Prince!

Something remained at the bottom of the bag and she reached in. It was another bag, a tiny one, containing a collection of keys.

Escape from the palace had always required careful planning, but this time there was the added problem of avoiding Hal. He would not criticise, but Andrela did not feel able to tell him that she intended, at her advanced and supposedly responsible age, to go once more on an 'outing'.

She sighed with relief when she turned the key in the garden door and slipped into the street. She hoped that she had been unnoticed. Bosron's population had grown and its streets were busier. Disappearing into a crowd might be easier, but joining that crowd from a gate that one wanted to be kept secret, was not. She had to concentrate hard, and for longer than she had done in the past.

Once she gained the square, things became easier. There were so many people, dressed in such varied styles, that even fancy dress might have passed unnoticed. A middle-aged woman in plain and rather outdated garments attracted no attention at all.

She studied the timetable of the public coach to Senby and was gratified to see that her estimate was reasonable. She had less than ten minutes to wait, provided the coach was on time.

It was a mere five minutes late, but some of those waiting were not patient and she heard many criticisms of the company, the traffic, the lack of planning and almost every other aspect of life in a busy city.

She listened, as she had always listened, for ideas, but nothing was suggested that she had not heard before; and discussed in Council meetings.

She was lucky enough to obtain a seat by a window in the coach, and she shut her mind to all conversation and stared out of it. She had been driven around Bosron and knew that it had changed and grown, but she had not seen it from the public's view. This was an opportunity.

The road had changed for the better as far as surface and width were concerned, but the countryside had suffered. Houses bordered the road for most of the way to Senby.

They passed the Great Hall, covered in posters advertising the many events that it was to host in the next weeks. Lord Campenden may have ceased to hold fancy dress balls, but at least one was forthcoming in the same venue. She smiled, but she stayed on the coach until it stopped in the centre of the village. She would find the steps at the far end of the street and stroll back along the beach. She had an hour before the coach returned to Bosron.

It was not as pleasant as she had anticipated. The water was high, the breeze was from the north and the cliffs hid the sun. She was cold when she climbed the steps back to the street. There were no coffee houses that she could see and only one hotel. She went there.

She was the sole customer in the small restaurant. They could serve her with coffee, but lunch was over, said the waitress and dinner was served only when they had guests staying.

Andrela accepted the almond tart with seaberry sauce to accompany her coffee, noting that it had been 'Today's dessert' on the lunchtime menu.

One waitress disappeared with her order and another came to wipe her table, though it was not strictly necessary. She was inclined to chatter.

Chapter 23

They were not busy just now, Andrela was informed, because it was the wrong season and there were no Big Events on at the Great Hall. That always brought custom, as did weddings. Why a couple should want to rise before the sun on their first night of married bliss, the waitress did not know, but it was tradition. Some of them came back, too, for anniversaries.

The woman moved to the next table, still talking. Some who came back were so mean and miserable that you wondered why they even noticed that it was their anniversary, but there were not many of those and some brought their families.

She sighed sadly. One of those had come every year until he died. They were *especially* pleasant. The wife had written to tell the hotel that they would not be coming again, not because they had been dissatisfied with the rooms or the service, but because her husband had been killed in an accident on board ship.

"I thought that was really kind of her, but then they were always thoughtful and appreciative."

The waitress smiled at the memory, moved to another table and stopped talking.

Andrela was not left without conversation, however, for her coffee and tart arrived a moment later and the bearer was also disposed to talk.

"Megar is too young to remember," she remarked as she put down the tray, "but that couple did not marry here. He came alone for a few years, before he brought his wife and their girls. It was always the same date, and he went to the beach to watch the sunrise. It must have been a woman, though."

She finished transferring the contents of the tray to the table and straightened up.

"I overheard one of the girls complaining one day, and her mother smiled at her so sweetly and told her that he loved them always, every day of the year, so they ought to allow him one morning to go and remember the one who taught him to love.

"Such a *sensible* approach. Perhaps they are sensible in Shyran – that was where they came from."

She nodded as she picked up the empty tray. "Enjoy your coffee," she said and walked away.

Andrela was glad that she had not felt obliged to answer. She was used to concealing her feelings in public whenever it was necessary, but she had not anticipated having to do so today. She had come in an attempt to recall her carefree youth and her lost love, not to grieve.

She spoke severely to herself as she sipped the hot drink. Many people from Shyran must come here, and Caston might never have returned.

She did not convince herself, however, and as she was leaving she stopped in the entrance hall to seek for a visitor's book. It was not difficult to find, nor was the entry that she sought. She turned back to the earliest years that the book recorded and sought for the date that she remembered so well.

His name was there, written in a hand that seemed suddenly as familiar as once it had been.

Caston Ambril had come here. Later he had come with Mrs Ambril and two daughters, and they had commented favourably on the service provided during their stay.

She turned the pages, year by following year. He had remembered her. He had come here to remember; to stand on the beach and watch the sunrise – every year until he had died and the entries stopped.

When she had paid her bill, she walked to the beach. It was afternoon and there was little sign of the sun, but she too stood and remembered how they had watched for the sunrise.

The voice startled her, though it was quiet and courteous.

"Good afternoon, ma'am. You have been standing here for a while. Are you not cold?"

She turned to the speaker, a young man whose dress and manner matched his voice. He was as startled by her face, as she had been by his words.

"Aunt Drela!"

She recognised Colly's second son, Jonal, from the appellation rather than his appearance. He had changed since she had last seen him and was no longer a gangly boy, but there were few in Eland who called her aunt.

"Why, Jonal, what are you doing here?" She greeted him easily when she gathered herself from the interruption to her reverie.

"I am just – being here."

He was clearly embarrassed and she was not, though she had only once before been recognised when on an 'outing'. Caston had been the first all those years ago.

She smiled and answered conspiratorially, "So am I, just being here; and I am alone and unofficial."

"I'm alone too," he said, and after a moment he added, "I can drive now, and I have the car."

She praised him and waited.

"There was a man drowned here last week. He swam out into the Bay on the ebb tide, so father sent me at ebb tide every day this week –,"

"To be there." She finished his sentence for him and he nodded and smiled in relief.

"Sometimes it must be hard to live up to that; though it is a wonderful motto."

He sighed and looked at her curiously. "Is it hard being a Princess?"

He spoke again, before she could answer. "Sorry, silly question."

Andrela shivered suddenly. She had stood too long and was cold, "I must go now, and you must stay. The tide has not turned yet."

She started to walk away thinking of her return and of Hal. She was sure that he would have discovered her absence and be waiting for her in the square. Suddenly she turned back to Jonal.

"It was not a silly question. Yes, it is hard sometimes being a Princess, as life is hard sometimes for everyone, but there are compensations."

Hal *was* waiting in the square. She saw him from the coach window, but she did not look at him as she alighted. He would follow her, she knew that. They did not need to catch one another's eye or make a sign.

She was obliged to walk the length of the palace wall, turn and retrace her steps twice before the street was clear and she dared to open the gate. She sighed with relief when she regained her rooms. She was no longer young. The difficult moments had been exhausting rather than exciting and she had no one with whom to share her experience.

She had learnt that Caston had remembered her despite a seemingly happy marriage, but she had also learnt that he was dead. Sometimes it seemed that everyone she knew was dying and leaving her lonely.

She shook off her desolate mood with difficulty and went into the garden to walk. Best enjoy it now, whilst it was still large and private. When she had only the nursery wing, her garden would be reduced in proportion.

That thought prompted a serious wander to consider how the land could be divided and what particular features of the garden she wanted to keep. An interesting discussion with the head gardener concentrated her thoughts on the future and the griefs of the past were temporarily forgotten. She felt that her time had been well spent, for a hedge was to be planted there, and one grubbed up in another place and her favourite roses were to be replanted in another bed where she could not only walk around them but would be able to see them from her new bedroom. The old nursery wing, she decided during this conversation, would in future be called the Royal Wing.

She asked Colly and Vealla to dine with her the next evening and they accepted. They did not mention her encounter with their son and neither did she. 'Being there' implied discretion and she was comforted by the thought that at least one of Colly's sons had inherited his love and care for humanity and his lack of chatter about its faults and failings.

They talked mainly of mutual friends and families. Political problems were avoided, but Colly did bring up the subject of her travels around her country. She had visited every place of note in her country and been welcomed there, but it had not been restful. She needed a holiday.

Andrela was uncertain. She was alone and visiting anywhere without the prospect of work emphasised her loneliness. She said nothing of this, but Colly knew her well and sensed her reluctance.

"Try a tour of the small places," he suggested. "Travel by sea and visit the little ports; the ones that rarely see their Prince. Eland no longer has a Royal yacht so you can hire a small and inconspicuous vessel; and it will take you away from the palace during the renovations."

"That is a very attractive idea!" exclaimed Andrela and she considered carefully.

"I hate seeing the palace empty, as so much of it is just now," she continued, "but I am dreading the upheaval of Council moving in and of the redecoration of the Royal wing."

Vealla added her encouragement. Jon, Jon Tesher that was, often talked of the small places that he had visited, declaring them to be at least as interesting as the major ports.

Over coffee and brandy, they pored over a large scale map and looked for suitable places for Andrela to visit on a holiday.

She set out a mere two weeks later. Numerous individuals and hire companies were eager to lend her a yacht and every small port that was contacted by her secretary was more than willing to greet her, accommodate her, organise a welcome for her or indeed do anything that would encourage her to visit them. She was a little overwhelmed by their goodwill, but sensibly put it down to the increased publicity that a Royal visit would bring, and not her own popularity.

Her secretary surmised that it was a little of both and planned accordingly.

The first stop was at Wenling on the north shore of Bosron Bay not far from Lairmouth. It had once been a fishing village, but long since the fishermen had moved their boats to a town with a market for their catch. Now it housed the wealthy of Lairmouth who liked its south facing beach and the easy access to the countryside beyond the cliffs.

She had never been there before, though she knew its claim to fame and was happy to travel up the little river and gaze at the spot from which the mock Galtish boats were said to have been launched on their way to fight at Felten. That port was now called Feltenare[*] in honour of the women who had helped to defeat the Galts.

---

[*] The Battle of Felten

The local historians praised her knowledge, the shopkeepers dressed their windows anew in the hope that she would patronise them and the mayor welcomed her warmly, but with a minimum of fuss.

She enjoyed her stay and set sail happily for her next visit.

At her third port of call, she wondered suspiciously how widely Colly interpreted his family motto. 'Been there and have prepared the way', seemed all too likely, at least with regard to herself; but perhaps his ancestors had done the same, in their own discreet manner, for their sovereign lords.

She was sure of it when they moored in the harbour at Nathesh. Her attention was on the crowd on the quay, but she did catch sight of the yacht that was approaching from the west. It was Jonal Tesher's vessel, or it had been when last she had seen it.

Her heart lifted. Here she was not remaining on her yacht. There was a hotel which had an excellent reputation and a suite suitable for her use. She had not wanted to stay there, but had felt that the population would feel slighted if she did not. Now she was glad. If it was indeed Jonal, she could invite him to dine with her. They would use the public dining room. Then there would be no impropriety, even in Westland eyes.

She went ashore with a light step.

This trip had been planned as a leisurely tour. Her welcome was warm, but there were few official occasions planned. She was able to discover the owner of the yacht, and as it was indeed Jonal Tesher, to invite him to dine with her on her free day.

He accepted, and they spent a very pleasant evening together. He did not try to hide the fact that, yes, he had been in contact with Colly and did know that she was planning to visit Nathesh and journey on to New Stannul.

He felt that she would be much occupied whilst in New Stannul and as warmly welcomed in that town as she had been anywhere in Eland. The very existence of the port was due to an Eland woman with vision, and she was perceived as another – as beautiful and as intelligent. Thus he had come here, in the hope that if he did meet her, they would have a little time to reminisce.

She protested. She was neither as beautiful nor as intelligent as Kaiealestria[*] had been, but Jon merely smiled and observed that there were different types of intelligence and different types of beauty.

He noticed, from inference rather than admission, that she was tired, worried and had no one in whom to confide, but he said only that this tour of hers was an excellent idea. The approval of the many who lived in the smaller towns in Eland, which she had reportedly experienced, was more important than the attentions of the sycophantic, and it was assuredly nicer. The poor cheered her for what she had done, the rich and powerful frequently wanted only to increase their influence.

"Some do," she agreed, "but by no means all. I can think of several of my lords who are content with their place and their income, though naturally they have their own opinions and do not always agree with me."

She laughed suddenly, and asked what *he* sought of her.

"Only a smile," he answered, and there was an undertone in the laughing voice that she did not understand.

She turned to the subject of his travels. She had heard of some of his adventures in foreign lands from his letters to Darmon, Pedan and Colly, but she wanted to hear them first hand, so he told her his tales and he answered her questions.

She was genuinely interested in the customs, the politics and the manner of government of the countries he had visited, and she commented on them, often backing up her opinions with examples from her own experience.

She had no amusing examples to cap his tales though and, whilst her seriousness did not diminish his admiration for her, it did not help him; and he suspected that it did not help her either.

He would have been delighted to know that *he* had helped her. She did not forget her responsibilities, but she did fall asleep that night with a smile on her lips and she slept well. It was no hardship to rise the following morning and prepare to leave Nathesh and sail to New Stannul.

It was her last port of call and she loved it. It was a town of all peoples. The Northern Westlanders predominated, but Elanders were there in noticeable numbers. So too were Regans

---

[*] The Beginning of Unity

194

and Zorrennans, and she saw many in the streets and the shops whose looks and language she did not recognise.

She loved the shops with their great variety of goods, the food, which had elements of traditional dishes from all over Erion, and the people who welcomed her warmly. Jon was right. She had little free time and though she saw him at a few functions and danced with him twice one evening, there was no chance of quiet conversation.

There were no ports of call on the return journey and she had plenty of time to think. She had no regrets about her trip. She had learnt more about her people and was happier about their future. They had come out to wave to her, but she now realised that in the small towns – and there were so many small towns – they were too busy working, living and occasionally playing to care much who ruled them. Peace, a reliable electricity supply and low taxes; that was what they cared about – and the weather.

New Stannul had been a revelation. Home to so many different people, far from the capital city, but ruled strictly by its Town Elders, it had seemed a happy and tolerant place. She rejoiced that her own Council had members from all the large towns and resolved to find some way of sending them to New Stannul, on holiday or on 'an investigation', so that they would learn how to work together in a similar way. That would be an achievement of which she could be proud.

Her chief regret was that she had spent only one evening with Jon. True, it would have been difficult to have spent more time with him, but he was fun; and it had been such a long time since she had had fun.

Perhaps, she thought dismally, that was because she was too old.

Chapter 24

The reorganisation of the palace was near complete when she arrived in Bosron and she was delighted with her new quarters. She had ample space, the interior decoration was even better than she had envisaged and the changes to the gardens had been started. Some things must wait for the appropriate season, but new hedges had been planted and old ones had been removed. She was pleased.

The papers that lay piled on her desk did not please her, but not all were official business. There was a letter from Annia, some notes from people whom she had met expressing their delight at having met her and a highly decorative card from Fidel welcoming her back. Even the business papers seemed lighter after that.

Alas, the evening brought a relay from Maldon. He was not comforting. He was critical.

She had not expected that her tour would be reported in Westland, but her visit to New Stannul had not only been noted, it had been photographed; and some parts, in particular the ball, had been relayed on the visi-screens. She had been seen *dancing,* and it was not yet a year since father had died! The whole country was appalled at her behaviour. She had disgraced herself and her family.

Andrela interpreted this as meaning that those whose opinions mattered to Maldon were appalled. Most of those would be in the Bordilen family.

She told him firmly that she had enjoyed herself and did not consider it essential to be miserable for a whole year or to eschew dancing because his father had died.

"He would not mind. I know that. Ours may have been a political marriage, but we did share the joys of children and the grief of losing parents and your brother. I miss your father, but that is no reason to wear a long face."

She thought of telling him that red-brown hair would understand, but did not. Instead she asked after her daughter-in-law and advised him not to take the Bordilen's opinions too seriously. If they spoke of 'the whole country' they meant their little clique. For certain Lady Bordilen rarely, if ever, spoke to anyone outside it.

To her great relief, Maldon did admit that that was so.

She then talked about her tour. She did not call it a holiday and she advised him to visit some of the small towns in Westland. They would welcome him, but he should not spend too long a time in any one of them. He and those entertaining him would find a short visit less tiring. She did not mention that it would also be less expensive. Maldon did not consider expense unless it was his own.

They were in better accord when they said goodbye and cut the connection.

Two weeks later, when she had settled into her new palace and into her usual routine, the post brought a surprise. One envelope contained two photographs of Delki in Regan, with a note from Jonal Tesher. It was brief.

"Standard pictures, but I thought that you might be interested."

She was. She knew Salima well enough, but she had never been out of its waters. She put envelope and contents in her personal drawer.

Others were added during the next few weeks and when they numbered five, she ordered a large map of northern Erion and put it on the wall. The pictures were brought out and pinned in the appropriate places. The notes remained in her drawer.

Fidel visited and stared at it with interest.

"Regan, Ligaria, Zorrenna – Easton then Venna in the south – and on to Changol." He traced the route with a finger. "Where next, I wonder?"

"Across the ocean, I expect," answered Andrela pointing to the great continent of Andea to the west.

"Maybe." Fidel did not think that likely. "He could as easily go south to Irrok, along the north coast, call in at some port in

Shyran and be back in Bosron around," he paused before he mentioned a date. It was the anniversary of Darmon's death.

"He was a close friend of father's, wasn't he?"

"Yes." For some reason Andrela found that prospect more appealing. "Yes, but the big anniversary service will be in Kaldor. The one that I am planning will be very small in comparison."

"Jon won't care about that! He likes informality and has no time for Westland's pompous aristocracy who will all be there. Besides, Mal is in no need of comfort and will be busy planning his coronation."

Andrela concentrated on the last phrase. There was plenty to discuss about Maldon's Coronation. The ceremony itself was not their concern, that would be as it had always been, but Andrela's position was new. She was mother of the new High Prince, but she was also a High Prince in her own right. It was interesting to speculate how her invitation would be worded and how she would be expected to dress.

As Fidel put it in his irreverent way, do you pander to Mal's sense of his own great importance, or do you stress your own high position and annoy him on his big day?

"I shall ask for advice," concluded the High Prince of Eland, but she did not say whose, nor did she say that she would follow it.

As the problem was not urgent, she did not ask anyone's advice immediately. There were other matters that required her attention. She did, however, feel happier when the next photograph from Mr Tesher arrived. It showed a castle in an ancient port on the north-west coast of Irrok.

She pinned it onto her map and tried not to look forward to the next one.

Fidel made it easier for her. He invited her to Winisham to see the University and to meet informally with his friends. She accepted with alacrity and had a delightful week.

She attended lectures, she met the speakers, she asked such intelligent questions that even the cleverest students were impressed; and she went to every social occasion that she could fit in. She ate and drank, she chatted and advised, she danced and she sang and even attempted to play the flute, though she was sadly out of practice. She enjoyed herself very much.

Her enthusiasm amazed her son as it did his friends, and their admiration made him prouder than ever of his mother. Better still, he knew that she was happy and had, for a few days at least, put aside the grief and trouble of the last few years.

When she returned to Bosron, Andrela was in better spirits than she had been for some time. She was ready to discuss the anniversary service with her Council.

To her surprise, they recommended that it be held in the Cathedral. A smaller church would not hold the numbers that they expected to attend. She did not argue. Most of them were planning to come with their wives and some of their children.

She had thought of a discreet, almost private service, but she was glad that she had not insisted, for two days before the date, Annia arrived in Bosron. Lord Pandour was with her and so were two of their children. Another ship brought Elizabeth and her husband. Her Ladies of the Bedchamber had come to support her.

Fidel arrived later the same day. He was not in the least surprised.

"You may not feel in need of support," he explained with a smile. "You manage everything perfectly, but it does take effort. This is an opportunity for everyone to show how much they appreciate you; and that, yes, you are widowed, but no, you are not entirely alone."

He was right, again, she thought, when she entered the packed cathedral. The aristocracy was there, the Council members from various towns had come with some of their townspeople, the merchants were well represented, a group of Fidel's friends were there, her household had turned out in force and she saw Jonal Tesher, standing with his friends from Westland. And there were also the ordinary folk of Bosron.

They did not cheer; it was not a day for cheering. Instead, they called down the blessings of Namier upon her. Their voices were muted, but there was no doubt about their good wishes. Had they not cared, they would have stayed at home.

She was near to tears when the service began. She had not expected such numbers and had made no provision for them, but she scarce had time to worry.

"I have booked the ballroom at the Grand for refreshments for our friends," whispered Fidel as they sat to listen to Lord Pandour, "and the Cathedral hall is open for everyone else."

Andrela had hardly time to whisper her thanks before Pedan began his tribute to Darmon. It was brief, but it did justice to every aspect of Darmon's life.

"We from Westland," he finished, "have come to join with your High Prince in her commemoration of her husband and the beginning of her journey out of official mourning. We wish her happiness, as I am sure that all of you who are here do also."

He was applauded; inappropriate perhaps in a cathedral, but those who clapped their hands were showing agreement, not praising his speech.

The ballroom at the Grand Hotel was not a scene of celebration, but it was convivial and concentrated on the future. The merchants looked forward to taking over their new premises and the Council to meeting in the palace. It would, said one Lord, be more convenient for the High Prince as she would not now be obliged to venture outside in inclement weather.

Fidel stored that comment to repeat to his friends. No one who had seen his mother in Winisham would believe her to be anxious about wind, rain or even deep snow.

Andrela joked about it too. She invited the Westerners and a few others to the palace to view the changes, and showed them around most of the newly transformed Royal wing with its modern conveniences. She also showed them the enlarged room where the Council would meet and the new offices though they were not yet finished.

"And there," she exclaimed triumphantly, "is the door that I shall use when the weather is inclement!"

There was general laughter, and Lord Geraish observed that Venlan was well known for his fear of weather, rain was definitely to be avoided and even fresh air was suspect.

"He is near eighty, though," said Colly, "so perhaps he has a point."

"But life must be dull, if he hardly ever ventures outside."

This topic occupied everyone until they took their leave.

The 'home lot', as Fidel irreverently named the visitors from Westland, stayed in Bosron for less than a week, but Jonal's yacht remained in the harbour.

Fidel was pleased. He liked Jon and did not consider him to be a Westlander. He had travelled so much that he no longer belonged anywhere. He was a wanderer.

"His home is in Dunnoura," said Andrela, "and I believe him to be very fond of New Stannul."

"He is not a typical Westerner, though."

"Neither are you, my son, and I am very glad of it. Nor was your father. Had he been, I might not have married him."

Her eyes twinkled and he laughed in return.

"I shall ask Jon about that."

Fidel did go to the harbour to see Jonal, but he did not ask about his father. He asked about his travels and during the course of the conversation he mentioned his own trips around Eland. Lake Warne was full of holiday homes, but there was plenty to do and see. He had friends too in Bosron, and they had spent a day at Angel Heights. That was nearby. Had Jon been there?

Jon had not, but, as Fidel admitted, neither had he until the other day when someone had suggested it. He had not realised that there was such a splendid view point so near to Bosron. One could see across the Great Bay to the north and the island of Shyran to the south – if the weather permitted. It was worth a visit and Colly lived not far away.

"Perhaps, my mother would like to go. She has never told me of the place, but she must have been there."

Fidel did not mention the details of the conversation to his mother and he returned to Winisham the next day. She was therefore surprised to receive an invitation from Lord Collingwade to join him and a party of friends on a trip to Angel Heights. They were to set out from Bosron, travel by electric car to Senby and take horse from there.

He added that he was aware that she had ridden very little whilst in the west, but she had been an excellent rider and he knew that she had been on horseback several times since she had returned home.

The reminder of the restrictions of Kaldor, his praise of her riding skills and the word 'home' were enough to persuade her. True she had not been to Angel Heights since that dreadful day when her brother had been killed. She had feared to go, as she had feared to sail past Shyran. That had been done now and her brother had been dead for many years. Caston too was dead and Darmon had never been there.

She would not forget any of them, they were all important in her life, but the hurt had dulled. It was time to dispel all her fears. She would visit Angel Heights again.

She bought a new riding dress for the occasion because Vealla always wore dresses. Also, she wanted to wear a bright colour, and trousers in vivid shades were neither fashionable nor flattering.

The dress she chose was in a swirly pattern of different greens. Very practical, as the sales lady had said, for it would not show the marks that were bound to appear when one came into contact with saddles, harness or hedges. She added that those always in the public eye had their difficulties. They may have servants at hand, but the burden of appearing as neat and fresh as if one just stepped from the dressing room, remained.

Andrela was usually suspicious of sales ladies. She respected their skills, but they frequently annoyed her. This one did not. She was pleased with her purchase.

She was not so pleased when she awoke on the day of the outing. It was raining heavily and she was glad that the first part of the journey was by car. She travelled with her bodyguard and a Mrs Fandray, whose husband was in the second car with Jonal Tesher. Colly was unable to organise the weather, but it was typical of him that he had arranged for two cars so that she had ample room and was not crushed against a man. Mrs Fandray, she had met once before, but they were not well acquainted. The lady, however, was good company.

They chatted inconsequentially about the scenery, Lord Collingwade and his family, the pleasures of the garden and the fine quality of the leather goods in the shop in the forest of Ament. They decided to visit it, even if the gentlemen were in a great hurry to arrive at Angel Heights for their lunch.

"I am sure that there will be time," said Andrela. "Colly will have arranged for all eventualities. He always does, and a half hour here or there will not disturb him in the slightest."

She was right. When they arrived in Senby they were obliged to make a decision. They could ride as planned if they thought the rain had eased, or they could travel to the Leather Factory by coach.

Andrela opted to ride and the matter was settled.

It proved to be a good choice. The clouds scudded northwards, the sky began to clear and a fitful sun appeared. The trees dripped water on them occasionally, but the way was broad and firm and the air smelt beautifully fresh. The gentlemen rode on the edges of the path closer to the trees. They became wetter than the ladies and so were quite happy to stop. The restaurant at the Leather Factory was noted for serving anything at any time and it was warm and dry. The ladies were able to browse and buy at leisure.

Clouds were gathering again when they reached Angel Heights and Andrela offered to walk with Jonal to the high viewpoint whilst the rest of the party organised lunch. Colly had taken a private room in one of the inns. It was, Andrela noted, the same one that Caston had chosen.

"We will not be long," said Andrela, "but if you wish to order the food, I will have whatever fish they have as a first course and a venison steak, rare. Buffalo will do if by any mischance they do not have venison."

Jonal echoed her choice and they began their walk.

Andrela was silent and Jonal regarded her thoughtfully as they made their way to the summit of the slope.

"Here we are," she said when they reached the highest point. "From here you have a splendid view. There is Bellue to the east, the Great Bay to the north, and Shyran to the south. On a clear day, some have claimed to have seen the north coast of the Bay, but not many. It is a long way."

He stared out to sea. Senby and coast lay below, but further on there were waves and mist.

"I have sailed round Bellue many times," he said, turning to the east, "but from here you can see more clearly how the coast has been eroded. Do people still live around the fort? In time it could be an island."

They discussed the strength of the sea and the slow but steady changes that it made. Eventually Jonal turned to the south; and Shyran.

He had been there. He had seen much of it and, in his view, it could not long remain independent. It was too small and it needed electricity. Some flat lands generated power from the tides. Nowadays there were few people who were content to scrape a living from the land. They wanted modern comfort and news.

He waited for her comment.

She had never thought of generating electricity from the sea. It was obviously possible. All that was needed was flowing water to drive the turbine; but Eland had its rivers and she had no responsibility for Shyran.

"I have never been to Shyran," she said at last, and they stood in silence and gazed at the long low island.

"Why not? It is not far."

She looked at him, seeking help, but he could not help her. She turned back to contemplate the island.

"I was going," she said at last. "I was going to be married. We were here; we had lunch in the same inn where we are to eat today; and after lunch we heard that my brother Fidel had been killed. I had to go back."

He sensed her distress and there was no one about to see them, so he put an arm around her shoulders.

"Will you manage?" he asked. "Colly could not have known."

"No. No one knew; and yes, I will manage. It is many years ago now."

She moved from his encircling arm and began to walk down the slope.

"Love can last for many years," he answered quietly.

She wondered at his choice of word. Why not 'grief'?

After a while she said, "I missed my brother, very much; but when he died, I was heir. I could not marry as I wanted, and now he, the one I wanted to marry, and Darmon, the man I did marry, are both dead. Those I love seem to die before their time."

"No one dies before their time," he answered soberly. "Some die young, some when they are old, but I doubt that love has much to do with it."

She stayed silent and after a time, he added softly, "And anyone blest with your love would surely have great reason to stay alive."

She could not answer and was almost glad when she felt a splash on her hand.

"Oh! A drop of rain!" she exclaimed in a completely different tone. "How very annoying that it should rain today and spoil the view! Yesterday it would not have mattered at all."

They hurried towards the inn, but she slowed before they reached the door and spoke. She had made her decision.

"Tomorrow I am busy, but the day after I am free. Will you still be here? Are you able to lunch with me?"

"Yes," he said and they went inside out of the rain.

The sun appeared as they were eating and the remainder of the day went as planned. It was most enjoyable. Andrela sang to herself as she made ready for bed and she gave considerable thought to her lunch with Jonal Tesher. He would eat anything and praise it, she knew that, but she wanted to offer something special.

She decided on 'peasant food', but delicately spiced and made with the finest of ingredients: fish soup, minced lamb balls with herbs, onion sauce and vegetables and a selection of cheeses with fresh fruit.

It was a great success.

They walked in the garden after lunch. The morning rain had ceased. Some leaves still glistened with damp, but the paths were dry. Andrela wanted to show him the changes that had been made.

"I did consider creating a 'children's garden', but there was not space enough. A proper 'children's garden' must have at least one big tree and plenty of hedges to keep it screened." She sounded regretful.

"You could not use it now," Jonal responded with sympathy. "In addition to all your other talents, you are a mother, soon to be a grandmother, and thus banned from a proper children's garden. Much better to use the space as you have. You will enjoy it for years."

She laughed. "*My* 'children's garden' would allow me in it," she declared. "I need the privacy to practice rope-climbing again, and running."

"Ah, yes. I remember how hard it was to beat you. I had intended, gallantly, to let you win. I decided, as I pounded after you, that you would not want that. You might rejoice in victory, but not if you won by concession."

He looked at her, affection mingled with his admiration.

"You do not think yourself less able, simply because you are a woman."

Andrela smiled. "No, I do not. All of my life I have been privileged. People looked up to me, because I was a Princess; so much so that no man ever actually asked me to marry him. The one who loved me did not dare, not directly, and all other proposals came via my father or via the Council, as Darmon made his."

"Did he not ask you in the proper manner?" Jonal was scathing. "How unfair and unimaginative of him. Perhaps he felt it inappropriate for a Prince. A man must drop to one knee," – he suited his actions to his words – "so that he is below his lady. She already has his heart, but he offers her his wealth, his position, his life, his all, when he asks for her hand."

"Not now," she said in sudden panic. "Maldon's coronation is in six weeks."

Immediately she felt awkward. She had assumed that he was about to propose and to stop a man at such a point was surely not tactful; perhaps even foolish. He might have been joking, but if he did propose, she realised suddenly that she wanted to accept. She wanted very much to accept, but not now. It would not do to upset Maldon's celebration by announcing her betrothal a few weeks before it.

Jonal stood up. He had forgotten about the coming great event in Kaldor. As a third son, he would not be invited to official functions, but Andrela most certainly would.

"Only six weeks! You will have to leave soon. You will be an important guest, staying at the palace, I assume, with Fidel."

"I have not made any plans yet," she owned. "I have been putting off the decisions. I have not even decided what to wear. There is something in the Westland regalia that is worn by the High Prince's mother, and Maldon will probably expect me to use it, but it was old and may not fit. Also, my subjects in Eland may not like that. It puts me too much in the west."

"It will also be heavy, grand and formal," said Jonal with a grin. "If you must wear something so uncomfortable, wear Eland regalia. You are High Prince of the country, after all."

"What a good idea!" exclaimed Andrela in delight. "Why in all Erion did *I* not think of that? And no one can complain, because I daresay that most other foreign rulers will turn up in their country's grandest robes *and* with their chests covered in medals that mean nothing."

"Do not cover your chest with medals," he advised with the bow that always preceded his elaborate compliments. "That would be a sad waste. If you do have a medal, wear it round your neck on a long ribbon so that it draws attention your figure, rather than conceals it."

She laughed, but she was flattered.

"I shall probably wear jewellery, State Jewellery," she told him, "but I shall send Fidel to you to ask for advice about his dress. He is as undecided as I was and fears that Maldon will find some ancient moth-eaten robe that was once worn by a younger brother."

Later she told Fidel something of their conversation and advised him to discuss his own worries about the Coronation with Mr Tesher. Jonal knew Kaldor and the Palace and its protocol, and he would not recommend any course that would lead to serious disaccord.

Chapter 25

Fidel was very happy to consult Jonal. He had talked over his problems with friends, but their advice had not been helpful. None were Royal and did not understand that an irreverent choice of garment, intended to cause mild annoyance to a brother, but worn in public at an important event, might affect a whole country. Jonal would.

Jonal did. He had also remembered that the coaches available for the Grand Procession to the Cathedral were limited in number and that not all were in a good state of repair. He was sure that Maldon would wish to convey his mother to the Cathedral in comfort and style, but it could present problems. It might help if the High Prince of Eland took one of her State carriages to Kaldor. That would ensure that she would have a conveyance that suited her.

"Jon knows trade," said Fidel when he told his mother of the conversation. "He can organise sea transport of the carriage and I can take the horses via the mountains."

Andrela had her doubts. She did not want to antagonise her elder son, but she did approve of the smart outfit that Fidel had purchased. It was fashionable and richly adorned. It indicated his Royalty without stressing that he was the 'younger brother'.

She also liked the idea of taking her own transport. She called Annia on the relay and arranged that her carriage and horses would be accommodated at the Pandour Town House. If all official arrangements were satisfactory, Maldon would not even need to know that they had made other plans.

Andrela travelled by sea and arrived in Kaldor a week before the Coronation Day. She was met at the quayside, though not by her son, and was taken to the Palace.

There she was welcomed by Lady Bordilen, who was in residence and had taken charge. Andrela was told in resonant tones that the High Princess was resting to conserve her strength for the 'great day', and that the High Prince was occupied with National Affairs.

The refreshments offered were accepted gracefully, but the room that was offered to her was not.

"I shall stay in my old home with Fidel," declared Andrela. "Mal told me only a few weeks ago that it had not been altered in any way and I always found it comfortable. It may need a dust, but that is no great trouble. My servants and Fidel's man can then be accommodated in the same wing, which will be more convenient for us and less trouble for the Palace staff at this busy time."

Lady Bordilen was not pleased, but all her arguments were dismissed.

Andrela had cooks and cleaners on the Royal yacht. They were being paid and might well be happier if they had work to do. Also they knew her ways. She and Fidel had naturally brought their own body guards and they too could stay in the 'new wing'.

"And I know well," continued Andrela in her sweetest manner, "that it is quite separate. If they wish to see us, Their Royal Highnesses may call on us or invite us for some specific occasion. Otherwise they will scarcely know that we are here."

Lady Bordilen conceded the point as gracefully as she was able, but she distanced herself from the decision when she next encountered her son-in law. To her surprise, he was almost indifferent.

"The place is there," he said, "and my mother is more familiar with the new wing than she is with the main palace. So is Fidel. I shall go and see her straight away. I expect that she will have brought everything she needs, but she may have forgotten something that I can supply."

"I will come with you." Lady Bordilen was quite determined. "I have looked out the robe that is traditionally worn by the Dowager Princess at Coronations and I will bring it. It may need some alteration. Your mother is not as slender as your grandmother was."

Maldon hid his sigh. He had been more in tune with his grandmother's formality than he had ever been with his mother's casual approach to protocol, but he had disliked their battles almost as much as his father had. He had hoped that this meeting with his mother would be free of such unpleasantness. Andrela *was* his mother and he was fond of her.

He greeted her warmly and was hugged in return. She acknowledged Lady Bordilen politely and disregarded the elaborate gown that hung over her arm. Maldon asked where Fidel was.

"He will be here tomorrow or possibly the day after. It depends. He is coming overland with my horses."

Andrela smiled at her son. He was tense, which was hardly surprising so near to his coronation. He would have little support from his wife as she was expecting a child and was unwell.

"I remember that grand carriages in good condition were in short supply when your father and I were crowned, so I have brought my own, with horses. They need not be used if they are not needed, but it would not be diplomatic to seat one of the foreign guests in a carriage with worn seats."

Lady Bordilen compressed her lips. Her husband's allies in the Assembly had allocated to the Dowager Princess a carriage with a very dilapidated interior. She was further annoyed when Maldon expressed his approval of his mother's arrangements.

"I will find room in the stables," he promised, "but they are rather crowded at the moment."

"No need. The carriage, the purple one that you and Fidel used at my coronation, has been taken to Pandour's place. Annia said there was room and they will house the horses too. I'm looking forward to seeing them both again – and their children."

As her son showed no sign of annoyance Andrela smiled warmly at Lady Bordilen and pressed home her advantage.

"Is that the regalia that Dowager Princess's wear?" she asked.

"Yes, it may need altering for you. The Princess Indola was so very slender."

"That was just as well," responded Andrela cheerfully. "I recall that it was much worn in places and that large tucks were essential to conceal the holes, as well as to make it fit; but it does not matter. I shall not be using it. This is such an important occasion that any lapse in protocol will be noticed by every journalist in Salima, so I must dress accordingly. I am High Prince of Eland which is a more important title than Dowager High Princess of Westland. I must wear Eland regalia."

She grinned wickedly at her son.

"I have no 'decorations' to pin on my chest and I can hardly wear my coronation robe. It is quite as over trimmed and heavy as yours is, but there is a formal suit used for the yearly Grand Meeting of Council that I have adapted for wearing with a skirt. I have brought that."

"Excellent," said Maldon. "And Fid. Has he something suitable? The 'younger brother's' regalia has not been needed for more than a century. Namier knows what it will be like."

"He has a very elegant suit, but it will take a cloak if that is thought appropriate, and he will ride or travel in the carriage with me. He does not mind. Whatever your advisors think is better."

Maldon smiled and some of the tension left him. He had been worried about his mother and Fidel. They were his closest relations and he wanted them to take part in his coronation, but neither of them had the same priorities as he did. He appreciated his mother's diplomacy.

Andrela was pleased too. She had not provoked a confrontation, not even with the Bordilen woman, and she had told Maldon of all her plans. They had not disagreed and that meant that Mal and Fid would have nothing to quarrel about. Perhaps their time together would be easy, as easy as it been when her boys were tiny. It was. The ceremonies and the social occasions connected with them, proceeded without serious problems. Andrela was honoured as both Prince and Princess and was complimented on her fine sons. Fidel was feted both as a handsome and unmarried man and as a Prince. Lady Bordilen had many grand moments as mother of the newly crowned Princess and Jonal Tesher remained in the background.

"I am of no importance," he explained to Fidel when that young man tried to include him in a celebration. "My elder brother, Lord Barre, has his place in Westland society, but I do not. I left it long ago. I am here to 'be there', as in Collingwade's motto."

He looked gravely his companion. "I think it a noble motto and one that he and his family live by. I have no such nobility, but I am here for your mother. I trust she will have no need of me, but I am here."

Fidel pondered on the lives of his mother and their friend. He also considered his own responsibilities and his somewhat frivolous approach to life. They were serious thoughts, but he did not allow them to intrude upon his enjoyment, and it was enjoyment, of his brother's coronation.

Jonal organised the shipping of the coach back to Eland, so he was 'there' in his own way and it relieved Andrela of a small burden.

She returned to Bosron via the land route. There was now a rail line for the first part of the journey, and she took that. It saved nothing, for her horses had to be led or ridden, but she felt that it would boost the use of such transport and it did not remind her of the other times, often sad, when she had travelled to the mountains.

She visited the valley where Lanchir was buried and scattered petals over his grave, but his spirit was long gone and the peace of the site was soothing rather than distressing. She went through the tunnel to Eland with a happy heart and she stayed for a few days in the places that she had so loved in her young and carefree days.

She was welcomed as she had always been, but she was also honoured. The valleys had visi-screens now and Maldon's coronation had been avidly watched. The High Prince of Eland had not disappointed the watchers.

She travelled slowly back to Bosron, taking the opportunity to visit the many villages that had sprung up along the route to the mountains. It pleased her to see her country thriving and it pleased the villagers to see their Prince.

Fidel waited at the palace until she returned, but once he had seen her safe home, he returned to Winisham to resume his interrupted studies.

Andrela was praised, too, by her Council. There were one or two matters to discuss, but first she was welcomed home and congratulated on her splendid appearance at her son's coronation. No one criticised. True, no one looked forward to the day when Prince Maldon would be High Prince of all Salima, but, as that would not happen until she were dead, it would have been tactless to mention it.

Having met her Council and found that there were no serious problems that needed her attention, Andrela enquired as to the whereabouts of Mr Jonal Tesher. She needed to thank him for arranging and supervising the transport of her carriage and indeed for the suggestion that she took it. It had been helpful to Maldon, had pleased everyone in Eland to whom she had spoken and it had allowed her to travel in comfort whilst she was in Kaldor.

She also wanted to share with him her small triumph over Lady Bordilen, but that would have to be done in private. Lunch again, she thought happily, if he were still in the environs of Bosron.

She discovered quickly that he was, because his yacht was in the harbour, but contacting him took her a long time.

How difficult was it, she asked herself crossly as she tore yet another sheet of paper into shreds, to ask a friend to come to lunch?

Eventually, she sent one of her attempts. It was very brief, almost curt. It listed three dates when she was free for lunch and asked that he come so that she could thank him in person for his help. She did not specify what help nor did her letter convey any of her hopes or her emotions.

His reply was equally succinct. He said only that he would be delighted to come and lunch with her at the palace, and he gave nothing more than the date and the time.

She did not care. He was coming.

She planned a more sophisticated menu than she had chosen for his previous visit; crayfish tails with salad, roast haunch of venison with accompanying vegetables, a fruit tart to follow and a delicately flavoured cheese should they still be hungry. She counted the days.

When he arrived, she was glad that she had not repeated the 'peasant food' of their first lunch at the palace, for he arrived carrying a bottle of Air Gold.

"Forgive the presumption," he said as he showed it to her. "I am sure that your wine cellar is well stocked with many fine vintages, but this is made by a friend of mine, and he makes so few bottles that it is not sold on the open market. I like it and would like to share it with you."

Andrela did not object. When she did sample it at the end of the meal, she found that she liked it very much, but she was aware that that moment was perhaps not the best time to pass judgement. The meal had been delicious and the wines that she had chosen had complemented the food beautifully. Mindful of his gift, she had not drunk deeply, but the company was as heady as the alcohol.

"Shall we walk in the garden?" he asked. "I saw the changes you have made last time I came to lunch, but I do not think that we finished our conversation."

She hesitated and Jonal smiled.

"We can take our glasses and what is left in the bottle," he said. "We were drinking Air Gold in the afternoon in a garden when we first met. Do you remember?"

Andrela remembered. She remembered both the day they had first met and the much later unfinished conversation he had mentioned. She picked up her glass and led the way outside.

"Did I thank you for your help in transporting my coach?" she asked. "That was the reason I invited you, but the discussion about this delightful drink has made me forget."

"I do not need thanks for that, but I do agree that this wine has some strange effects. It lends wings to the mind."

They walked slowly along the path, in accord, but each with their own thoughts.

"It was just here I think," said Jonal suddenly, and he took her glass. He set it down with his own on a low wall and led her two steps further.

"Here, I am sure. Here it was that you told me that no one had ever proposed to you in person, only via 'official channels'. You deserve better."

The ground was wet, almost soggy, but she did not stop him from dropping to one knee or from speaking.

"Andrela, my Princess, my loved one," he began, "you have had my heart since the day we met, but I could not ask you then. Now, you have fulfilled your duty. You have been true and faithful and you have borne an heir for Salima. My lowly status is now irrelevant, and I can ask the question that I so wanted to ask long ago."

His tone changed. Light-hearted, formal, amusing Jonal became impassioned.

"Oh, my love, my only love, my dearest one, will you marry me?"

He stretched out his hand and she took it.

"Oh, yes!" she answered and she stood in silence savouring the moment.

Suddenly, she laughed. "How could I refuse such a proposal? But do get up. The ground is still damp from yesterday's rain."

He stood up, put his arms around her and drew her close. She leant her head against his chest.

"Have you really loved me since the day we met?" she asked wonderingly. "That was years ago."

"Yes, it was years ago; but I was not then an acceptable suitor for any woman of rank, certainly not you. Nor am I now, but we are older, too old for children, and it matters less. Then, Darmon was perhaps the only man you would have married; and he wanted to marry you. He may not have loved you, he did not love anyone at that time, but you were the answer to his problem."

He kissed her gently. "Over the years, you have been the answer to many of his problems. I know that. He wrote to me; via Ped, to lessen the risk of interception. We were friends, good friends.

"I did not want to damage our friendship, nor did I want either of you to know then that I loved you. It would not have helped. So I went travelling."

Andrela returned his kiss.

"No, it would not have helped, then. Now," and she looked up, smiling at him with a tenderness he had seen only when she had held her children, "now, it will help a great deal."

After a while, she drew back from his embrace, frowning.

"But will you be happy living here in the palace?"

"Half here, half at my much smaller and less formal place in Dunnoura? We could vary the route between the two so that you can visit all parts of your princedom as we travel between our homes."

"I would have to go south sometimes," she answered, the frown only slightly less anxious.

"Thirds then. No, that would be too generous to the south which is smaller. They can have a month. The north can have two, Bosron four and Dunnoura four. Will that suit?"

Her frown disappeared. "And the other month?" she queried laughing.

"Will be mine," he said and kissed her.

She did not answer, she could not, but she approved: of his words and his action. They would work out the details tomorrow, or the next day, or the day after that. There was time.

Hal was walking around the garden. There was little danger, but he was paid to keep alert and to watch. He saw them together and changed his route. He could watch equally well from further away.

He smiled as he walked. His fellow guard was competent enough, but he had always considered the Princess Andrela to be *his* responsibility.

He had seen her grow from a mischievous child to a lively young woman. He had known of her secret 'outings' and had sensed when she had fallen in love. He had been there when she returned after her brother's death. He had guarded her at the funeral, on her first visit to Westland and on her wedding day.

Westland security had eventually accepted him and he had watched over her at Naming Ceremonies, State functions and social outings. He had been at all the family funerals, her son's wedding and no fewer than three coronations. He had taken care of her.

He had enjoyed the return to Kaldor for the last coronation. He had seen his children again. They were grown now, but it had been good to see them. Family meetings had been short and expensive since he had come back to Bosron.

Now he would have more time. Now he could retire.

He knew Tesher, second-hand, but well. He had made thorough enquiries.

The man had been Prince Darmon's friend. He was reliable, he was experienced, he was trustworthy and he was honest; and he loved the Princess Andrela.

He would take care of the little Princess who had become the High Prince of Eland. She would be safe with him and he, Hal, could leave her in his care.